DECEPTIVE NIGHTS

NIGHTS

BY

SYLVIA HUBBARD

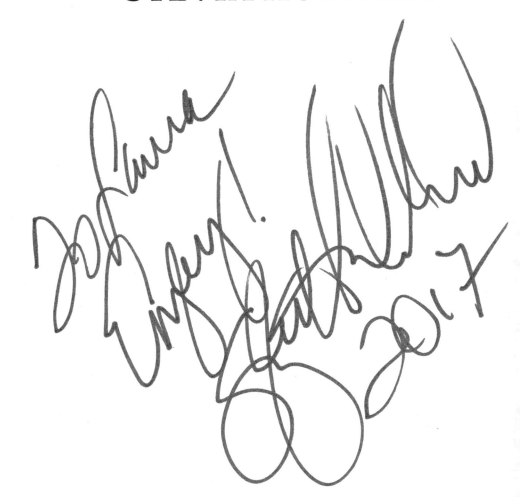

Deceptive Nights © 2005 Sylvia Hubbard

Cover design by Sylvia Hubbard

HubBooks Literary Service Code
111001-1221:E101005-1538

Available in Tradeback and E-Book

Visit her website at:
http://SylviaHubbard.com

Reprinted with CreateSpace.com 2009
ISBN is 1442199822 and EAN-13 is 9781442199828

Also available wherever eBooks are sold.

Updates and related books listings can be found on author's
website at: http://SylviaHubbard.com

Thank you in advance for supporting this author's literary endeavors. Tell others, leave reviews and read more of this author's books.

Other Books By Author:

Dreams of Reality *
Stone's Revenge*
Stealing Innocence 1& 2
Road To Freedom
Dark Façade (I/R)
Mistaken Identity (n)
Drawing The Line (I/R)
Baby Doll (n)
Red Heart (n)

*These books can be ordered at the any bookstore or on the author's website.

(I/R) Interracial Romances
(n) Novellas

More   books   available   wherever   books   are   sold.

Chapter 1

At one point she knew when her eyelids were getting heavy and would be impossible to keep them open. Soon as she realized this, Phoebe changed positions in her chair. Exhaustion ran through every vein of her body, but she was determined to get through this very long day.

"...And furthermore, we have seen a seventy percent improvement in the turnaround time..." the co-owner of P&B Communications LLC, Madeline Porter said into the speakerphone across from Phoebe to Lansing's FIA office. Her heavily made up face was picture perfect.

Unlike Phoebe, who stuck to eyeliner and a light shade of lipstick, Madeline prided herself on covering every centimeter of skin from her hairline to almost her collarbone. Phoebe couldn't imagine the job the woman had to do every morning and every night.

"I do commend your staff on the fine job, Madeline, but there are reports that we are still missing," Leslie Cross, supervisor of the Lansing FIA office said over the speaker.

Madeline motioned for Phoebe to begin taking notes. "How many?" Madeline asked.

There was a brief silence, before Leslie responded with, "Seventeen to count. Phoebe has done an excellent job as your new manager finding the other two hundred."

Phoebe immediately straightened herself at the mention of her name and looked at Madeline trying to seem as alert as possible. Looking through her folder of many notes, she pulled out a specific list. "Leslie, I spoke with, Kyle, your assistant yesterday. Eight of those aren't on our system. Five of them were partial dictations that were dumped and the rest were purged off our system due to the time delay. I know this is an inconvenience for your doctors, but we have found over eighty-five percent of the reports that were lost due to the system shut down."

This was an old subject. Three days before she was hired the recording network had shut down due to severe electrical power outage. The server was literally struck with a bolt of lightning frying the main drive. What had saved them was that the back up hard drive had dumped all of its files onto the C-drive of the tower, due to current pulses directing the information in the wrong direction. It was supposed to dump it back in the main network hard drive to replenish it.

The day had been saved when Phoebe went in the C-drive by mistake thinking it was the main network and recovered all the information. She never told anyone it had been a mistake, she just said she had a hunch.

The prior manager had been fired two days prior for losing the majority of reports from another account and mismanaging the office.

Madeline Porter immediately promoted her to office manager and Phoebe had benefits for her kids.

Next, Phoebe was aiming for a car, but needed every paycheck to pay her bills her ex-husband had decided to run up using her name and other personal information. Phoebe was just lucky she had never given Daniel Newby their children's personal information too or he would have tried to make their credit bad like he had done hers.

After the meeting was over, Madeline wanted to discuss other things, but Phoebe had millions of other things to do. Still she sat there and took notes while Madeline rattle on about things. When that was over, Phoebe immediately got back to work. Simon poked his head in her office at lunchtime. "Eat yet?"

She looked up at his innocent yet charming face and smiled, "No, but I had some peanut butter and fruit?"

"For lunch? Are you still on that diet?"

"No pain no gain," she said, now concentrating on her computer screen as she answered as many emails as possible. "Yes, I'm practicing control over food, plus that was all I could grab this morning."

"How about some soup, my treat?" he suggested.

"I guess. Make sure it's not tomato and bring me wheat crackers, not saltine."

He winked a light green eye at her and disappeared.

She sighed sitting back and dialing her home. Her mother, Patricia Green answered as expected. "Hi Mom. I'm going to be working late again."

"Again, Phoebe? I thought we agreed to a three day a week late hour. This is number five this week and I know she'll make you work the weekends."

"I know, but this is important, Mom."

"It's always important."

Phoebe sighed not able to give her mother a good excuse. "I promise I won't do it again, but you know how I'm trying to catch up from the last manager, who was the one responsible for not doing their job and I want to make a good impression to Ms. Porter."

"I think you have gone above and beyond making a good impression to your boss," Patricia snipped more to herself. "Alright, I'll pick up the kids. You be careful and if you need me to pick you up, just call. Don't take the bus home if you don't have to, Phoebe."

Phoebe wouldn't dare use her mother for just a ride home from work when she could catch the bus right in front of her home from Downtown Detroit where she worked.

As she replaced the receiver and got back to work, she was glad her mother was there for her. They were best of friends more than anything.

After Daniel left her six months ago - six months after she had the twins - to go his own way since there wasn't any more money from her father's inheritance left. Phoebe had been distraught over being left alone. He had simply been using her, yet that had been her life story.

Mike, her high school sweetheart, had used her for the car her father had gotten for her in high school. When Mike had wrecked the car, he left her.

Harris, a college sweetheart, just needed a place to stay for free and someone to pay for all his music equipment. After that he left.

Daniel, who had convinced her to marry him, had used the twenty thousand dollars she had gotten from her father's trust fund after college expenses were paid for had used it to buy his car, his clothes and new women, then left her.

That had been the last straw for Phoebe. She had decided to hell with men and devoted her time to raising her children. No other man would ever use her unless she got something in return for her own self.

Chapter 2

It was seven when Phoebe walked out on the dark mid-November streets of Detroit. A cold river chill encircled her, making her to hurry and close the ankle length brown coat, and pull her cheap thick wool hat on her head with her matching gloves over her hands. Her job was a block away from Cadillac Square. The walk did her well. She walked past the Renaissance Center, the Millender Center, then to Cadillac where all the buses came. Well most of them. She could catch the Gratiot straight home. It dropped her off at the corner of Grinnell on the east side and her mother's house was on the corner from the bus stop.

Phoebe hurried along down Jefferson to get to the bus stop. Detroit was on the brink of exploding into a world-class city. With the casino's coming into town, and General Motors moving into the Renaissance Center, the city was making changes. With this in mind, Phoebe often saw limousines in the nightlife of Detroit of visitors to the city or citizens of the city living it up. Parties, business functions, and even just casino runs often drew these people who loved to spend their money on absolutely nothing in Phoebe's opinion who could use the money to pay off her own debts her ex-husband had run up.

She had come to ignore the fancy cars and limousines that drove by or pulled up beside her and keep walking, yet when one came to a stop next to her as she was waiting for a red light, then didn't moved even when the light turned green, she gave the back window a very grim frown then sighed tiredly. 'Probably a little teenager showing off to his friends with his rich daddy's money,' she assumed. Phoebe really didn't care. Men being attracted to her no matter what age, race or financial status at this point in her life didn't matter to her anymore. She didn't want to be bothered by them at all.

The limousine finally turned just as the light turned from yellow to red. She proceeded on to Cadillac Square not giving the limousine another thought.

****

The well-dressed three men sitting in the chamber of the limousine all were silent. Different thoughts running through all their heads, but one was able to read the most troubled man's thoughts. All were quite handsome and very successful in their own rights.

"What was that about? Did you know her?" Desmond White asked his friend from inside the limousine as it drove on to the Renaissance Center. They would be staying in the hotel for the night.

Lawrence Ripley, Jacoby Walter's best friend and blood brother, chuckled to himself knowing full well what was going through Jacoby's head. Earlier in the night when the dates Desmond had promised to bring them from out of town had fallen through, and then Lawrence was unable to get suitable overnight dates for them, Jacoby had been pretty pissed off or probably just horny.

"Aren't there any good women anymore who just want a one night stand?" Lawrence had said. "Makes me want to stop the next women on the street and offer her five hundred dollars just to get some pussy."

Desmond, who was always the consciences one in the bunch, said, "With the diseases going around and the needs of women changing you can't expect a good one anymore."

"I'm willing to bet I can buy a good one," Jacoby announced, who loved to gamble. He hated to sleep alone and it really wasn't sleep he wanted either. The way he was feeling he would spend a whole grand to get a good woman underneath him. Damn, he wished he were back in Lansing about now where he had a woman just waiting for him to call her. It was a simple arrangement he had there. He could just go over her house, make love to her and leave. They didn't have to speak, and they didn't have to stay the whole night if he didn't want it. No strings-attached was their relationship and neither discussed it any further.

Desmond changed the topic to business to ease the tension. Hell what did Desmond care, he was about to get married. Something Jacoby at thirty-three had longed for, but was too damn picky and selfish to do it. The woman was either too dumb or just couldn't satisfy all his needs.

Sheryl Cobb, Desmond's fiancee was perfect for Desmond. She was so together and they made a perfect couple.

Jacoby couldn't find one like that. He seemed to only attract the ones that were interested in joining bank accounts with him. He never had real chances to get out. He was usually always doing business. The woman he slept with whenever he felt the need or she called him up for a good time was about the only woman right now in his life and he had no real feelings about their relationship. She provided a way for him to release himself with any hassles. He didn't want anything more with her. True she was an older woman, but he knew he would probably never find a younger woman who would want an arrangement like the one he had with his older woman.

The limousine finally arrived at the hotel and let them out. Horny and tired, Jacoby went quietly to his room mumbling a goodnight to his friends, who had opted to stop in at the bar near the lobby of the hotel.

Why was that woman standing alone on the corner? What had made him pay attention to her? Even though he hadn't got a very good look at her face, she looked a little over twenty-five, attractive, voluptuous in the right places and... Something. He couldn't put his finger on it.

Her stockings. No, not stockings - Tights. He hadn't seen a grown woman wear white tights. It seemed so little girlish, innocent, and somehow sexually arousing? It was strange for Jacoby to note something like that.

Jacoby then thought Desmond would have had a cow if he had offered that respectable woman some money for a night a pleasure.

After a cold shower, he laid in bed staring up at the wall too horny to sleep. Just as he decided to flick on the television to watch infomercials, his phone rung

"Why didn't you do it?" Lawrence asked on the other end.

Jacoby chortled. He should have known Lawrence would be poking around in his head. The best friends knew each other like the back of their own hands. "Because it wouldn't have been fair to you. She didn't have any friends with her and I definitely didn't feel like sharing tonight. I wanted something all to myself."

Lawrence joined in on the amusement. "I just had to ask."

"Hey, if it's fate, I'll see her again then I'll know next time what to do," Jacoby teased, knowing he'd never see her again. "Tonight I'll nut off."

"See you in the morning," Lawrence forced out through his laughter.

After hanging up the phone, he seriously thought about it, and then went to the bathroom to get his washcloth. Making the room dark, he calmed himself and pictured her face on a thick fully breasted body riding naked on him. She threw her head back and moaned those sweet helpless high-pitched moans of pleasure licking her lips.

She knew just how to ride him too - real slow. Gripping him tight, leaning over so her large nipples hung over his mouth and he suckled them as if they were the last ones he would ever have. He could feel himself getting closer so he rolled her over never missing a stroke and pounded his body against her. She took his large thick member deep inside her, loving every last long thick stroke. Her juices surrounded him, her heat enveloped him, and she begged for him to fill her with himself.

"Sweet honey," he whispered as he erupted deep inside of her.

****

When his heartbeat returned to almost normal and he had gathered his wits, physically he felt just tired, emotionally he still felt unfulfilled. In order to satisfy that need he knew he needed the foreplay and the sigh of pleasure he would hear from the female after it was over.

Yet amazingly, all through his fantasy he had focused on one face - that woman standing on the corner. Usually he wouldn't concentrate on the face. Hell in some of these fantasy episodes, he did twenty different women. Why had he concentrated so hard on keeping the face the same? He could have some unfulfilled fantasy about really having sex with a strange respectable woman.

It didn't matter, Jacoby told himself as he shrugged it off, using the washcloth to clean himself. It didn't matter at all. Even if she was here, he would be done with her then ask her to leave. He couldn't imagine sleeping with just anyone. He didn't trust any woman enough to actually go to sleep with them beside him. They either wanted to rob him through the night or think he wanted to marry them in the morning.

Women always wanted something for a piece of their pearls. Whether it was money or a wedding ring, no one just gave it away anymore. He didn't want a free ride, but why couldn't it be his decision on what to give them instead of them making the decisions?

He slept soundly. Tomorrow Jacoby would visit with Lawrence in his Detroit office. Lawrence was vice president of a small firm with two offices in Lansing and Detroit. Lawrence took care of the computer side of operations of the business selling software and hardware, while his cousin took care of the other part like the customers and employees. Lawrence wasn't a very personable person. Matter of fact, the only person who could put up with him was Jacoby. Everyone else called him an anal jerk. Lawrence was also going to meet a client in Detroit about restoring a computer's software they had installed a while ago, but the server had been struck and now the software wasn't acting correctly.

Desmond had offered to accompany them, not to meet with the clients, but to find Sheryl a nice gift. While Lawrence and Jacoby were meeting with the client, Desmond would be out shopping.

Chapter 3

The twins weren't asleep when she came in the house. They were quietly playing in their rooms, except when they realized she was in the house, and then demanded she picked them up. Too tired, she knelt down to them and hugged them both.

Patricia came out the kitchen with two food bottles. "I was just getting ready to lay them down for the night."

"I appreciate this Mother." She hugged her mother. "You are a lifesaver."

"Go get ready for tomorrow, dear. I'll finish getting them ready for bed, then you can go tuck them in," her mother ordered.

Phoebe kissed her mother's cheek and took her orders. Going upstairs to her room, she undressed immediately hating the dreaded tights she had to wear everyday to work. They felt awful against her skin, but catching the bus in the winter chill with plain stocking on was horrible to her legs and she hated her skin getting too dry from the cold weather in Detroit.

Looking at the mirror, she first studied her face.

Her mother always thought Phoebe was beautiful with her oval face; deep almond skin with wide expressive dark burnt orange eyes, full moist lips and a pert nose sloped downward. Phoebe always thought her one hundred forty five pound body was too much, but to Patricia it was just the right size. She wasn't too skinny or too fat.

Turning around to study her backside, she noticed all her stretch marks were almost gone. Phoebe had gotten them in her fifth month of pregnancy and drowned her skin in vitamin E since them. More came, but not so harsh. She still had a slight discoloration and silvery lines underneath the small bulge of her stomach. When she stood straight the bulge almost disappeared.

Forget it, she told herself. Her last ten pounds were the hardest to get rid of and if she did lose them, he wouldn't come back – they never came back. They had gotten what they wanted from her and that was it.

That didn't stop her from getting on the floor and doing her fifty sit-ups with her thoughts still on men leaving her.

When she was done with her exercise, she pulled her permed, black, earlobe length hair in a tight ponytail, and then wrapped it for the next day. Washing up quickly, she put on her favorite red pajamas.

Standing five feet four and a half, she figured herself to be good to the eye of any man, but it wasn't what was on the outside that bothered her much - if she didn't think too hard about the extra ten pounds. Phoebe possessed voluptuous breasts (more than a regular handful) and backside. Before pregnancy she had been a nice 34C cup. Now she was a 38D and one size up than her usual ten since high school. Twelve wasn't so bad, she guessed just on the brink of being a plus size. Even though no man was around to encourage her or compliment her, she refused to let her body go to waste. With the DeproVera shot, which she highly enjoyed not because she was sexually active - which hadn't happened in two years - but because it kept her period away, she still had gained weight all over.

It was inside that made her upset. As much as she promised herself she wouldn't allow a man to use her again, she was scared she wouldn't listen to what she wanted and do the same thing over again. Phoebe knew she needed to become stronger and really make a stand when it concerned her mental happiness.

Yes, she would be open to dating, but she wouldn't let a man come into her life ever again, use her like a piece of tissue and then throw her away. She needed to really resolve herself to using the men just as they were using her.

Closing her eyes, she did her affirmations to herself out loud. "I am a good woman and any good man would find me a pleasure and joy to be around. I will never let a man take anything from me without getting something in return before giving it away ever again. I will not let my past or any man take away my joy. Happiness in my life is my number one priority." She said a little pray, asking for a good man would come into her life and for inner strength. Lastly, she prayed for a financial solution to all her debt problems.

When Stephen and Stephanie were sound asleep, she joined her mother, who had fixed a plate for her at the dining room table. The home was just like when she was a little girl. Her mother hadn't changed a thing, and the furnishings in the home were kept in good condition through the years. Phoebe had learned from her mother how to keep a good house and how to raise good children. The twins were highly intelligent and very obedient. She was blessed with good children and thanked the Lord every day for giving her the patience of being a good mother so that her children would be well taken care of.

At the other end of the table, her mother had the bill book open as always trying to keep everything all paid up, even Phoebe's own debts were listed in there. Her father, before his death, had made sure Phoebe's college expenses were paid up and the mortgage on the house her mother lived in was paid off, but not the funeral expenses and other bills like the family's credit cards and the car note.

Phoebe had not known about this stuff until after Daniel had taken off with the money. Guilt surrounded her at not being able to help her mother out, which was why she tried her best to help her mother out by paying the bills with her own check after she paid daycare and paid a little off on her own debt. Usually she just gave the entire check over to her mother, trusting Patricia to make all the decisions about the household finances.

Hopefully in the near future, Phoebe's diligent prayer would be answered soon. Somehow.

"If I sold the apartment building, I could have enough to pay the taxes," Patricia surmised with a mentally tired sigh.

"Mom, you need that to pay for the other ones and your other expenses. You can't and you won't do that," Phoebe protested. "You know that apartment building meant a lot to Daddy."

"Well, five thousand dollars isn't going to drop in our lap."

Phoebe sat back in her chair. "Just give it a little more time, okay?"

"We've only got four months with the taxes, honey, before they take everything away. I really don't want to file for bankruptcy."

"I'll figure something out. Just another month, okay, I'll ask Madeline for a raise or an advance on my check. Maybe I'll look into more child support from Daniel. I'll figure out something, Mom, before you get rid of what is important to you."

"This isn't your business, Phoebe. I should not allow you to sacrifice your life to help me out when you have so much of your own going on."

"I don't mind. Helping you out is beneficial for both of us. You're helping me with the kids, Mom. It's the least I can do.

Patricia put the subject to rest. In truth, her mother did need her help very much and it was a joy for her mother to have the grandchildren around. Tomorrow morning, Phoebe would be driving with Madeline up to Lansing, and then taking the Greyhound back to Detroit.

Phoebe had her own car, but she insisted her mother use it because Patricia picked up the children more. Plus, she didn't mind catching the bus. It saved her a lot of money than paying for parking downtown, which was very expensive.

Her mother always told Phoebe to get out more socially. Patricia would encourage her daughter to find more friends, but Phoebe always avoided this with different excuses. Patricia then started suggesting church social functions or to get in touch with old friends. Phoebe constantly just put it off, devoting all her time to her children, her job, and the home without the least bit of anger or frustration.

Phoebe loved unconditionally, which made her a good target for men who wanted to use her, but with time and her repeated prayers for strength, she knew that she would forgive and forget and maybe try again. One day.

Chapter 4

Lawrence picked Jacoby up bright and early. After breakfast, he took Jacoby to the clientele office also in Downtown Detroit. A young man named, Mr. Bowen greeted them at the door explaining, "The office manager isn't in today, but she's left detailed instructions and I will be able to assist you on any questions you might have."

Mr. Bowen showed them to the room where the server was so Lawrence could get to work. While in there, the young man called his boss, who had taken a trip to Lansing, but wanted to speak with Lawrence as soon as he arrived.

Lawrence had explained to Jacoby, "I was told the office manager hired here recently is a highly intelligent young lady - Every just rave about her constantly. The office manager single-handedly saved the company's largest account."

"You sound as if you were eager to see her today," Jacoby said with a nudge.

"I was pretty impressed with how she was described," Lawrence admitted. "I'll have Mr. Bowen show you around after I get done with this phone call."

Jacoby was pretty impressed by the operation and how smoothly everything ran even without the office manager being there.

"Is she old?" Jacoby asked the office assistant.

The young man gave him a look as if he should know whom the office manager was, but then answered after a brief hesitation. "Oh no. She's young. She just really loves to work and work hard. Our turn around time deadline has been made continually because of her."

Jacoby's pager went off. "Can I use the phone privately, please?" He had left his phone in the limousine.

"Sure," Mr. Bowen said, showing him to an empty office near where Lawrence was working.

Jacoby saw on the door it had the office manager's name on it. "She won't mind me using this office, will she, Mr. Bowen?"

"Oh no," the young man assured him. "Don't worry. Just dial nine to call out." He closed the door to give Jacoby privacy.

He went over to the phone and dialed his lawyer, who had just paged him. Jacoby was presently buying out a small research firm located near Davenport, Ohio. He was also going to put his corporate offices in the downtown area of Detroit. Abraham Blue, his lawyer was setting up a meeting for the buyout and Lawrence was going to arrange the video conference tomorrow afternoon to make the deal final. Instead of Jacoby flying down to Ohio, he could stay in Lawrence's Detroit office and discuss it through fiber optic lines.

As he was put on hold for Abraham, Jacoby noticed the pictures of the two children sitting and smiling the most beautiful smiles. Immediately he could tell they had to be identical twins although of different gender because of what they had on and how they looked. Their eyes were so expressive and wide. He could just imagine the mother with the same beautiful eyes and smile. If he really concentrated he could just imagine him, the happiest man in the world with this beautiful family.

"Jacoby!" Abraham's deep rumbled voice came on the line suddenly. "Sorry to keep you on hold."

"That's quite alright. My thoughts were elsewhere."

Abraham continued talking and Jacoby turned away from the pictures. The mother had to be beautiful to produce the twins. Intelligent, highly self motivated as Lawrence had described her, but would she be great in bed? Even though Jacoby had personal dealings with Madeline, they didn't discuss each other's business when they were together. So that's why Jacoby had never heard of this fantastic office manager. They never discussed anything when they were together.

Jacoby forced himself to concentrate. What the hell did it matter, he wouldn't marry her. With two beautiful kids like that a man would have to be stupid to leave them.

All the good women were taken and she seemed like a good one. She was definitely taken - married or not.

****

Cold, hungry, and tired she walked the eight blocks from the Greyhound Station to her job where she had some crackers in her desk drawer. She didn't realize she shouldn't have refused Madeline's offer for food until after she was well on her way back to Detroit. They had eaten breakfast with some clients, but after that they had been in meetings the rest of the day.

She stuffed the crackers in her mouth until she almost choked, then forced herself to swallow. Stuffing what she had left in her purse, left out the office and tracked back down Jefferson heading to Cadillac Square, still tired, hungry, and cold. Phoebe had called her mother from the bus station to let her know she was back in town and was going back to the office to see what kind of day everyone had without her. Since there was nothing on her desk, she figured Simon would have the list of stuff for her to do tomorrow.

Right now, she felt she didn't want to think about work until she had a good night's sleep. While talking to her mother, Patricia told her the mail had delivered a bill from the tax office again and she had been denied the loan on the apartment due to her credit.

Phoebe, of course told her mother not to worry about it. Things would work out eventually.

Phoebe hoped.

Chapter 5

Was it fate? Hell, it couldn't be said more plainly.

Jacoby had left Desmond at Lawrence's city apartment, The Jeffersonian, which had a lovely view of Downtown, the river, and Canada. Jacoby was too tired to go to any club and drink. He just wanted to get to the hotel to sleep his misery and horniness away.

There she was, standing on the corner this time across from where the limousine had stopped at a light, yet nevertheless the same young respectable woman. He decided the best method would-be to get out and approach her. He told the driver to follow her.

She was coming across the street and he stood on the corner to wait for her. "Excuse me, miss," he said.

Phoebe looked up at him, hesitating before stopping. "Yes?"

He made a note she actually put an "s" at the end of her word, so she was somewhat educated or at least very articulate. "Are you headed home?"

"Of course, are you lost?" She looked up at him with brows up, very warily.

"Somewhat for words. I stay at the Ponchartrain."

She gave him a "what-do-you-want" glare clutching her bag tightly too her.

"I want to know if you'd be..." his voice trailed off. "Look in no way do I think you-" He sighed frustrated and never before felt so confused and flustered before in his life.

He seemed to be a very confused and flustered man. What he wanted was still a mystery to her and she decided to help him out. "So you're not lost?"

"No. I've never done this before."

"Talked to a stranger?" she guessed teasingly.

"Can I give you a lift, I saw you last night and it's so cold. I felt since I saw you again, I should ask."

"Why do you think its fate?" she teased. "You must be from out of town." She smiled the most breathtaking smile, leaving him mesmerized.

Yes, he wanted her, he determined at that moment. "So you'd like a ride?"

"I was born at night, not last night mind you. So I don't want a ride." She started to walk away, but Jacoby smoothly moved in her way.

****

Quickly, he said, "Miss please a moment. I don't want to offend you-"

Phoebe cut him off. "You haven't yet. Do you always speak this way?"

"What way?"

"Beat around the bush. What do you mean offend me?" she asked suspiciously. He was quite an attractive man and his embarrassment only made him cuter.

She watched as he took a roll of bills out his jacket. Hundreds! It looked like thousands of them. "I want you to be with me."

With a look of insanity, yet hope, passed through her eyes as if he were the answer to her prayers. Phoebe stayed dead silent and frozen until she heard footsteps approaching behind her.

Moving toward him, she covered the hand with the money using her own and held it against her chest. "You can't go around flashing that much money around, sir." Two strangers passed by them going on down the street not paying them any mind.

"It's Jay," he introduced himself abruptly.

"Have you lost your mind?" she asked incredulously.

"No. I saw you last night and I want you still."

Why did his words send tingles through her? Compose yourself, Phoebe. "Put that money away before someone comes and shoot us both."

He was not one to give up so easily. Plus, if she weren't the least bit attracted to him, she would have walked away after giving him a sound slap across the face. "How much?" he asked putting a handover hers keeping her close.

"You have no idea who I am," she said exasperated.

"Then tell me your name."

She sighed. "If I tell you will you put the money away?"

"Maybe."

She decided to give him her middle name. "April."

"So how do I propose, April, into just speaking with you?" he questioned.

Phoebe looked at her watch. "Speaking with me?"

"Ten minutes of your time to just interest you in what I would like to offer. One hundred dollars for ten minutes."

He was either crazy or desperate!

"Ten minutes of my time for a hundred dollars?" she questioned in disbelief.

"Ten minutes to interest you." He started to touch her cheek, but inches from her skin, he realized how forward it might be, so he withdrew his hand, but noted that she didn't move away from him almost touching her. "If we're not interested with each other in ten minutes, you'll still have one hundred dollars."

A cold breeze went straight through her. She was highly interested, but it seemed so crazy. "I'll time you," she warned.

He handed her a bill and opened the limousine door. "Not until we're inside."

Warily, Phoebe moved past him and ducked her head in the limousine. "Wait!" She stood up again out the car. "Give me your ID or something."

He pulled out his wallet and passed her an American Express Gold card. "Is that good enough?"

"I guess." She clutched it tightly in her hand, then ducked into the limousine and moving over so he could get in next to her. "Are you hungry?" he asked.

"Ten minutes," she warned again. "And tell your driver to head to Cadillac Square."

He instructed the driver immediately, and then put the divider up for privacy. She had her arms wrapped around her waist practically sitting across from him for distance.

With a hesitant look on his face, he seemed to not know how to really begin, but started off saying, "I guess I should get to the point." He answered her previous question. "Yes, I could have had any woman on the strip, but they were not you."

"Flattery will get you nowhere. What makes you think I'm not diseased or something?"

"Are you?"

"No!" she said insulted he would think so, but she had asked for it so she shouldn't be so touchy. Plus by taking his money, it had initiated the fact that it was possible for her to be bought for with a price.

"Neither am I, so we've gotten that out the way. I'm willing to take any precautions necessary to ensure safety. I just want to know how much."

"I can't believe you are not crazy. You must be. You can't go around and ask ordinary women this."

"You are certainly not ordinary, April and I know this which is why I'm willing to make it worth your precious time." A very serious look came on his face and Phoebe found herself short of breath with his intense gaze. He continued yet this time his words were slow, with a little bit more clarity and there was a strange huskiness in his voice. "I want you, April."

He was even better looking in the light, she thought. "And how much is worth my time, Jay?"

"One thousand."

"Plus the hundred?"

"Of course." He could see the dancing of her eyes. She needed or wanted the money badly, but was desperately fighting with her conscious. "Just think of this as a business deal."

"Business?"

"Certainly." He sat back. "I have something you want."

"No. You have something my mother needs, but she wouldn't dare take you up on your offer. I did promise to help her even though I'm well off with my job." She tried her best to sound as if it didn't matter.

"So if your mother didn't need the money, you wouldn't consider me at all."

"Of course not," she said very insulted. "I wouldn't sell myself, that would be unmoral."

"Yet now you're in the situation which could benefit us both."

"True."

"Then how about it?"

She looked at her watch. Two minutes left as the limousine pulled near the bus depot.

He noticed the ring on her left hand. "Married?" There was disappointment in his voice.

"No, divorced," she answered.

"Even better. Two hundred more."

"I don't-"

He cut her off, "Three hundred."

"Stop that," she insisted.

"Then accept," he declared taking her hands into his. "I promise to be gentle and so good to you. Just one night. No one will know." He could see the fight draining from her. "Let me give you this," he whispered in her ear.

She shuddered and he watched triumphantly as the effects of his words broke down her barrier. "I'll do it, but under one condition." Her throat went dry and she forced herself to swallow.

He frowned wondering what she could possibly want.

"No strings attached. This is strictly business nothing more."

"Of course." Jacoby smiled with relief and pulled out the amount agreed upon. "Can I take you to my hotel?"

"After I make a phone call."

He handed her his cell phone and turned it on for her.

She shook her head pushing away the phone. "I'd much rather use a pay phone." The less he could contact her the better off she was. Her mother really needed this money, but she refused to let this be known to anyone how she had gotten it.

"And how do I know you won't run off with my money?"

She handed him the money he had initially given her. "You can give it to me upon my return. I'll be right back," she promised.

He watched her get out and walked to the pay phone across the street. Phoebe called her mother. "I met an old friend from high school at the bus stop. I'm going to have dinner with him." She rehearsed this line ten times before calling.

"That's wonderful."

"I'll be home soon."

"No, take your time. I insist." Patricia sounded too happy. "I won't wait up for you and don't you dare worry about the children."

Her mother knew her too well, but despite the fact she trusted her mother wholeheartedly, she would still worry. "Thanks Momma." Phoebe hated lying to Patricia, but she needed to do this.

After hanging up with her mother, she called her own personal voicemail and read off the American Express number off the card along with the expression date. She wanted to make sure if anything happened to her, someone would be able to trace it to him. Hopefully, it wouldn't come to that, and she prayed that this would be the easiest thirteen hundred she would ever make.

Turning back to the limousine, she saw the driver outside the back doors waiting on her. Getting back in the limousine, she sat right next to him.

Her windblown, French rolled hair made her look so untamed and sexually arousing and those expressive eyes, which boldly met his in curiosity, turned Jacoby on immensely. Having her here in the flesh after last night's fantasy was very thrilling to him. He wanted to touch her all over, feel her move underneath him and produce that groan he had too vividly imagined her making.

His arm moved behind her head and he leaned slightly into her. "I thought we would seal our bargain with a kiss."

She gently pressed her fingers against his lips to stop him. "Before we do that, Jay, you should tell me what kind of woman you are expecting. No one pays this much for anything without some expectations."

He smiled liking her strategy. "Responsive, slightly aggressive - not dominant, eager to excite, very willing to learn and open to suggestions."

"You're describing your perfect lover."

"Oh yes." His breath was increasing.

"Keep going," she urged him. The limousine was becoming hot with her thick coat on. So she unzipped it slightly.

He immediately drew his eyes towards the fullness of her breasts. "Don't like sloppy kisses."

"Me neither," she agreed.

"I like them long though and very thorough if you know what I mean."

She saw how his eyes moved slowly up her neck to her lips. Her tongue snaked out slowly and unconsciously with the tip to wet the dryness.

"I like to touch and I love foreplay of any kind," he continued.

She smiled, blushing knowing fully well what that meant. "But of course with the proper protection," she reminded him.

He leaned even closer. "When can we seal our bargain?"

She looked deep in his dark brown eyes then down at his sensuous lips. Lord, he'd probably make her forget everything. Control Phoebe, she warned herself. Leaning closely, she whispered, "Soon."

'Was she playing games or being a tease?' he wondered.

They pulled up at the hotel and the driver helped her out. She graciously thanked him and followed her "date" into the hotel.

As they walked to the front desk to retrieve any of his messages, she said, "Can I make a request?"

That distrustful look came to his face again, but he still nodded. . She couldn't run from him, which she hadn't asked for yet.

"I'm slightly hungry. Something light will do for now."

He smiled with relief, "Soup?"

Phoebe nodded. "Sure, but no tomato. I'll wait here." She sat down in a chair near the desk to give him a little privacy for his messages.

After requesting his messages, he ordered for the kitchen to bring up room service. Every once in a while he kept looking back at her as if she would sneak away. Phoebe had to wonder why he didn't trust her or was it that he didn't trust any woman. Maybe he had gotten hurt by a number of many women too many times. He was a strange, yet handsome man.

She put any machinations of anything longer than tonight of this man out her mind and prayed she would not regret her decision.

"They'll send it up right away," he said coming back.

Possessively he took her hand in his and led her to the elevator. Her gripped tightened a little just as he pushed the button for the eleventh floor as if she were bracing for something.

When the doors closed, she opened her coat all the way and then turned to him. "I'm ready to seal the bargain," she said in a most seductive tone, making his manhood twitch with excitement.

Moving awkwardly to her five foot four, yet nicely thick in all the right places frame, he had to lean down from his six two height to meet her lips, but hell if it wasn't worth it. Touching her lips with his seemed like a relief.

Her body instantly leaned against his and her arms moved around his neck as their lips joined for the first time. Her lips parted inviting his tongue in and he enjoyed the oral sweetness. His large arms encircled her tightly deepening the kiss.

Suddenly, she was nudging him away and reluctantly he let her stop the kiss.

"This is our floor," she reminded him.

Jacoby couldn't believe how alert she could seem while he just seemed to want to lose it all. Her look of amusement to his arousal exasperated him, as he hurriedly led her off the elevator down the hall to his room. He had the card key in hand before reaching the door.

Soon as they were inside, he drew her into his arms again and proceeded to resume their initial kiss. She could feel his bulge press against her belly and now she too became eager. This man was pure intoxication and it was taking every effort not to be overwhelmed by him, but damn if he wasn't turning her on completely. Pulling off her coat, letting it drop to the floor, she hastily worked on the front of his pants.

The whole act of lovemaking seemed to enliven her all at once. Especially since she hadn't had it in so long and Daniel had taught her so much. No longer was she the shy innocent girl of twenty-four. She was twenty-seven and fully capable of pleasing a man in any way shape or form.

This man in particular, whom she found highly attractive and erotically arousing.

No woman had over undressed him yet before he knew it, she had his pants down and quick as lightening with the sweetest caress of her fingers against the tip of his manhood, she broke off the kiss again dropped to her knees and enveloped him deep into her oral cavity. He groaned rolling his eyes up into his head enthralled by her warm deliciously wet mouth against his member. He was amazed at how deep she could take him and just watching her made him want to come.

'Not yet,' he told himself grabbing her shoulders, pulling her up and kissing her even more passionately.

"Lord girl, you're going to kill me," he murmured through his kisses.

She giggled, "I'm sorry. I couldn't help myself."

"Don't ever be sorry," he growled, tackling her neck with his lips.

She whimpered in pleasure yet drew him close, loving his mouth on her body. There was a knock at the door. She gasped, but he didn't care.

Jacoby felt could eat later. He could eat her and be full.

"Jay," she warned after the second knock. "Our food."

"Eat later," he murmured, capturing her lips again. He couldn't get over how good it felt to kiss her. She was so responsive and willing.

Another round of knocks came and then someone on the outside said, "Mr. Knight."

Jacoby huffed angrily and moved away.

She laughed at his frustration. "I'll take a shower."

"No!" he said irritated.

Standing up from the bed with him, Phoebe kissed his cheek. "Yes, Mr. Knight," she said, using the name she heard from the outside of the door assuming him to be that man.

Hearing his name on her lips made his manhood twitched.

"When you're done with room service, you can join me," she told him seductively.

The thought of her all wet turned him on immensely. "Hurry up. I'll be in there in a second," he promised, turning on a light switch so she could see. They'd been in the dark the whole time.

She gasped seeing the actual size of him, then closed the bathroom door and leaning against it to compose herself.

Jacoby ran a nervous hand through his short cut fade after fixing his clothes somewhat. Why did he feel this night was going to be special? She was not the first. So what if she aroused him more than any woman had ever and had a mouth he could kiss forever. She was erotically fantastic and he had yet to touch her inside.

Calmly he opened the door to the servant who pushed in the cart of soup and fruit, with some champagne. After tipping him, Jacoby quickly undressed. The shower had been going for five minutes already and he could just imagine herself all soaped up.

He carefully laid his jacket over the chair with a slight tilt so he would know if anyone touched it and specially put his wallet and other pocket necessities on the table next to the bed very carefully also.

Quietly, he entered the bathroom just in time to see her washing the soap off of her. He stepped inside right behind her startling her.

With no words needed she moved to him and pressed her body against his. Their lips joined instantly and she moaned that special moan as their tongues met and his hands moved down between her legs to enter her softness. It was warm and wet just like he imagined his other hand cupped her full breast and then his lips moved down to suckle the large dark nipple. She gasped his name as he quickly moved her around until her back pressed up against the wall and the water bounced over his back.

Phoebe closed her eyes drowning in electric pleasure running through every vein in her body. He switched breast repeatedly, each time bringing cries of pleasure from her.

She couldn't believe how wanton he made her feel and she didn't care. Right now, she was on the brink to having an all time unbelievable orgasm. It had definitely been too long since a man had touched her like this. His mouth left her breast and began a decent to her belly. He briefly paused nibbling at her navel and letting the tip of his tongue trail down to her soft thatch of hair.

Her body froze suddenly. She realized his destination as soon as he started to part her legs wider. She dropped down to her knees, not caring if her hair got wet, to stop his venture. "Jay, we do have an understanding don't we?"

He frowned a little confused by the serious look in her eyes. "Of course."

"With caution," she reminded him.

Raising a brow of offense, he questioned dubiously, "You're going to deny me tasting you?"

That sounded so erotic to her ears and sent warm chills down her spine. Gathering her sanity, she said, "You don't have to." Standing up knowing that answer should have sufficed, she also added, "You're just doing it because you feel guilty because I did you. Men shouldn't feel that way."

Jacoby wanted to get mad, but then couldn't because she looked so sure about it. He had never met a woman who actually thought the idea of a man giving her pleasure orally was strictly prohibited. "Who put that thought in your head?" he asked out loud standing up and putting both hands on her shoulder to stop her from moving or looking away. His tone of voice was brusque and harsh.

She stiffened in defense. "What thought?"

"That a man using his mouth on you was merely an act of guilt."

"I don't know what you mean," she denied as she gently pushed his hands away and got out the shower trying to avoid his intense gaze.

He could tell that was a lie as he too got up and turned off the water. Jacoby didn't want to call her a liar, yet he did want the truth. Just not right now, he was positive they had more time to find out about each other.

She got a towel, but instead of drying herself off first she dried him off. He felt like a king as she took her time. It felt so good, but he knew she was purposely trying to make him forget their conversation. It almost worked.

The more she denied him though, the more Jacoby wanted to do it. It was the most confusing predicament he had ever been in. He wasn't use to being told no and now that he had, he didn't like it one bit. "What if I told you I wanted to taste you?" he insisted.

"I would deny you." She pulled gently on his arms for him to step closer to her.

He took the towel from her and began to dry her off.

"You don't have to," she said as he nudged her to turn. Although, she did love the feel of the rough towel against her skin, she was just not use to this.

Reaching around her body, he gently cupped a full size breast and used his thumb to rub the peak to life. She leaned against him reaching behind him caressing both of his firm buttocks.

While planting soft kisses on her neck, he turned her around. "You won't change your mind, will you?"

"No." She knew exactly what he was referring to. "And no amount of seducing will change my mind, sir. You do remember our deal. All precautions will be taken."

"But you took me," he debated.

"But you did not come in my mouth," she pointed out.

"Then I could have." He wrapped the towel around her body, tucking it slightly under her arms.

"Only if I had swallowed."

He enjoyed her bluntness. She didn't have that silly high-pitched giggle and blush all the time like other women her age, which was why he had always chosen to deal with older women. "Would you have swallowed if I had come?" he asked.

"No. I don't know you that well."

At first he frowned real hard because he thought that was just idiotic, then he saw the teasing light in her eyes and hooted with laughter. She was quite a fascinating woman.

Pulling him out the bathroom, she led him to the large king size bed, but paused as she looked around confused and surprised. The only light in the room came from the two candles on the wheeled table of food that had two chairs pulled up to it. There were two silk robes lying across the bed with the hotel's emblems on the right breast.

Even though they had spent a great deal of time in the shower, the food was still hot. He couldn't believe how taken aback she was at the setting. This act of kindness seemed to break down her barrier and he knew he could probably drop to his knees and taste her until the sun came up if it was his choosing, but he would respect her modesty about the subject although he didn't understand her logic about it.

"You did this?" she asked turning to him.

"I arranged-" He didn't get any farther. She flung her arms around his neck and kissed him so hard he though she would inhale him.

"Make love to me," she ordered breathing hard.

"Aren't you hungry-"

She pressed a finger against his lips to stop his thought. "Make love to me, Mr. Knight, right now." She let the towel fall to her feet and pressed her nakedness against his own feeling his arousal against her stomach.

Jacoby was never one to refuse a request like that. He couldn't stop himself from touching every inch of her and in turn, her hands were just as veracious. Somehow they made it to the bed, with him sweeping her down under him and moving between her willingly open soft supple thighs. She was like a hellcat and he could smell her arousal so vividly.

"Protection," she reminded him in a sweet whisper in his ear.

He nodded reaching for his wallet by the bed and pulling out a condom.

She snatched it from him, tore open the package and quickly put it on. "Now!" she urged spreading her legs wide, and then wrapping them around his waist.

All he had to do was guide himself in. Yet she took him by surprise by Her body arching her body hard and he found himself driving deep into her. Jacoby grunted hard from her tightness and she gasped in pain and pleasure feeling how thick he was completely inside of her.

"Would you like to continue on your own?" he managed to tease.

"Will I have to?" she asked, gripping her muscles even more tightly against him.

It was his turn to gasp at the control she had. Lord, she was going to kill him. He began to move inside of her slowly. Their rhythm seemed awkward at first since, he wasn't use to a woman being so responsive, but soon he was driving into her with such skill it was as if...

He didn't want to realize it himself, but they were very compatible when it came to sex. Even with the rubber on it was evident she could affect him. He usually had to go a long time before he came when he wore protection, but Jacoby now found himself on the brink of an incredible peak.

Phoebe was so enraptured by his touch, his movements, his wonderful rod; she paid little attention to her body's control. She could actually feel him getting ready to come, but she wasn't ready for it to end. She had come several times already, but she wanted this last one to last for at least one more for her.

Knowing he was distracted by the europium of moving inside her, she released her legs and with the quickness laid the left down and bumped the right against his hip hard making him lose his balance as she rolled on top of him.

She didn't miss a stroke as she began to immediately move him deep inside of her.

This was not happening, Jacoby told himself closing his eyes. It was a dream come true! He gripped her nipples tight and held on as she rode him to orgasm just the way he like it.

She threw her head back moaning with pleasure as the vibrations from shaft titillated her insides, making her final orgasm burst forth like a geyser. Even her fingers trembled as she held on his shoulders enjoying the ride. Soon the powerful wave began to subside to tiny shudders as her muscles spasms died down.

Phoebe collapsed against him enjoying the fullness inside of her. He was breathing just as hard and even though the room was a mild temperature, they were sweating heavily. Carefully, she masked her disorientation by their experience. She had never orgasmed past once with Daniel, who had been a great lover. Daniel was the one who had taught her how to really orgasm with a man, but he also had broken her heart. She didn't want to get her heart into anymore messes. Sex and love were two different things she forced herself to believe because she couldn't stand to get her heart involved anymore with any man.

Slowly, Phoebe moved off of him. He was still sensitive, which was why he threw his head back in pleasure. Gently she took off the condom and put it in the waste can beside the bed after she wrapped it in some Kleenex located on the bedside table.

Putting his hands behind his head, he half watched her enjoying her special attention, as she went to the bathroom. He could see her with the wall mirror on the bathroom door as she washed herself up thoroughly. She washed out the cloth again, and then came out the bathroom to the bed with the cloth in hand.

Kneeling between his legs, she washed his groin area with the utmost care. Jacoby laid in amazement as she finished cleaning then returned the cloth back to the bathroom and laid down next to him waiting for his response.

He had a gleam of pleasure in his eyes. Usually Daniel rolled over and went to sleep after making intense love or watched television while she got him a beer.

Pushing the covers away from himself, he got up and circled the bed. She visually inhaled him, taking in the broad shoulders, the tightly defined muscled chest, a rippled washboard stomach, powerful arms and legs, and a great butt. He could do commercials for the Bowflex machine with his body, but she had a feeling he was much more than a model. He carried himself too arrogantly so he must be an executive of some type. Truly a wonderful specimen of male.

Daniel wouldn't come close to him with his beer belly, hairy flabby chest, and lanky thighs.

"Are you always this bold?" he asked, sitting on the edge of her side on the bed. He placed one hand on each side of her thighs.

"Bold?" She raised a dark brow letting the covers drop to her waist. "Do you really think I am?

He chuckled deeply and sensuously sending warm shivers through her nerves. "I just wanted to know if this was all an act?"

Damn his mind couldn't be happy with his body. Yes, this man was a true thinker. Even as she could tell his body was completely sated, looking deep in his eyes clearly told her, his mind was far from it. "If it is, are you getting your money's worth?"

"Definitely." He pulled the tray closer to the bed and plucked a grape from the bowl of fruit with fresh juice around it. She opened her lips to allow him to put it in. It was still cold to her amazement and so sweet to taste.

He handed her the cream beef soup and watched her eat. "How do you know how to please a man so well with your mouth?"

"I pleased you?" she asked, smiling as if he had bestowed a million dollars on her.

"Indeed. Which is why I'm giving you a chance to eat so you may have enough strength to do it again?" At the thought of her just doing it made him rise a little to life.

"Again?" She licked her lips. "That would mean more money," she teased, not thinking he would take her seriously.

"No doubt." He was dead serious. Jacoby knew he would want her again and had every intentions of compensating her.

Phoebe couldn't believe he took her seriously and she really didn't want to talk about money right now. Agreeing to this she hadn't realized he would actually be such a good lover, but he was. Handing him the bowl almost empty, she licked her lips and decided to answer his earlier question. "Daniel, my ex-husband kind of taught me. I read books and sort of studied lovemaking to make him stay. He would stay for a while and then another woman would come along. When my father died and I got the money, he married me only to get his hands on it, but as naive as I was I thought he loved me. Now he's gone with my money, forever, and left me with the babies."

"Babies?"

"Just two."

"That was the reason for the phone call?"

She nodded. "My mother would have gotten worried to death."

"I understand. So Daniel's never went down on you?"

She rolled her eyes to let him know she was getting tired of him trying to talk with her about the subject. "Of course not. He said men only did that because they felt guilty about women doing it to them and enjoying it. He didn't feel guilty for anything."

He looked quite offended. "It's not guilt at all. It brings me pleasure just as it does you when you do it to me."

"We won't discuss this," she said firmly. "I've told you no. We are taking precautions. Plus that's only something people in love do. Daniel just probably never loved me, I guess." She shrugged offhandedly as if this didn't bother her and then chortling to herself, she said out loud, "Stupidly it took me two babies and a divorce to see this."

Why he wanted to know all about her was beyond even him? Jacoby pushed this thought away reminding himself this was a one-night stand and he would probably never see her again after tonight. Yet, deep inside he wanted to.

Taking a juicy piece of cantaloupe he slid it into her mouth making the juices run down her chin. He pushed away her hands that tried to stop it; instead he used the tip of his tongue to capture the sweet drip along her chin and following the path back to her mouth.

She chuckled. "I never thought eating fruit could be so erotic."

"You should see what I can do with watermelon and whip cream."

She laughed now, but was immediately stopped as his mouth tackled a sensitive spot in her neck.

Soon they were pushing the covers away and he was feeling every inch of her with his hands. Twice he tried to move his face between her legs and she diverted him with either a kiss to his own nipples and a bold fondle to his groin.

It drove him insane to know she had the upper hand at all times, yet still he made love as if there were no tomorrow.

Chapter 6

Several hours later, Jacoby suddenly stirred and realized she was missing from the bed. Looking around the room he saw she was nowhere to be found. Cursing under his breath he looked at the time and saw it was about four in the morning.

"I'm sorry, did I wake you?" she asked coming out the bathroom fully dress.

"You're leaving?" he asked surprised, sitting up and turning up the lamp that had been dimmed previously.

She even had on her coat and her hair looked untouched. "It's late. I need to be home."

Jacoby was gripped with a sense of urgency not to let her leave, but he couldn't force her to stay. "What if I wanted to see you again?"

"When you came back in town?" she asked. "Maybe."

He reached for his wallet noting it was in the exact same place he had tossed it in when he had gotten the second condom out. This ruled out any possibility that she was not a thief.

Phoebe watched as he took out his business card and three thousand dollars, and then handed the bills to her. Never in her life had she ever seen this amount of money in her life and as desperately as she needed all of it, she had to be honest and reasonable about this. She counted out fourteen hundred and placed the rest back on the table on the table. "Our deal was for fourteen hundred."

"But we went twice," he disputed with a wicked wink.

Fighting the urge to smile at just the thought of that delightful experience, she said as seriously as possible. "I'm already feeling awkward taking this money and I really was teasing when I asked for more money, Mr. Knight. Plus you gave over the amount if I was really expecting that money."

"Can't I tip?"

She sighed tiredly. "Can I be unbusinesslike for a second?" Her left eye twitched in slight exasperation.

He nodded eager to hear what she had to say.

"You've given me a most pleasurable night. I've never been made love to so completely in my life and I thought no man would be able to surpass Daniel, but you have shown me it isn't only the man to make lovemaking fulfilling it is also me and that I don't have to worry about lovemaking but other things in order to keep a man, when I thought all this time that was why Daniel left me." She placed four hundred dollars on the table. "I don't want any extra from you because I feel I would be ripping you off. I just want to go with what you originally offered."

"But-"

She put a hand up to stop him from speaking. "I won't argue about this Mr. Knight." Checking her watch she gasped. "I really must go. If I stay another minute I will be in a world of trouble."

"Your number. Can I have it?"

She hesitated a bit giving him a very cautious look, and then went to the desk to write down ten digits on the hotel stationary. Coming back to the bed she handed it to him, but when he took it he also took her wrist and pulled her down in the bed in one swept. Her lips were captured in the fall by his own in mad passionate kiss that left her completely breathless and the hardness pressing at her side clearly indicated if needed he could definitely go for another round. The wicked look in his eyes clearly told her if she was interested he could take her up on any offer.

Blushing like a schoolgirl liking the effect she had on him, she reluctantly pushed away standing up. "Good night, Mr. Knight."

"Don't you mean good morning?"

"All the more reason to get out of here." She hurried out the door.

Jacoby cursed under his breath several times before burying his face in his pillow. Why did he have this sinking feeling he would never see her again? Why did he feel he should have done more to make contact with her? Dinner? They could have had dinner or lunch, hell he should have insisted she stay for breakfast. It didn't matter to him that he would have to pay for her time. He would have stayed in town for another day if it meant-

What the hell is wrong with you? Jacoby asked himself suddenly. Did he really think she wanted even anything to do with him? It had taken too much of his energy to get her to agree to spending a little time with him. She was too much work and on top of this, she didn't want anything more to do with him. The pile of money on the table clearly told him that.

Furthermore, he knew absolutely nothing about this woman. Everything she had done could have been just for show. She just knew his likes and had acted upon his wildest dreams, which he had told her in advanced.

As much as he tried to convince himself that he did not want another thing to do with her, Jacoby couldn't. Whether it was a show or not, he found himself hooked to her and wanting more.

Chapter 7

Just as Phoebe knew, her mother was sitting in the chair by the door curled up in a deep sleep. Phoebe figured Patricia had tried to stay up as long as possible and if awake when Phoebe came home, would have rushed upstairs and pretended not to know what time Phoebe came in because Patricia still had on her shoes and her bed robe was closed securely about her.

Quietly closing the door, Phoebe snuck past her mother and went upstairs to her room. As soon as she took off her coat, she went into the twin's room to check on them. They were sound asleep. Her daughter was snuggled up close to her son, who snored quite loudly for a two year old.

Just as she was going back in her room, her mother called her name from the bottom of the stairs. "Is that you?"

"Yes, Momma," she said quietly.

Patricia came up the stairs and gave her a worried yet relieved hug. "Are you okay? Is everything okay at work?"

"Yes, Momma." She yawned and stretched in an attempt to get out the hug.

Patricia looked her over and frowned worriedly. "Are you sure you are okay, Phoebe?"

Phoebe huffed rolling her eyes heavenwards. "Yes, Momma. I'm fine." She went in her room with Patricia following her. "Why do you keep asking me that?"

"Because you have your shirt on backwards."

Phoebe looked down to see her tag sticking out the front of her shirt and blushed profusely. Covering her eyes with her hands in embarrassment, she plopped on her bed. "Oh Momma, I can't believe what I did. I didn't want you to know. I'm so ashamed of myself."

"Why? Just because you had sex? What's to be ashamed of?" Patricia looked as if Phoebe had won a million dollars.

"If you only knew what I did tonight, Mother, you wouldn't be so happy."

"I only care that you look like a light bulb. I never seen you glow like this before in my life."

An unladylike snort came from Phoebe as she fell back on the bed and closed her eyes. "You really don't understand, do you?"

"I know that even if you didn't come in here with your shirt on backwards, I still could have known some handsome man ravished you." Patricia knelt down and began to take off Phoebe's shoes. "He was handsome, wasn't he?"

"Too handsome, Mother."

"Did you have fun?"

"Yes, too much fun. I almost didn't want to leave."

"You could have stayed you know. I would have understood." Patricia sat beside Phoebe on the bed. Sitting up, Phoebe leaned her head on her mother's shoulder comforting in the feel of having her mother there. She really needed a friend right now and Patricia was definitely being that for her.

Yet Phoebe was terrified that if her mother knew she had taken the money for sex, things would change. She wanted very much to be honest with her mother, and she wanted very much to just get that money out her pocket and place it in her mother's hands, but she didn't want to see the shameful look in Patricia's eyes when the truth was known. So Phoebe bit down on her lip hard and waited for Patricia to finish interrogating her about the night hoping it would be over soon.

"So give me all the juicy details," Patricia said. "Who is he? Where did you meet him?"

"Well we didn't get into all that he did, but I suspect he does some business thing by the way he dresses and carries himself." Another yawn escaped her, this one on purpose, longer than all the others

"Alright, you can go to sleep. You don't have to tell me twice." Patricia got up not at all upset. "I'll question you tomorrow about everything." Kissing her daughter on the forehead, she left out the room.

Phoebe didn't even bother taking off her clothes. As soon as her head hit the pillow, she was out like a light.

****

"You look like shit," Simon said as he poked his head in her office.

"You do too and I bet you got some rest last night," Phoebe snapped.

He crinkled his nose and brought himself all the way in the office. "That is not my bright and cherry Phoebe. Did you leave your spirit at home?"

"I lost that spirit last night on my exhaustive trip home from Lansing. I really can't wait for this weekend."

"It's only Wednesday."

"And I feel like a train wreck," she snipped.

"You look like a train wreck," he agreed.

She couldn't help but laugh knowing the bags under her eyes must be huge. "Don't you have work to do?"

"Oh now you want to act like the boss, huh?" he teased then pulled out some papers from behind his back. "Madeline faxed these over then called me and let me know to expect the computer engineer to come back today to install some new software. The computers haven't had one glitch since he fixed them yesterday, and now he said he just needed to install a program he wrote to make sure what happened before doesn't happen again. Won't that be great?"

"Yes. Let me know when he gets here. I have to sign his bill and personally fax a copy of it immediately over to billing so he can get paid as soon as possible. Madeline told me to make sure I took care of his billing because he was very important to her."

Simone gave her a crooked salute and then left out. Putting on her reading glasses, she looked over the papers he had handed her. More work to do by the end of the day, she told herself and put it in her end of the day basket. Her desk was piled high with reports and other information she needed to get done by the end of the day or the month or the year. Either way it was a lot of work and it seemed the piles never got smaller. The last office manager had not turned in a lot of the reports needed by the head office in Lansing and the task was put on her shoulders to get everything updated. She was working overtime and not getting paid for it, yet her job pride from the completion of getting things done.

Yes, Madeline was working her like a horse, but Phoebe figured she would be able to at least say got this office running like a well oiled machine.

Phoebe looked up from all her work about one that afternoon to take a mental break.

Coming into work had been a bad idea because since she awoke this morning at eight and came in an hour late for work, she found that if she didn't think about work, she was thinking about him. Cursing to herself, she looked back down at the black and white print in front of her and forced her concentration back on work.

Chapter 8

Going up in the elevator with Desmond and Lawrence, Jacoby's mind was a thousand miles from them.

"That's a first," Desmond noted quietly to Lawrence.

"What?" Lawrence questioned.

"If I didn't know any better, I would say Jacoby was daydreaming."

"You don't know any better," Jacoby snapped, hearing the amusement in Desmond voice and the chortle from Lawrence.

Lawrence said, "Yes, he was Desmond. He's been like that all morning since I had to drag his ass out of bed."

"I would have much rather stayed in my bed," Jacoby growled.

"Serves you right staying up all night with that pretty little thing I saw leaving at five this morning," Desmond said.

Lawrence chortled more with a surprised look on his face. "I see why you didn't want to join us last night. Was this planned, Jake?"

"That's none of your damn business," Jacoby snapped. "Fuck off."

Desmond and Lawrence looked at each other and laughed not at all taking Jacoby's attitude serious. Desmond said, "So was she good as she looked?"

Jacoby heisted for a moment, then smiled more to himself. "Better."

All three of them burst out in a round of laughter. It was always good to discuss these things out loud and they enjoyed listening to each other's exploits with women, but for some reason, Jacoby wanted to keep this more to himself, but at the same time shout from the ceiling about the pleasurable night he had experienced.

"So please relish us with details," Lawrence encouraged as they stepped off the elevator, heading to the office of his client he had visited yesterday.

"I'm not going to kiss and tell," Jacoby insisted. "I think I want to keep this to myself."

Desmond frowned. "You've never wanted to keep it to yourself before. You're usually criticizing the woman from head to toe negatively."

"Well this time was different," Jacoby admitted shrugging. "I just wish-" He stopped himself.

Lawrence stopped walking and turned to Jacoby studying his friend's features for a moment. Desmond looked curiously on as Lawrence and Jacoby's eyes met as if they were sending each other telepathic signals.

"Where the hell did you meet this chit?" Lawrence finally demanded to know after the pause of silence between them.

Jacoby bit his lip as if to keep the information to himself, then he finally admitted, "You remember the respectable woman on the corner?"

"You saw her again?"

"Yes. It was like fate." He frowned not understanding it himself.

Desmond suddenly grasped what was going on. "That woman accepted money for sex?" His voice was a little bit too loud and people walking by looked over at the three handsome men who drew enough attention on their own without Desmond being so loud over what they were talking about.

"Tell the whole fucking world, Dez. Can't you whisper, ass?" He looked back at Jacoby narrowing his eyes. Lawrence interest was clearly peaked. "She was very beautiful now that I think about it. I was tempted to offer her myself, but I didn't think you were serious."

Incredulously, Jacoby admitted, "I was shocked that she took the offer. I mean when I first approached her with the offer in mind, I thought for sure she was going to slap me in the face, but this serene look came over her face and she accepted as if I was answering her pray."

"And once you got her to the hotel room?"

Jacoby became excited in his speech as he said, "She was a dream come true, man. I have never met a woman so uninhibited about herself. She was so incredible in bed-"

"Alright that's enough bragging," Lawrence snipped. Clearly he was jealous for Jacoby for not taking advantage of the situation. Both of them knew, Lawrence had seen the woman first and had drawn Jacoby's attention to her.

It wasn't like Lawrence to take a woman so personally, but Jacoby had never expressed interest in a woman like he had this one, so Lawrence knew something was pretty special about her.

"Don't you have an appointment with this client?" Desmond questioned Lawrence.

"Nothing set in stone, but let's hurry up and get this over with so we can get back to Lansing."

Jacoby could tell Lawrence was not in a good mood anymore, but for the life of him he couldn't imagine Lawrence actually being jealous that Jacoby had taken advantage of the opportunity that had just practically fell in his lap last night.

As they proceeded to the office, Lawrence decided to interrogate Jacoby trying to sound as nonchalant as possible, but Jacoby knowing Lawrence all too well could tell there was some hidden motive behind his questioning. "Did you get her digits?"

"Yes and I told her when I was in town again I would look her up."

"So she lives in the city? What's her name?"

"April."

"April what?"

Jacoby became defensive and annoyed. "I didn't ask for the last name."

Desmond intervened. "You sleep with an incredible woman and you don't even know her whole name."

"It's nothing new, Desmond," Jacoby snapped. "Just because you're getting married doesn't mean you have to act so high and mighty. Before you met your woman, you were sleeping around like a wild mutt."

Desmond snickered. "Then maybe you both need to find a woman like mine to understand how sick all of this sounds."

Lawrence and Jacoby gave Desmond a lethal glare, clearly telling him to keep his opinions of the lifestyle they chose to himself, but of course Desmond wouldn't take either one of them seriously.

"Jez, you guys, why don't you lighten up and get some rest. You're both acting as if someone rained on your parades," Desmond encouraged them.

At this time, they arrived at the office and that skinny guy with the pretty eyes greeted them again.

"Glad to see you finally came, Mr. Ripley," Mr. Bowen said. His voice was full of sarcasm, but that didn't get Lawrence out of his moody disposition.

"I just came to get this in the system then I'm out of this city with the quickness, Mr. Bowen," Lawrence gruffly.

Mr. Bowen led them back to the server and left them to do what they had to do. Desmond, who had assisted Lawrence in writing the program assisted in the upgrade and the testing. The whole process took about ten minutes. Upon completion, they were all eager to leave. Jacoby hadn't said one word to anyone and still looked a bit peeve at Lawrence. Lawrence was still moody about the latter conversation they had discussed out in the hallway before entering the offices. Desmond seemed amused about the entire situation.

Jacoby could have stayed in the limousine while they did all this and waited until they were done with the upgrade, but he knew the office manager would be up in the office today and he really wanted to met and speak with the mother of those two beautiful children. Plus, all the nice things Lawrence had said about the office manager had piqued his interest and she sounded like a very interesting person. Lawrence had never met her personally himself, but had spoken to her over the phone and found her to be a very vivacious professional, hardworking person. She had single-handedly whipped the failing transcript division into shape and was working like a horse to keep it on track. Jacoby found women like her to his liking and even though she did have extra baggage, he still wouldn't mind trying to see if he could get to know her better since he would be moving here.

She seemed like a nice woman he could spend some dinners with her, while he was in town while he spent his nights with April. The thought of last night flowed into his mind and he became semi-hard thinking of her. Closing his eyes and concentrating, he tried not to think about it, but found that difficult to do.

He should have asked for the office assistant to take him in to meet the manager, but he didn't want to seem too overzealous to meet her when he hoped that she would at least make an appearance with Lawrence and Desmond there. Plus, he had always known he had a formidable presence and being alone with her might intimidate her.

Once Lawrence and Desmond were done, they found Mr. Bowen in the front of the office and Lawrence handed his bill to the office assistant. Mr. Bowen held up his hands as if he were at gunpoint.

"My manager would kill me if I took those from you, sir."

"Then who the hell should I give them too?" Lawrence snapped.

Desmond intervened again. "Calm down, Law. He didn't sleep with your girl, Jacoby did. You're jumping down the wrong man's throat."

Jacoby stepped to Desmond as if he were about to do some bodily harm. Desmond stepped back immediately.

"Remember we're suppose to be professional gentlemen," Desmond quickly reminded both of his friends. "Let's act like this until we are at least in private." He took the papers from Lawrence's grip and turned to Mr. Bowen. "If you aren't suppose to handle it, then who do we give this paperwork too, sir?" he asked politely.

Mr. Bowen narrowed his eyes distrustfully at all three men as if he couldn't believe the way they were acting. "I was about to let Mr. Ripley know before he jumped down my throat that I'm to instruct him to give them to the office manager as soon as he is done with the upgrade. She'll be back any second now. She just called from the elevator. She got tired of waiting around for you to come and went downstairs to get her something to eat. I just spoke to her from the elevator on the phone." He looked down at his watch.

"What if I don't have a second to wait?" Lawrence snipped.

"You were late, Mr. Ripley. As I said, she'll be here any second. The rest of the office personnel have gone home as you can see because it is after five." He looked at Lawrence very disapprovingly. "We thought you would be here before quitting time."

"I didn't expect the delay I had, but I didn't have an appointment set in stone."

Mr. Bowen looked like he wanted to argue more about the subject, but decided against it seeing Lawrence wasn't in the mood and looked quite dangerous.

"So you'll be leaving?" Desmond asked.

"Yes. I was on my way out the door as you were coming in, but I trust you in the office alone until she returns." Mr. Bowen looked past the three men out the glass lobby doors and smiled relieved. "Ah ha, there is she stepping off the elevator now."

All three men turned around to look at the voluptuous woman walking tall and straight with an air of confidence about her that one couldn't help but to notice.

"Damn she's fine!" Desmond noted out loud. "That's the beauty Madeline's been bragging about?"

"Yes," Mr. Bowen said proudly. "She's the office manager."

Desmond looked over at the shocked expressions on Lawrence and Jacoby's faces. "Now that's the woman you should have slept with Jacoby," he teased.

Lawrence gave him a look as if he had lost his mind. "You dumb ass that is the woman he slept with! Don't you recognize her?"

Desmond's eyes grew wide like saucers as he now gave the office manager a second look. "Well I'll be damn!

Chapter 9

Stepping off the elevator, she gave the glass office doors a brief glance to see the three tall men with their backs to her. They stood over poor Simon's short height like giants and she couldn't believe how incredibly big they were even from behind.

Someone called her name to the right of her to say good-bye and she looked over that way seeing it was one of her typist coming down another hallway. She waved to them just as she was two feet from the glass door entrance into the office.

Immediately, she dragged her eyes to those gorgeous framed men who had now turned around to greet her and she stopped dead in her tracks dropping her food to the floor as her eyes grew wide as saucers.

She couldn't move as she meet those beautiful intense cinnamon brown eyes that just twelve hours ago was ravishing her visually. Lord no, he was not standing there looking as though he wanted to choke her.

Simon stepped in front of the three men with a wicked smile on his lips and opened the door for her. "Ms. Green, the computer expert is here. He's all done." Simon bent down and picked up her dropped sandwich. When she still didn't move, he took her arm and pulled her inside the office.

One of the other men with friendly handsome features, who was the only one smiling out the three, said, "This is quite awkward, isn't it?"

"Awkward?" Lawrence sneered. "Jacoby, did you know she was the office manager here?"

Jacoby finally broke eye contact with Phoebe to look at Lawrence. "Does it look like I knew?" He looked back at Phoebe even more angrily. "You lied."

"I never lied," Phoebe defended herself. "We never got into our jobs."

"How could you do this?!" he asked incredulously.

"That's none of your business," she stated angrily.

Jacoby looked at his friends and then looked over at the office assistant, who was soaking this up like a soap opera. He grabbed her arm and dragged her into the nearest office slamming the door behind them to give them some privacy.

Once the door was closed, she snatched out of his grip and whirled around at him.

"You told me your name was April," Jacoby accused her.

"It's my middle name," she defended.

"I don't believe this! I don't believe that you're the same woman I slept with last night. How could you accept money for sex?"

She stood akimbo. "That's none of your business, Mr. Knight. I have my reasons."

"Do you do this often?"

"No and you know I don't," she snapped offended.

He shook his head. "That's the point. I don't know anything about you. I didn't until last night. I heard about you running this office, but I can't put you being the same woman I was with last night together. That's two different women." He said it as if that was an impossible fact.

"Does the fact that I'm the office manager here bother you or the fact that I accepted money for sex bother you?" she asked confused.

He ran a frustrated hand through his head. "Both," he admitted calming down. "Because I still want you."

Those words were like fire to Phoebe's senses igniting heat to her groin. Turning away from him to gather her equilibrium, which had been thrown off by his words, she said in an unsteady voice, "I didn't have any intentions of seeing you again."

He moved up behind her and gently rested his hands on her shoulders, speaking softly near her ear. "But you gave me your number," he pointed out.

Her voice was stronger and full of sarcasm. "It's not my number. It's a dummy number. I lied."

Jacoby turned her around. She really expected to see him angry at her deceit, but he looked amused down at her. Even with her heels on she still had was a couple of inches shorter than him. In this light, he was a nice deep almond shade that her fingers and mouth long to just touch, taste...

"Then it is fate, Phoebe Green that I came here today," he declared, smiling as if he knew what she really wanted to do to him.

Breathlessly, she said, "There's no such thing as fate for me, Mr. Knight, only bad luck."

He chuckled huskily, looking as if he wanted to eat her alive. "I can stay in town tonight for you." His arms moved around her waist and molded her body against his.

She gasped at his hardness that she could feel through his clothing on her stomach.

"We could have watermelon and whip cream." He raised a hopeful dark brown brow and those cinnamon eyes were tender, making her insides feel jittery with excitement.

Trying to keep a straight face, she said, "You are crazy."

"Only about you right about now, Phoebe." His warm lips pressed up against hers molding to them.

It felt so sinfully right kissing him like this and Phoebe wanted to take him up on that offer so bad, but the thought of giving herself to him was so wrong. Breaking the kiss by turning her head away and pressing her hands against those broad thick shoulders, she fought to control the situation. "No."

"Speak up you two!" Desmond muffled voice shouted on the other side of the door. "We can't hear you."

Jacoby cursed loudly and released her, seeing she was again in control of her wits when he wasn't. Again he ran another frustrated hand through his hair. He released her not wanting to force her. "I want to see you again, Phoebe."

"No!"

"You've got to be kidding me, dammit."

"Don't you curse at me. I'm only making the right decision for the both of us." She went to the door of the office and opened it.

Lawrence, Desmond, and Simon almost fell in. Phoebe gave his friends and her office assistant an exasperated look before turning back to Jacoby to say, "This conversation is over with, Mr. Knight. Don't try to contact me. There are no strings attached to our business." She took the papers from Desmond and snatched the pen from behind Simon's ear.

Looking at Lawrence and Desmond as she handed the papers back, she said, "Thank you for your service, Mr. Ripley. Madeline is grateful to have you as a source for our computer needs."

"We're glad to be your source, Ms. Green," Desmond said highly amused.

She moved past them and went to her office not giving Jacoby another look.

Desmond asked Jacoby, "Does she know who you are?"

Jacoby walked angrily past them and went to the elevators. Lawrence and Desmond followed soon after.

"So that's it. You're not going to find out more about her?" Desmond inquired.

"No. She said she had no intentions of contacting me." Jacoby pulled the hotel stationary that had her number on it out his pocket and ripped it in little pieces.

"Does that mean you have no interest in her?" Desmond asked.

"It means she doesn't want anything to do with me or weren't you all listening at the door?" he snipped, tossing the shred of papers in the nearest garbage container.

Desmond nudged Lawrence. "Hey, now she's free game Lawrence."

"I don't want used goods," Lawrence said nonchalantly.

"Used goods never stopped you before," Jacoby bit out.

"This is different. Now that I know the kind of person she really is I'm not interested."

"That's a load of shit and you know it," Jacoby spat just as the elevator doors opened.

It was a good thing the car was empty. They all stepped inside and Jacoby waited until the doors closed to finish what he had to say. "You have no idea the kind of person she is. You couldn't handle her even if you had her."

"Are you speaking about yourself?" Lawrence asked amused.

Jacoby shoved him against the wall he was so angry. Lawrence shoved back. First were about to follow, but Desmond tore them apart pushing them on either side of the elevators.

"This is crazy. She's just some girl. The both of you are acting like she's the last girl on earth."

"Shut up, Desmond!" Lawrence and Jacoby sneered.

Desmond sighed confused. "Look, let's just get back to Lansing in a professional matter, before we kill each other."

"Fine with me, as long as that ass don't say shit to me," Jacoby growled.

"Same goes here," Lawrence hissed.

Chapter 10

As soon as the door to her office was closed and locked, Phoebe leaned on the back of the door to catch her breath and get control of herself. She was shaking all over felling hot and cold at the same time, but either way there was the flush of tingles in every part of her body.

The urge to make love to him again was quite powerful, but she fought it with all her will. She couldn't allow herself to give in to the pleasure he could give her or she was sure she would lose her heart to him. No, she had to find someone she was clearly indifferent to because she needed to have control.

Jacoby clearly had an aura about him that she was drawn too and she was terrified he would be another Daniel.

A soft knock at her door sent her heart racing again thinking it was Jacoby, but then Simon's voice came across.

"They're gone. I just saw their limousine leave. You can come out now."

She opened the door partially and looked at him with narrowed eyes.He looked as if he were about to burst out laughing. "Shut up," she snapped, coming out the office completely turning off her light.

"You slept with him?"

"That's none of your business and if you know what's good for you Simon, you should keep your business to yourself."

Simon giggled wickedly. "Then I shouldn't tell you the juicy gossip, Latrice told me."

Latrice was Madeline's assistant in Lansing. Simon and Latrice were constantly on the phone with each other gossiping back and forth about each office's going-ons. Latrice knew all of Madeline's personal business and loved telling Simon about it. Simon could keep a secret if you made sure you told him it was a secret, but he often shared some of Latrice's information with Phoebe even though she didn't want anything to do with office gossip.

Yet the way Simon was giggling, she knew it was something she should pay attention to. "What Simon?" They walked out the office together and he locked up as she pushed the elevator button.

He came over to her and leaned real close to her with a devilish glint in his pretty green eyes. "Remember a couple of months ago, Latrice said Madeline's got herself a love slave and it's a friend of one of our suppliers?"

Her face became a frightful gray.

He continued on taking her silence as not remembering what he told her. "Remember when Madeline got drunk at the Christmas party and was telling us how she got her bootie calls with a tall dark man. How she would just call him up and he'd come over and do her, then leave. They wouldn't talk. Just do it. He was like her love slave. Remember?" Simon finally looked at her as the doors opened and she didn't step in. He then realized her silence was because she didn't remember. Her silence was horror. Horror at knowing exactly what Simon was going to say.

"It was him?" she asked in a tiny voice.

He nodded confirmation.

"How do you know?"

He spoke as if she should know this already. "Latrice has sent me photos of him coming and going into the Lansing office from her phone. I recognized him the moment he stepped foot in here yesterday, but I was surprised he returned today."

Phoebe felt so sick to her stomach, she ran to the bathroom to relieve what little contents she had inside.

Chapter 11

His phone was blowing up. Madeline had called Jacoby five times since he had come into town.

Desmond was probably the one who alerted her that they were back in town. He was usually the one who spoke with the clientele for Lawrence.

Jacoby finally answered her call a little after midnight picking up the receiver with a quiet, "Hello."

"How was Detroit?" Madeline asked quietly.

"Same as before," he answered.

"Were you busy? Because I wasn't."

"No."

There was a long pause at this point. Usually when she asked this question, he would say, "I'll be right over." This time was different. His body wasn't into going over there tonight.

Madeline took the initiative and said, "Why don't you come over and join me for a little fun?"

There was another long pause, before he said, "I'm tired. I would be useless, tonight, Madeline."

"You won't have to do any work. Just lie back and let me take care of you."

Again more silence before he said, "No thanks. I'll call you later." He hung up and tossed the phone over on the couch not bothering to replace it on the base and then he went to bed after a long cold shower. He was hornier than a dog in heat, but Madeline couldn't satisfy his desires about now. No one could, except Phoebe.

He cursed to himself.

About thirty minutes later, Lawrence called. "I just got a call from Madeline," was the first sentence out his mouth.

"Yeah?" Jacoby asked, with a matter of fact tone of voice. "It is kind of late for clientele to be calling you, isn't it?"

"She was calling to discuss how things went in Detroit. She wanted to know if the upgrade went okay." There was silence on the line for a moment. Lawrence continued, "I told her it went great." A pregnant silence and then Lawrence said, "She asked about you." Jacoby didn't respond. "She asked me how were you and how did things go for you in Detroit?"

"What did you tell her?"

"I told her things went great. Everything was fine."

Jacoby cursed under his breath. "Do you think Desmond opened his big mouth about the incident?"

"No, but who's to say that office assistant want. He looks like a faggot gossiper if you ask me," Lawrence sneered.

Again Jacoby cursed. "She's going to get fired you know if Madeline finds out."

"What make you think Madeline doesn't mind sharing?"

"She doesn't. There's no strings attached, but I think she will take an exception to the rule when it's her own office manager. I don't give a shit at how good Phoebe is at running her office, she won't like it that I'm fucking her too."

"It was only one time," Lawrence said. "I think you're making a big thing out of nothing."

"I don't think I am," Jacoby said very concerned now over Phoebe. "I should drive down there tomorrow and tell her about Madeline and I."

"Why? What does she need to know about it?"

"Because I think she should."

"Are you listening to yourself, Jacoby? The girl doesn't want anything to do with you. I know this is hard to believe, but why should she care on whether you were intimate with her boss? You'll spread unnecessary business around the office and she'll hate you more."

Jacoby had to admit Lawrence made a little sense.

"Do you think allowing Phoebe to know this information is going to make things better between the two of you?" Lawrence questioned.

"I just need to see her and let her know."

"If it's so important for her to know, why don't I tell her? Madeline mentioned she needed me to go down tomorrow and supervise the installation at her new apartment in Detroit."

"Madeline is moving to Detroit?"

"Sure. She getting a lot of clientele that would make it easier for her to work in the city and do business in the city. Why shouldn't she move to Detroit? You and I will," he pointed out. "In any case, when we spoke tonight she asked me to go down tomorrow and personally supervise the installation then setup some things."

"You usually send a technician for things like that," Jacoby pointed out suspiciously.

"Yes, but she asked me to address it with my personal attention and I want to make her happy because when it's time for us to having lunch with the rich and powerful we both have to remember Madeline made it all possible."

Jacoby had a feeling that last statement was meant more for him than for Lawrence sake. It was true Madeline had gotten Jacoby and Lawrence many appointments with a lot of their clientele and had swung a lot of business their way. Lawrence was really trying to say, "don't fuck up with the goods for a little piece of pussy."

"I'll speak with Phoebe," he said to Lawrence. "I want to tell her myself about Madeline if she doesn't know already, but I won't be able to get down there until Sunday."

"I'll stick around and you can tell me how it goes. I'll be staying in Madeline's apartments on the river."

"I'll call you when I get in town." He really didn't want to speak with Lawrence anymore about Phoebe. He truly felt Lawrence had his own hidden agenda, but he didn't want to even think about what it could be. "Talk to you later, man."

Hanging up, he stared up at the ceiling wondering how was he going to let Phoebe know that he and Madeline were lovers.

****

Phoebe had come home and immediately went to her room. Patricia probably assumed her daughter had a hard day at work and needed a few minutes alone, but when Phoebe didn't come out after dinner, she knew her mother was going to start to worry.

Patricia came in the room to see Phoebe buried under the covers in her bed. Her clothes were thrown around the room and the lights were out. "Phoebe, what in the name is wrong with you?"

"I'm exhausted, Mother," Phoebe mumbled under the covers. "Can you put the kids to bed tonight? I'm so tired I can't move a muscle." In truth, she had just finished throwing up once again just from thinking about what she had done.

"Of course. I figured you would be. I don't see why you just didn't call out today and stayed at home for some rest."

Phoebe peaked over the covers at her mother. "You know I only use my sick days for the kids."

"Well, I need to speak with you about an important matter that happened at the bank this afternoon." Patricia said sitting on the bed next to Phoebe.

"What's wrong?" Phoebe asked.

"They posted a debit to our account of a thousand dollars. I let them know it was a mistake."

Phoebe sat up abruptly. "What?! Why'd you tell them that?"

"Because neither one of us had that kind of money to put in the account and you know I'm an honest woman just as I have raised you to be. I wasn't going to use money that wasn't mine, Phoebe."

Groaning in misery, Phoebe said, "It was yours, Mother. I put it in there this morning."

"Where did you get money like that from?" Patricia demanded to know.

She took a breath to prepare for the lie she was about to tell. "It's a loan from an old friend. Let's just leave it at that, but now we can just pay some of the taxes and don't you worry about paying it back. I'll figure something out for them and I have as long as I want to pay it back."

"You shouldn't have done that Phoebe. I'll help you," Patricia insisted.

She shook her head. "No Mother. I won't have you give me a dime. What you do around the house and for the kids is worth its weight in gold. I have plenty of time to return the money so I don't want you to worry about."

Patricia kissed her daughter's cheek and gave her a big hug. "I've got sandwich and soup on the stove. Get some rest and we'll talk more later. I'll straighten things out at the bank about the overage."

"Thank you, Momma," she said gratefully laying back down very blessed to have a mother like Patricia who was so understanding, although she had a feeling Patricia didn't believe her story about the loan, but Phoebe knew her mother wouldn't press the subject. Patricia would give Phoebe time to come out with the truth eventually.

Phoebe just didn't know when she would be able to tell her mother the truth. Closing her eyes, she felt the vile deep in her belly rumble and she knew in a moment she would be making another trip to the bathroom to throw up what was left in her stomach. Her thoughts went back to all those late nights with Madeline at the office. Madeline would tell her about the wonderful lover she had and how he could make love all night long, satisfying all of Madeline's needs. Once Madeline had even joked Phoebe could borrow him to relieve some of the stress in her life.

Well, Phoebe had certainly taken Madeline up on that offer. Her stomach rumbled in displeasure and she knew the only reason she was sick to her stomach was not because she had a very wonderful night with Jacoby Knight. The truth was that Phoebe couldn't believe she had slept with Madeline's lover and the worst part was she wanted to do it again.

Covering her mouth to avoid a mess, Phoebe rushed to the bathroom again before she let it out on the floor.

Chapter 12

Arriving into work extra early, Phoebe was able to get a lot of paperwork done. Simon arrived at his usual time and she went straight into his office to speak with him privately. With a serious nature about her, she immediately got to the point.

"I know you're the town crier about the office, but I would appreciate you keeping that little incident that happened yesterday to yourself."

Simon nodded. "I won't if you tell me all the details. Did he really offer money to you for sex?"

Her eyes narrowed. They had been listening at the door. "Yes, and you know the debt I'm in. How could I refuse almost three thousand dollars?"

"Hell with that kind of loot, he could have had all the women in Cass corridor."

"Well we did do it twice," she admitted.

Simon gasped.

"But I didn't accept it all. Not even half because my conscious was bothering me about even accepting anything." Phoebe continued offhandedly. "He wanted to do it again, but it was four in the morning. I couldn't be away from the twins another moment."

"Damn girl. You could have paid off yours and mine if you had stayed there any longer and gotten every dime from him."

She chuckled a bit relaxed now that she had someone to share the moment with. "It was great Simon, but it won't happen again, especially now that I know who he really is."

"But you said it was great. Don't you want it again?"

"Yes, but I don't want to get emotionally involved. I don't want to get hurt like I did with Daniel," she said.

Simon smacked his lips. "He's not Daniel, Phoebe."

"Yeah, I know, but he makes me feel too much and I can't handle that. I can't be in control when he's around. You saw me yesterday. I looked like a scared deer in the headlights when I saw him."

"It could have been just shocked."

"No Simon. I lose myself to him. He's just that good and it's not just his lovemaking I'm attracted to. It's just something about him draws me to him."

"So you won't be dating or seeing anyone."

"I'll find a man I'm physically attracted to only. I don't want the emotional luggage I get. No man's going to break my heart again," she said determinedly.

"When do you think you'll ever get over Daniel?" Simon asked seriously.

"When I feel like I don't have to worry about the man I'm with breaking my heart and when I know he'll be a good father to the kids. He'll love them like they are his own."

Simon sighed wishfully. "You deserve happiness, Phoebe. Not the crap you're getting now."

"I know, but good things come to those who wait." She left out the office and went to work.

Later on that day she got an email from Madeline to make sure the office was in tip top shape by Friday because she would be having a poker party with some friends and clients. Phoebe ordered the catering and made sure the room would be extra clean for the party. Madeline also mentioned in her email a technician would be working at the apartment today that Madeline was planning to use on the weekends in the city.

Phoebe wondered would her lover follow her down on some weekends? Would he come to the office and would she have to pretend she wasn't interested in Jacoby when he was around with Madeline? It would be difficult, but Phoebe could do it. Maybe the more she did see Jacoby with Madeline, maybe she would be able to put her feelings to rest about him.

As she was preparing to leave, she caught a figure at her doorway and at first thought it was Jacoby, but as she faced the large frame she smile at Lawrence in greeting. "Is there something wrong with the computers that I don't know about?" she asked.

"No actually." He leaned against the door frame of her office, crossing his arms across his chest. In a tailor-made suit for him, he was a very handsome man. His build was similar to Jacoby's, except he was much more brawnier. "I was in town doing some things to Madeline's apartment and I realized I hadn't had breakfast or lunch."

"You were working that hard?" she asked.

"I almost broke out in sweat."

She laughed at his teasing.

This seemed to encourage him more and he came into the office. "Since I'm in town for the night and I'm famished as hell, but I hate to eat alone, I was wondering would you be free for dinner."

The smile she adorned quickly faded and she broke eye contact packing up her things quickly and putting on her coat. "I don't think that's a good idea, Lawrence considering yesterday's events."

"Well, I figured you needed a load taken off and I figured I need the company of a nice young woman of just dinner. That's all I would like and it's my treat."

Phoebe found him to be quite charming and indeed handsome, but she wasn't emotionally attractive to him, but would it seem she was going out with Lawrence to try to get closer to Jacoby. That wasn't true at all. She did need to get her mind off of Jacoby and Lawrence would be a wonderful distraction. Plus she didn't have to worry about being emotionally involved with him. He would be a perfect distraction.

Meeting his deep brown chocolate eyes, she smiled warmly. "Let me finish straightening up and make a phone call to my mother about my children, then I'll let meet you in the lobby."

He looked happy and relieve in the same instant. "Thank you."

When he was gone she called Patricia's cell phone to let her mother know she was going to be late tonight.

"Is this the same one?" Patricia inquired, without even knowing why Phoebe would be late.

Phoebe evaded the answer. "Mother, please."

"I'm not mad. I love it. This time, though, make sure you call so I won't worry."

"Yes Mother. Do I have a curfew too?" she teased.

"Shut up girl." They both laughed.

She hung up and joined Lawrence in the lobby. "Before we go any further, I need to know some things."

"Ask me anything," he prompted, not looking the least bit worried about what she was going to ask.

"Are you doing this because of what happened between Jacoby and I? And do you expect something more than what you are saying?"

Lawrence answered casually, "No. I'm doing this because I need the company of a nice intellectual lady such as yourself for dinner and nothing more. I don't expect anything, but good talk and a good meal. Is that too much?"

"No, it isn't." She hesitated before she asked him her next question. "Does Madeline know?"

Understanding crossed his features. "You knew he was her lover?"

"I found out after he left. Simon knew."

"If she knows, she didn't find out by us. Desmond finds this all too amusing and I don't spread my friend's business around to other people. Jacoby won't tell. It would ruin his Lansing bootie call, if I must be vulgar about it."

"I wouldn't want to ruin that," she snipped more to herself.

"What about Simon? Will he tell?"

"No. Simon's a good friend. He'll keep it a secret," she assured him.

"If there isn't any more, then may I have the pleasure of the evening with you?"

Phoebe looped arms around him and allowed him to escort her out.

****

Jacoby was surprised to see Madeline standing in the doorway. Her slender frame was adorned with the latest Donna Karen suit, her hair looked as if she had just stepped out of a beauty salon, even when they had been intimate, he had never seen Madeline look bad. Her make up never ran or smeared. She was a very beautiful woman of fifty and still had a few tricks up her sleep to excite a man with her body that was like a thirty year old.

Even as he thought of their kinkiest nights, it did nothing to stir his manhood at that moment. Frustrated that his life would never be the same now that he was hooked on someone new, he looked down at his work as she came in the room.

"You busy?" she asked, sitting in front of his desk casually.

He took off his glasses and rubbed his eyes. "Not really. Just wrapping up the Davenport deal."

"So everything worked in your favor?" she asked proudly smiling.

For some reason actually sitting there now having a conversation with her now, he felt as if he were speaking with his mother. "Yes, actually it did." He leaned forward to give her his full attention. "Thank you for the contact, Madeline."

Maybe he could do her the favor of giving her one more night. "Let's grab lunch together."

She put her hand up. "I have an appointment in an hour. I just came here for you to tell me exactly what happened in Detroit."

Jacoby froze wondering what exactly did she know about yesterday's incident. Looking at the clock, he knew Phoebe wouldn't be at the office and since he didn't have her number there would be no way he could contact her. Damn her deceitfulness. How could he warn her if he didn't know how to contact her?

To stall, he asked, "What do you mean?"

"I mean we planned on being together when you returned from Detroit. You couldn't keep your hands off of me the night before you left and now, when you come back, I can't get the time of day from you. Now either a piece of your anatomy has come up missing - which I highly doubt, or you've met some drop dead gorgeous woman who could rock your universe better than I."

He took a deep breath in reprieve. Madeline didn't know what happened, but she suspected pretty damn close. Still he pretended evasiveness. "I don't understand what you mean."

She leaned forward. "Cut the shit, Jacoby and let's act like adults. I'm too grown for games. What happened?"

After a pregnant silence feeling a little bit relieved that this could end with a decent amount of maturity, he admitted, "She's drop dead gorgeous."

"I figured that much. Young?"

"Yes. What does this mean for us?"

She stood up and came around the desk. Leaning down, she kissed his cheek. "We'll always be friends, Jacoby."

"Thanks Madeline."

She cupped his face and pressed her lips against his, but he didn't respond. Moving away, she looked highly disappointed. "If you ever change your mind, don't forget me."

"I won't," he promised.

"We can have lunch Monday in Detroit. You will be there won't you?"

"I intend to. Abraham Blue will be there to finalize Davenport."

"Will your offices be ready by then?"

"There is a slight asbestos problem on the floor I'm on in the David Kahn Building, and I won't be able to go in until next month."

"Don't you have appointments already set up? Where will you meet them?"

"There are a lot of restaurants downtown, I think I can mange."

"That's ridiculous, Jacoby. I have two empty back offices in the Detroit layout. You can pay me back later for the usage." She looked through her bag and handed him a gold key and an electronic card. "The gold key is for the office itself, and the electronic card is my extra parking space."

"I don't think this is appropriate, Maddie," he insisted.

"It's fine, Jay." Standing up she kissed his cheek one more time and headed for the door. "Make room for lunch Monday afternoon. You and me." With that, she was gone.

Looking down at the keys in hand, he wondered how was he going to explain this to Phoebe? A black book on the end of his desk caught his eye. He knew this was Madeline's handy scheduler and he quickly reached for it and flipped to where she had her employee's listed. Phoebe's number was circled in red and her address followed. Quickly writing it down, he closed the book just in time as his door opened again and Madeline came back in.

"I thought I left it." She came to him and he handed her the scheduler. After blowing him a kiss, she left.

He looked down at the number and address smiling.

Chapter 13

Dinner was great and she even allowed him to take her dancing as well. By ten that night, Phoebe was exhausted, yet happy and relaxed. Lawrence was nothing but a gentleman and she allowed him to take her home instead of returning her back to the office. He walked her to the door and she kissed his cheek.

"Thank you for taking my mind off my troubles," she said.

Taking her hands in his, he said, "Thank you for giving me a very enjoyable evening." He leaned over and kissed her cheek.

She smiled up at him and then quickly went inside. Patricia came from the living room where she had been sneaking a peak. "He's cute," were her mother's first words.

"Thank you, Mother." Phoebe shed her coat and stretched. "I'll go check on the kids and meet you in the kitchen, okay?"

Patricia nodded.

Phoebe even changed after kissing the sleeping twins, before joining her mother who had made warm milk for the both of them at the breakfast nook.

"He looks nice too."

Phoebe agreed. "He was and I did enjoy myself. He just wanted to talk. It was so nice."

Patricia frowned. "Why do I have a feeling he isn't the same man you were with the other night?"

"Because he isn't, Mother and I don't want to speak about that anymore. Did you get the bank all straighten out?"

Patricia nodded, but there was a look of worry in her eyes.

"What's wrong?" Phoebe questioned getting upset knowing that look meant something was terribly wrong.

"There's a problem still at the bank." She pulled out an overdraft and handed it to Phoebe.

She didn't open it, but merely put the envelope on the table. "What's the problem?" she asked.

"There's a two thousand overdraft, not including the fees."

Phoebe jumped up. "How did it get overdrawn, Mother?" she asked incredulously not believing after all hey had done to get the bills down this could happen.

Patricia looked just as disheartened. "Someone withdrew the money."

Their eyes met and both knew who had done it.

Patricia explained, "When they investigated it, it seemed even though Daniel's name was taken off the account, he still had a card to the account. It was easy for him to get to an ATM and withdraw the cash."

"Now we're even deeper in debt and the taxes still need to be paid off by Tuesday." She stood up and paced deep in thought. "Where are we going to get that kind of money? We can't possibly take out a loan at a bank." She stopped suddenly knowing who she must ask.

"Whatever you are thinking Phoebe, the question is no. Don't do it."

Phoebe turned to her mother quite perturbed that her mother could read her thoughts. "There's no choice in the matter. We need to get the money as soon as possible and we don't have anyone or anything we can depend up for financial support."

Patricia stood up and stood in front of Phoebe to stop her daughter from pacing. "I don't want you getting the money from where you got it from before. Whoever gave you that money changed you, honey. You haven't been yourself. You're withdrawn and upset and you don't sleep right. I don't like the person you become. It feels like when you were trying to get over Daniel."

The scared look in her eyes returned and Phoebe felt helpless. "I have to, Mother. I have to get the money."

"No!" Patricia said adamantly. "I'll lose it all, but I won't lose my daughter. Not again Phoebe. Not ever."

Phoebe turned away gripping the kitchen counter to stop the shaking that wanted to envelope her and send her to crying. Her mother was trying to back her in a corner. They needed the money really bad and Phoebe knew only one person she could get the money from. "With the overdraws and the taxes, there isn't any guarantee that he will even have that amount of money as quickly as we need it, but I have to try, Mother."

Patricia held her daughters shoulders tightly. "Whatever you had to do to get that money, Phoebe, it wasn't worth it. He's not worthy. We can lose it all if we have to."

"Daddy worked too hard to give us that. He wouldn't want it to be sold. It's all we have left of him, Mother and I don't want you to lose it." Phoebe knew the property meant a lot to her mother and she would be distraught over losing.

"Not like this. We'll try another bank, another credit union. Something, anything. We'll figure out something else," Patricia said desperately.

Phoebe kissed her mother's cheek with serene understanding. "Do what you must, Mother. I won't let you lose the properties." She pushed gently away and went up to her room to find the card Jacoby had given her that night.

Chapter 14

Jacoby couldn't take his eyes off the phone. He had been staring at it for the past two hours as if staring was going to make the thing dial Phoebe's number. It was ridiculous to even think that, but he couldn't muster up enough courage to call her. All she'd do was shoot him down again. She had made it very clear she wanted nothing to do with him. Knowing that she didn't made him want to find out why. Never had a woman just out right ignored him. They usually played hard to get, but they just never said they didn't want anything to do with him.

Until Phoebe.

Being used for just sex didn't sit too right with him. True she had needed the money, but usually younger women wanted a ring, commitment, and/or some emotional attachment to him.

Until Phoebe.

Taking a shot of Jack Daniels, he used the back of his hand to wipe his lips, then headed to the phone looking at it as if it were ten feet tall. Jacoby had memorized the number and he had every intention of staying on that phone with her until she agreed to see him. Hell, he'd be willing to pay a hell of a lot more money just to get her back in a hotel and being that same woman he had wanted to make love to all night.

Just as he was about to pick up the receiver, the phone rang. It was probably Lawrence or Desmond. Right now he didn't want to speak to neither.

"Hello," a soft voice said on the other line.

Jacoby couldn't believe his ears. "Should I pinch myself?" he asked simply.

Her soft nervous laughter was sweet music to his ears.

"What do I owe the pleasure of this call, Phoebe?"

Silence came which he didn't want to hear from her. He wanted to hear her voice, not her breathing, but he didn't want to push it. She might hang up. Damn why did he feel like a teen boy speaking with his first girlfriend? He was nervous, sweaty, and off balanced all at the same time.

"This isn't a pleasure call, Jacoby." That serious tone in her voice was there again and he found himself a little annoyed at the sound of it.

"Are you pregnant?" he asked sarcastically.

She snickered. "No."

"Good, because I was going to say that was impossible."

"Really? You can't have children?" She actually sounded concerned.

"Long story," he only said thinking her concern was probably faked.

"I didn't know."

"Of course you wouldn't."

More silence from her.

Jacoby knew something was wrong and he wanted to broach the subject about Madeline, but he just couldn't find the courage to address the topic with her. "This isn't like you," he said.

"What do you mean?" she asked.

"It isn't like you to beat around the bush."

"You're right." This time the silence was only brief. She took several deep breaths and Jacoby could just imagine her biting her lip and wrinkling her cute brow. "I should start from the beginning."

"I'd rather hear the short sweet version."

"I need some more money." The words were forced out.

It was his turn to be quiet.

His quietness must have unnerved her because she went into explanation. "My ex-husband...he took it all. He took more than all, he wipe me out so completely, I don't think I'll ever pay it all back in my miserable lifetime. It's all my fault though. I should have canceled his card, but I forgot I gave him one. I wouldn't be doing this if my mother didn't need it."

He stopped her. "You're only doing this for your mother?"

She hesitated before answering, but didn't hide the truth. "Yes, Jacoby."

Again he was quiet. Knowing he wanted to be with her in an unimaginable way, it was quite difficult to accept she was only doing this for her mother. For the first time in his life he wanted more, but he was too stubborn to admit. "I don't know if I want to help you, Phoebe."

There was a pregnant pause on the line until she finally said, "I understand. I just thought I'd try." He could clearly hear the deep disappointment in her tone. "I appreciate the consideration-"

He cut her off harshly, "I just said I don't know, I didn't say I wouldn't, Phoebe."

"Jacoby, if I've said anything other than the truth, then I'm sorry."

"You shouldn't be sorry for saying the truth if it is the truth. You should always tell me how you really feel." He sat down on his soft leather beige and closed his eyes wishing she had said something different. She didn't speak knowing he was in an emotional fight with himself. "How much?"

Again she hesitated before saying, "Ten thousand."

"That's all?"

"What do you mean that's all? That's too much."

He chuckled relaxing. "I spend that much on shopping trips to New York, Phoebe. I thought for sure you would ask for much more."

Her tone was belligerent, "Well us peasants don't see past check to check like you people do."

"Don't be like that," he coaxed patiently. "I'm not trying to make you feel bad for asking."

"Then what are you trying to make me feel, Jacoby."

"Just that. I just want you to feel."

She didn't respond to this and he knew she wouldn't. No emotional attachments in her life. He remembered her saying that to him, but he didn't think those words would be his own downfall.

"If ten grand is a lot of money for you, how do you intend to pay it back, Phoebe?"

"You can make it a loan."

"Paying out money like that and getting nothing back in return instantly is a disappointment to me. I like instant returns."

"I couldn't pay you back fast, Jacoby. That's why I had to turn to you." The frustration in her voice was evident.

"How about we strike up a deal?"

"What kind of deal?" she asked warily.

"Meet me at my hotel tomorrow at eleven in the morning in the lobby."

"You know I have to work," she said disappointingly.

"You can call in."

"I have too much to do."

"Then I guess borrowing this money isn't important, is it?"

The sigh was more upsetting than anything, but Jacoby was going to have his way. It took this much of her own stubbornness to get this far. He wondered how much could he push her before she broke down and allowed herself to have some kind of feelings.

"Is it going to kill you to have one day off?" he questioned when she didn't answer right away. "Maddie works you like a slave horse. You need the time off anyway. Should I pencil you in?"

She forced out her answer, "Fine." Sarcastically, she asked, "Is there anything I should bring?"

"An honest and open disposition and a smile." He hung up the phone smiling to himself.

Minutes later, the phone rung again. Desmond wanted to know about the meeting they were suppose to have together tomorrow afternoon to design the installation of his offices.

"I want to reschedule it. I'll be busy in Detroit tomorrow morning."

"Detroit's just a two hour drive, you can get back in time."

"I plan to be busy the whole day."

"What hell kind of appointment do you have?"

"That's none of your business, Desmond, and if you were a smart man you'd keep it to yourself and just say fine Jacoby, when do you want to reschedule?"

"What are you trying to hide? You know I'm a nosey bastard."

"That you are, but I'm not going to tell. Monday is good for me."

"It will have to be in Detroit. I'll be there to finish off Madeline's installation and help Lawrence check out her set up at her apartment. Swing by around the end of the day and we can have dinner."

"That's fine with me. I was going to be in Detroit all next week anyway."

****

Phoebe hung up the receiver and laid back on the bed closing her eyes. What the hell was she doing? Doing this was not a good idea. Her mother was right. Phoebe was taking a chance on becoming emotionally involved with Jacoby and that was definitely something she didn't want to do.

"I don't approve of this," Patricia said at the door. "Is he going to help?"

"Yes, he will." Phoebe didn't bother to open her eyes. "When you get a chance tomorrow can you close the entire account? Call me on my cell phone with the new account information and I'll have the money go into the account by the end of the day."

"I don't like it, Phoebe, and I wish you had told me how you got the money the first time. I would have never allowed you to do it."

"I'm a grown woman, Mother. You really couldn't have stopped me if you wanted to."

"I don't want you to do this for me. This is no better than…"

Phoebe opened her eyes and looked at Patricia standing akimbo in the doorway. "What? A prostitute? You always told me in life you make choices. Some you regret, and others won't faze you. Either way you choose those pathways to get by in the world and you have to live with them. I'm choosing to do this and it won't faze me, Mother. This handsome man with a lot of money wants to make love to me. He wants to give me pleasure and he will pay for it. I don't mind it and I won't allow it to affect me."

"Whether or not you know it, Phoebe, it does affect you. I see the difference at what he makes you feel and what he does to you. What about the other man? Can't he help? Don't you have some obligation to him?"

"Lawrence is the last person I have any commitment to, Mother. I like him, but not in a sexual way. He just wants to be friends."

"That's crazy," Patricia. "Unless that man is gay there is no way you can say he wants to just be friends with you. You are beautiful inside and out and any man is a fool to hurt you or use you."

"He's not using me, Mother," Phoebe insisted, knowing Patricia was speaking about Jacoby. "If anything I'm using him. I don't want to be emotionally involved with anyone right now."

"But the heart wants what the heart wants."

Phoebe closed her eyes again. Her father use to say that all the time. Pulling all her wits about her like a shield to protect her, she said coldly, "I don't think I have a heart anymore, Mother."

Patricia didn't say anymore. She left her daughter be for the rest of the night.

Chapter 15

She spoke with Madeline at six o'clock that morning. Phoebe lied with the excuse that one of the twins was ill and she needed to stay at home in case their temperature became worse. Madeline told her to keep her cell phone on in case she needed anything. Simon could handle everything, but he seemed very disappointed and very reluctant to take over the responsibilities of the office.

Taking a long hot shower, she washed up thoroughly and then put on a sweet smelling perfume she always loved to wear. Donning on black velvet mid-thigh length dress and matching shoes, it felt odd to wear something like this on a Thursday morning, but wearing the dress did make her feel quite seductive.

Going to the mirror, she turned around to see the outline of her underwear. Biting her lip indecisively, she removed them and tossed them in the hamper and then looked back in the mirror. With no stockings, her legs still looked smooth and toned. Her heels made them look even more attractive and she almost couldn't wait to see his expression when he saw her. Sweeping her deep brown hair in a clip, she allowed the curls to dangle all about her head giving her a wild seductive look.

Just as she was about to call her cab to get downtown, the phone rang. She hesitated before answering, praying it wasn't him canceling.

"How are you, Phoebe?" Lawrence asked on the other line.

She relaxed. "Great, now that I hear your voice," she teased playfully.

He laughed genuinely. "Now that's what I like to hear from you. You definitely know how to make a man feel wanted. I was planning on bringing lunch over and keeping you company for a while, but how about dinner. I could bring it over for you and the kids."

"Lawrence, that's so sweet, but my son's acting real itchy," she quickly lied. "I've been away from home so much, he probably just needs some Mommy time."

"Are you sure? I really don't mind."

"I insist on a rain check, Lawrence."

"Well, I do need a favor for this weekend. I've asked Madeline's permission too."

"What kind of favor do you have that I need Madeline's permission to fulfill for you?" Phoebe asked.

He chuckled deeply. "I have a client whose having this awesome birthday party for his five year old grandson complete with a circus and on a ranch. I would like the client to swing my way and if I show up for the party he invited me to attend with two of the most beautiful twins in Detroit, I am positive he would love me to death."

She laughed knowing he was complimenting her children to earn some brownie points with her. Knowing that she could read him so well, enforced her belief that she could control herself when it came to Lawrence and he would be a better catch than Jacoby with regards to her heart even coming close to being involved. "When is the party?" she asked.

"This weekend in Harper Woods."

"That's a bit of a way."

"Well, that's why he's sending his boat to deliver us up there and bring us back. Plus, we can leave Friday night and get back by Saturday night all rested up."

An overnight with Lawrence as company. It did seem a bit too much. She knew him, but only over the phone when they spoke.

He could sense her dilemma. "I'll be the perfect gentleman and I even requested separate rooms to be set up at his guest house for us. Madeline's going to allow you to leave early to get home and get the kids ready."

"Can I bring my mother? To help me with the kids."

"Of course. I don't mind. The more the merrier I always say. So I can pick you up tomorrow night about seven?"

"Yes," she said. "It's a date."

"I like that."

She said her goodbyes and hung up with him wondering if Jacoby had told Lawrence anything about her. Lawrence didn't seem like he would be interested in her good girl type of from all the times he had spoken to her in the past, so his sudden interest in her could be construed with wariness. Matter of fact, he had been all business, although he could be attracted to her now that he had seen her for the first time at the office. Men seemed to garner interest in her visually initially because she was impersonal most of the time. Shielding her true self had become second nature since Daniel left her.

With this pushed to the back of her mind, she called for her cab and nervously waited to go downtown to the hotel. When she arrived in the lobby, it was five minutes early and she took a seat near the front desk. After two minutes, she couldn't be still enough to sit and stood up looking at the front doors to see when he came in.

Large hands pressed on her side, and his body moved against hers from behind her suddenly. Lips caressed the side of her neck just under her ear, sending warm chills down her spine. She knew it was him without even looking behind her.

"You smell beautiful," Jacoby whispered in her ear. "You smell good enough to eat, Phoebe."

Facing him, as his arms encircled her waist, she looked up at his handsome face and her breath caught in her throat. Seeing him again, made her body tingle all over. She had missed him, but was too proud to admit it. Moving her arms around his neck, she softly said, "And will you be tasting me now?"

"In public? Don't you think we'll cause a scene?" he teased.

With a throaty sensual laughed, she returned the jest and suggested, "Kissing me on my lips?"

He raised a deep cinnamon brown brow in wicked amusement. "I wasn't thinking about those lips."

She blushed deep red as his mouth captured hers fully. Her passion quickly came to equal his and by the time he moved away and looked down in her eyes, he could tell she was very happy to be there. Taking her hand, he steered her into the elevator and prayed no one would be in there.

Unfortunately, others came on the elevator. She moved in front of him, and he pressed his hardened manhood against her full apple-bottom. She took his hand and moved it under her dress from the rear to let him know she was bare as a newborn baby. He softly groaned behind her and she could tell he really wanted the elevator to hurry up. Once they were on his floor as soon as the elevator door closed, he swept her up and carried her to the room kissing her face, neck, and chest. He almost kicked the door down and slammed it closed once they were inside.

"You're going to break the door," she giggled amused by his eagerness.

"Fuck the door," he snarled, laying her on the couch kissing her as if it were going to be his last. She reveled his passion with her own, practically tearing his clothes off and entwining her legs around his waist.

Through his anxious kisses, she fought for control knowing if they didn't stop he would lose what little control he had.

"Wait, Jacoby," she whispered desperately.

He groaned again, but didn't stop meaning he heard her, but was too far-gone to do anything. He was fighting with her zipper in the back of her dress trying to get it down, but it was being stubborn. Cursing under his breath, he gently nudged her back and pushed her dress up until she was fully exposed to him.

It was her turn to groan as his finger pressed deep into her wetness. She gripped his shoulders digging her nails into his shirt, as her body exploded from his single touch and when he began to maneuver his hand sending ripples of pleasurable waves all over her body, she exclaimed her joy to the heavens, not wanting him to ever stop. Throwing her head back, closing his eyes, she screamed at the top of her lungs.

Jacoby knew this was his opportunity to catch her off guard as he moved down and replaced his mouth over her hot liquid fired womanhood. His arms encircled her thighs and locked around her hips to keep her in place, as she seemed to scream her pleasure even louder.

Tears streamed down her face, she was so overcome with emotions as he pushed her body to the utmost pleasure. There was no fight to stop him. He had drunk that away and replaced that with the urge to never let him go.

Even after her orgasm, he didn't stop giving her pleasure with his lips and in that moment she knew he enjoyed it and it made the act even more intimate. This man had found a way to join so close to her that she knew she would never be able to resist him. He had the control and she relished in giving in to his wonderful mouth never wanting him to stop.

Jacoby knew at that moment he had branded her and he felt like the king of the world. Seeing her body at his mercy was powerfully arousing and as she wrapped her arms around his neck and kissed his lips tasting herself on his tongue, Jacoby had no doubt in his mind when the day was all over, she would be his.

Now there was no barriers with their lovemaking and Jacoby was sure he would know she was lying if she said she had not felt something for him. As he joined with her, bringing her to even greater heights he relished in every touch every feeling she gave him and knew he would want to make love to her forever.

Once he expended himself, joining her in their own private heaven, Phoebe covered her hands over her face.

"Why did you do that?" she asked looking up at him.

"Why shouldn't I have?" he asked innocently.

Shaking her head, she closed her eyes. "We're supposed to be using precautions, Jacoby," she scolded.

Lightly kissing her neck, he chuckled pulsing deep within her. She gasped at the sharp tingles that hit her. "Caution went out the door hours ago, Phoebe."

Looking through her fingers at him, she frowned. "What's that suppose to mean?"

"If you were so cautious, young lady, you would have never accepted my offer that night in the first place."

Defensively, she said, "I've never done that before in my life and you know my reasons."

Sarcastically, he said, "Oh yes, your mother." Moving away from her abruptly, he stood up from the couch. "And if you were so cautious this time, why didn't you insist we use protection."

She smiled thoughtfully. "Actually that was the furthest thing on my mind."

Helping her up, he narrowed his eyes suspiciously. "You have nothing to be embarrassed about, Phoebe. This is all very natural."

"No it's not. People don't make love with their clothes on."

He gave her a look of pure exasperation. "Whoever put these crazy notions in your head on what people are suppose to do when they make love Phoebe should be shot."

"Would you do the shooting?" she teased.

"Gladly. Whatever you believe or have been told about how to properly make love, I wish you would throw them out the window, at least when you are with me. I can't believe someone would distort you with rules about lovemaking. When you're with someone you make the rules up as you go."

She warily allowed him to take her hand and guided her up a small round of stairs off in the opposite direction of the bedrooms. He glanced back at her and chuckled at the perplexed expression on her face.

"You really should start trusting me, Phoebe. Have I done anything to harm you?"

"Not yet," she said warily, but she was definitely teasing by the silly smile on her face. "I'm not holding my breath though."

"You don't have to because it will never happen." He came to double thick oak wood doors that were closed. Jacoby pulled her in his arms. "Can you promise me something just for today?"

"Maybe." That distrustful look was still in her eyes.

"Just for today, could you act as if you were the happiest woman alive and trust that if just for today, you'll have the full attention of a man who wants you to experience the greatest pleasure there is." He gave her a peck on her nose. "Now let's get all clean again, then we'll eat."

She blushed at those words.

"I meant food," he said, seeing her turning red, with a gently tap on her posterior.

Opening up the double doors, she gasped at the beautiful black marbled tub filled with bubbles and smelling like honey musk. He had to nudge her a little bit for her to enter the room that seemed almost sacred as it was decorated with candles and flowers.

"You did this for me?" she asked spellbound by the romantic notion again. "Why?"

"Why not?"

She shook her head still not believing he had gone through so much trouble. "This is unbelievable." Sitting down on the edge of the tub. "Why Jacoby would you go through so much trouble to arrange this? You don't owe me anything and you're definitely not sorry for anything?"

He snorted annoyed narrowing his eyes at her. "Is that your ex-husband wisdom again?" Reaching behind her, he calmly unzipped her dress, which came down quite easy now that he wasn't in such a rush.

She flushed remembering what he had asked her to do before. "It's hard to change from what you're use to."

Kneeling down at her feet, he took off her shoes, then guided her to stand up. With a tug on her dress, the soft velvet fell to her feet. He planted soft kisses on her stomach.

Her breath caught in her throat at the pleasurable sensation he could cause within her by doing something so simple. Swallowing hard and licking her dry lips, she said, "Even I find it rather strange you would go through so much trouble for me when I didn't ask for it or expect it, Jacoby."

He looked up at her. "That's why it was done. I wanted to do it for the effect it would cause."

"So you do these things to see me surprised?"

"Were you?"

"Yes."

"And did it make you feel something?"

She only smiled not answering the question. "Is that what you are trying to do?"

He stood up and handed her a thick terry cloth robe to adorn then began to undress himself. Phoebe found herself watching him reveal every inch of skin closely admiring the muscles and tone of his body, which he was not a bit ashamed of. While he undressed he spoke matter of fact, as if he was discussing the weather.

"I realize that we both were in the same rut. Feeding off the hurt others had done to us, but I also realized something else. In order for anyone to experience the thing we call life, one must experience the terrible hurt and the pain life gives so that we can also truly experience the unbelievable happiness life delivers."

"Does that mean I make you unbelievably happy?" she allowed to slip out.

"I wouldn't have asked you back if you didn't." He checked the water. "Are you ready?"

"For what?"

"To take a bath."

She frowned looking at him as if he had lost his mind. "Together?"

He pulled her to him. "Trust me, you'll love it."

Phoebe watched as he slipped himself into the water, and then looked up waiting for her. "When are we going to talk?"

"Soon as you get in." He patted the space in front of him.

Filled with hesitation, she took off the robe and stepped into the water. He guided her down until she was sitting in front of him with her back resting up against his large chest. She was stiff as a board.

"Phoebe, you should relax." He chuckled at her uneasiness.

"Why?" Phoebe asked uptight.

He took a sponge and began to wet her arms and stomach. "That's what baths are for."

She tilted her head back and looked at him in an awkward position. "You really don't expect me to relax with you sitting right behind me."

"It's not like I haven't seen anything, Phoebe." He kissed her pouting lips.

She straightened back up. "Point well taken, Jacoby." After a thoughtful moment, she said, "Madeline's going to fire me when she finds out about this."

He nudged her to lean forward and began to wash and massage her back at the same time. "Madeline and I had an arrangement. I wasn't seeing anyone and neither was she. Now that she knows that I have an interest elsewhere - and she doesn't know who and she didn't ask - she understands that it is the end of our arrangement."

"Then you don't know how serious Madeline took your arrangement. She told me things and she was very fond of you. Just because you thought differently, that doesn't mean everything is fine."

He pulled her back and began to spread soap all over her chest, arms and stomach. Phoebe's body was very relaxed but her brain wasn't. "We're friends and only friends. We spoke about it and I think she took it quite well."

"Madeline's very good at hiding her feelings. Especially when she's been properly dumped. I've seen it before. I really don't see why you had to tell her about us. This wasn't planned to happen again."

"Whether I saw you again or not, after being with you, Phoebe, I had a different outlook on everything and would have still ended the arrangement with Madeline."

"She'll still fire me."

"Then you can work for me."

Again she tilted her head back in the awkward position. "You don't pay very well," she snorted.

Jacoby burst out in a booming laughter immediately catching her meaning. He laughed so hard, Phoebe had to hold on to the sides to keep from sliding in the water. "Oh damn. I haven't laughed like that in years, Phoebe," he said through his laughter wiping the tears off her face. "Your sense of humor is truly refreshing, but in no way was I speaking about our situation right now. I was speaking of a real job."

She turned her whole body around to look at him. "Our situation would have nothing to do with a job with you?"

"I don't mix business with pleasure, Phoebe. I find it a very bad combination."

"I don't sleep with co-workers. I find it in very bad taste. I couldn't work for you."

"So you'd be fired and that's it."

"I'm good enough. I believe I can find another job."

"But with no references then what? You think Madeline's going to give you a good reference?"

"I've had temp jobs before her. I can use those."

"Everybody is going to wonder."

"Are you trying to make me feel better?"

He stole another kiss with that same look of amusement in his eyes. "Work for me and you'll never have to worry about that. I assure you I wouldn't be hiring you because I feel I owe you. I'll hire you because I know you are a great employee. If this distances me with Madeline, I really don't care. I would value your skills, unlike she has done and kept you just over broke."

"What's that suppose to mean?"

"It means, you should be getting paid more than what she pays you."

Defensively she asked, "How do you know what she pays me?"

"Let's just say the old girl loves to brag about your skills and how cheaply she had to acquire them."

There was still perplexity in her eyes.

He sighed tiredly. "I don't want to get into anything right now, Phoebe, but if I were you, go see how much the other managers were getting paid before you. Right now, we'll drop the subject and speak of other things." He handed the sponge over to her.

She began to wash his chest and arms just as he had done her. "So now we can talk about the loan?"

He rolled his eyes heavenwards exasperated. "Do you ever just enjoy the moment or are you always business?"

"What moment am I suppose to enjoy?"

"Lovemaking always has its afterglow. If you'd relaxed you'd feel it."

"There we go talking about feelings again. I think you do enough feelings for the both of us, Jacoby. Before we go any further we should talk about this loan," she demanded.

He leaned forward and rested his head against her chest to indicate for her to do his back. As she did this while kneeling on her knees, he said, "I have the money, what else is there to discuss, Phoebe?"

"How I plan to pay you back?" she stated obviously.

"Hopefully with money," he teased.

"Jacoby, I'm being serious," she said in frustration rubbing hard on his back.

He looked at her. "Fifty dollars a month. Is that reasonable?"

"No. I'll be paying you back for the rest of my life."

A wicked smile touched his lips.

She sat down pushing him back to look directly in his face. "You are not taking this serious enough."

"You have enough seriousness for the both of us, Phoebe," he shot back sarcastically.

Phoebe didn't like him taking her words, turning them around so they could benefit him. "Fine, I'll pay three hundred a month. Will you adding a percentage to that?"

"No."

Frowning, she asked, "How do you expect to make any money from all of this? No one just makes loans for the fun of it?"

His amusement quickly returned as his hands came up to cup her breast. "Trust me, I'm having a lot of fun." His mouth attacked the pert dark nipple that seemed to cry out for his touch.

Her breath became erratic and the room seemed to spin. Phoebe held on to his broad shoulders for support as he moved over to attack the other aureole. She could not believe taking a bath would be so indulging and just as he had said relaxing.

Hours later, they winded up in the bedroom famished. He ordered room service and laid next to her under the sheets to await for the food to get there.

When she sat up and looked down at him, Jacoby chuckled knowing she was about to try to get back to business. Putting his hands behind his head, he pretended surrender.

"We are never going to get anything done if you continue to distract me," she said trying to sound angry.

"What more do we need to discuss, Phoebe?"

"Are you always this playful?"

"Only when I'm enjoying myself immensely."

"Are you often in the habit of giving loans out?"

"Actually, no. The last loan I gave out was to help Desmond and Lawrence open up their company. They borrowed over half of million, which was why I wasn't so thrown off when you ask."

"You are use to people using you?"

"I get my money back from them. Especially since I own twenty percent of their company in as a silent partner. I occasionally tag along with them on appointments, but I really stand back and let them make the money. They are quite good at doing that." He gently rubbed the back of his knuckles against her cheek. "You aren't using me, Phoebe. I think it was a very fair trade off."

She snorted. "Sex for that amount of money?"

"I don't see it as just sex." He stood up hearing someone at the door and put on a robe. "I see it as nice companionship, plus you'll pay me back. Although I do love the interest on this loan much better than any loan I've ever given out." Again he stole a kiss from her before leaving out the room.

In frustration, Phoebe laid back and stared up at the ceiling. She had to admit she was having a wonderful time, but all of this came at a very high price. If she wasn't so businesslike and serious it was almost easy to forget why she was with him today and if he kept up this wonderful demeanor and easy going character, she would find herself very much in love with him.

Sitting up again, she looked around the room to see a briefcase sitting on the table. Would that contain a little bit more of the answers she craved to know about him, but was afraid to ask?

Getting out of bed and putting on the robe he had given her earlier, she walked over to the briefcase and opened it. There were lots of files and important documents, plus sundries, but nothing to really pinpoint on his business. From what she read, his company was small, yet it handled large clientele with lots of money and spent abundantly on marketing research.

"Did you lose something?" he asked from the doorway holding a tray of food and staring at her his eyes filled with curiosity.

"No I didn't." She closed the briefcase guiltily and sat down on the bed. He set the tray down beside her and reached in his pocket in his robe.

Pulling out a check and handing it to her, he said, "Were you looking for this?"

She read the check in the amount of ten thousand dollars made out to her from his personal checking account. Looking at him, she admitted, "No. I was being nosey if you must know."

"What did you want to find out?" He sat on the other side of the tray he had brought.

"Where did you get the money from? Your company's not that prosperous."

"Indeed, but my father was a wise investor when I was born and decided to buy lots of stocks in my name. My portfolios pretty thick and with lawyers and smart accountants my father makes sure I'm never wanting anything. I see him and my mother on holidays like Christmas and Thanksgiving, once and a while Easter and I get a call and a present through the mail on my birthday. I was sent away to military school and he bought my way into Yale by being a very generous donor to the college. I practically raised myself, but that's alright, I find my life in Michigan where my mother was raised quite satisfying. I'm running my own business while my parents, decide to track all over the world for the rest of their lives. I figure I'll get a phone call when they die telling me to come pick up their bodies and bring them back here to bury. They've already bought plots on the family cemetery on the outskirts of Lansing. I'll take you up there when I get a chance if you're interested. Is there anything else?"

If that was not the most depressing thing she had ever heard. How could a man so rich in wealth have such a dreadful existence? She couldn't imagine her parents leaving her to other people to be raised. What about his values and morals and what about that motherly and fatherly love she just couldn't imagine not having? Warm tucks in bed, wet kisses to the forehead, tickles until you passed out, and hugs that just never stopped.

"So why can't you have children?" she asked.

He hesitated before answering, and as he spoke his words were slow and careful as he were controlling everything around him. "I was four and my parents were preparing for this huge Christmas party. About three days before the party I told my parents I wasn't feeling well. The nanny had gone to visit her family and my mother insisted she could watch her own child until the woman returned in a week. I tried my best to stay out of my parents' way and I understood how important this party was to them, but I had the worst fever and by the next day it was worse. I was throwing up and I was dizzy. My mother gave me some medicine and sent me to bed, but I guess in all the holiday excitement I was forgotten and by the time they discovered me I was near death on the floor of my room laying in a pool of blood filled vomit and a temperature of one hundred and two. They said I had to have been there for about three days before they found me and took me to the hospital. I had no idea how long I had been on the floor. Either way, I didn't wake up until a week later and so weak I could barely breath on my own. They said I had fried a few brain cells. I had to learn how to walk and use my right hand all over again. I was in the hospital recovering for over a year, and my parent swore I would never be left alone with them again. They didn't find out until I was ten that I was infertile. I could produce the testosterone, but I couldn't make them swim. A lot of people told me to hate my parents. It was all their fault, but they were so filled with so much guilt, I couldn't hate him. They've always been there for me when I have called upon them. They always return my phone call and anything I've ever wanted they have given me. What more could a child ask for from two people who were never ready to be parents? They carry around the guilt that they can't be parents by staying away from me as much as possible and allowing other people who can naturally nurture raise me. Besides, there are other options. I mentored in college and I taught class for a while. If I get married, adoption or foster parenting is also a good choice."

"You don't seem mad at them?"

"I never was. I love them. They were always wrapped up in their world and I knew this from almost the beginning of my life. I understood this and me becoming sick was just not in their plans. I don't blame them, and I don't blame myself. It's just one of those things that happens. Life gives you lemon and you make lemonade, right?"

She shrugged. "So you have a lot of money?"

"Enough. I'm not a needy person. I've never been - A trip to New York once a year and I live in the family house in Lansing. My business makes enough money to pay for my traveling and business necessities and I don't indulge in a very expensive life style of partying, drinking, and so on like Lawrence. Going into my private funds in the past ten years has been little to none."

"I'm sorry about sneaking," she apologized.

He shook his head. "No problem."

"I can't believe you gave this to me in a check. I thought you might give it to me through a bank transaction."

"That felt too impersonal. Too business. I wanted to give it to you, but I didn't want to walk around with that amount of money. Is this check not sufficient?"

It was perfect. This amount of money would secure the debt Patricia and she were in and very well have enough to give the twins a very enjoyable Christmas.

"The check is sufficient." Her stomach broke the somber mood by growling quite loudly.

"I take it you're hungry?" he asked.

She said teasing, "Just a little."

He picked up a piece of watermelon in one of the bowls on the tray. "I have a confession to make, Phoebe."

After taking a bite, she asked warily, "What confession?"

"I didn't ask you to my hotel room to make love to you. I really had plans to speak just business then offer you more money if needed for you to make love to me. I really just wanted to see you again. Yet now that I have you I would like to keep you here until the sun goes down. There's really no strings attached to the money. If you pay it back then fine, if you don't I won't hunt you down for it."

"I take this amount of money very serious."

"I don't, so please don't think of yourself as a prostitute."

"I was kind of finding it kind of kinky," she teased.

He chuckled sensuously. "Well, I brought a bottle of whip cream too. Would you like have desert first?"

She smiled wickedly and nodded.

Chapter 16

Patricia was standing at the door when Phoebe arrived home in a limousine driven car that evening about eight o'clock. The disapproval in her mother's face was quite evident, but Phoebe waved this away and kissed her mother on the cheek as she came in the door.

"He didn't bother to ride home with you?" Patricia asked.

"No, Mother." Exhausted she sat down in the nearest chair and stretched. "He was in bed when I left if you must know."

"Are you hungry?"

Phoebe giggled more to herself. "Oh no, we ate when we had time."

Patricia looked with even more disapproval.

"Oh Mother, the man is insatiable if you must know. It's like the more he gets the more he wants and in between he made me feel the same way."

"So you like him a lot."

Phoebe shrugged. "I don't know what I feel if you must know."

"I don't like him, Phoebe."

"You don't know him enough to not like him."

Patricia huffed and left the room not wanting to discuss the subject any further. Phoebe relaxed and stared at the wall thoughtfully. After they had eaten finally, he had called up for her to have a massage and then they played checkers in just towels on the floor of the front room. It had been an even more interesting experience.

By that time, she had grown accustom to being undressed in his presence and near the end of the night, there was no place on her body he did not know. The same had went for him and she delighted in finding new places on his body to touch to excite him.

Just as he had asked her, as soon as the sun had started going down, he had called the hotel desk to bring the hotel's limousine around to take her home. All his promises that he had made this day, he had kept and she had really felt like a queen as she rode home. Thoroughly loved through and through.

Phoebe decided she had enough energy to spend some quality time with the twins and afterwards gave them a bath.

When she tucked them into bed that night, her son gave her an extra special kiss.

As usual Patricia had set out some warm milk on the table for the both of them when Phoebe joined her mother in the kitchen after leaving the twin's room.

"What are you doing for the weekend?" Phoebe asked.

"Nothing," she said waving her hand away as if there were a pesky fly around. "I did want to take the twins out somewhere. They have been pretty patient for the past couple of weeks lock down in this house."

"I wanted to take them on a boat treat, then go to a birthday party. Lawrence invited."

Patricia brightened up. "Will you have to do any more meetings with this other man? Or can you now concentrate on Lawrence?"

"Who I chose to spend time with and how I spend time with are my business and my prerogative, Mother."

"I know and in no way would I dictate how you chose to spend your time, but I don't want to see you hurt again."

"I know you care, Mother and it's very much appreciated." She touched her mother's hands and smiled warmly. "You are very much appreciated."

"Thank you, Phoebe," she said very glad to hear her daughter say that to her. "Sometimes mothers need to hear that they are appreciated in some kind of way."

****

Just as Jacoby arrived back in Lansing, Lawrence called him from Detroit on his cell phone.

"I called your house and office all yesterday and you didn't answer. Desmond said he hadn't seen you either. Where'd you run off to?"

"I was out of town."

Lawrence chuckled. "You came down to christen Madeline's new apartment with her? She had mentioned she might invite you down."

"No, I wasn't with Madeline." Jacoby made no attempt to go into detail on his whereabouts. Jacoby thought Lawrence was being too nosey, but Jacoby was being very evasive. He didn't think he should let Lawrence know he had seen Phoebe again considering how Lawrence had acted the first time he had told him about Phoebe and him being together.

"I just wanted to speak with you about Phoebe," Lawrence said casually.

Defensively, he asked, "What about Phoebe?"

"I just wanted to let you know there are no hard feelings between us. You got to her first and maybe it was fate talking to me telling me that I had better start listening when fate starts talking. Phoebe's a good woman and I missed that opportunity, but I'm not missing any more opportunities like that again."

Jacoby assumed Lawrence meant he would be jumping a lot more bones when he felt the need to instead of waiting around. This wasn't unusual for Lawrence. He loved sleeping around with women and keeping the notches on his bed quite full.

"I didn't feel any hard feelings or guilt about what I had done, Lawrence. I was just worried you thought I had moved in on a staked claim when there was nothing to say you had laid claim to her. I would never move in on someone I knew you had an interest in."

"And do you still have an interest in her?"

Jacoby pretended innocence not wanting Lawrence to know just how much he felt about Phoebe when he wasn't sure about his own feelings. "There's a considerable interest, but I don't want to press anything. Maybe when I'm in town I'll look her up."

"But didn't she say she wanted nothing to do with you?" Lawrence reminded him.

"True, but that never stopped me before. I'm sure I could change her mind."

"So it could be just a one night thing then."

"For now. Maybe more if she wants more to do with me."

"And if she doesn't, you'll be moving on?"

Again Jacoby had that weird feeling Lawrence was up to something. "Of course. I wouldn't force the issue. I don't have to force myself on any woman, never have and never will."

"Good...I mean, fine. I was just wondering." He changed the subject about something else, yet Jacoby felt uncomfortable the whole time he was speaking with Lawrence, because now he was sure Lawrence was up to something and he felt he should speak with Phoebe directly about his concerns. "I'll be seeing you Monday," Lawrence assured after some more small talk.

"No doubt," Jacoby assured him very eager to return to Detroit again.

"Desmond told me of your move planned for this weekend. I'd help you, but I'll be seeing some clients over the weekend in the thumb."

"Don't worry. Even without an office assistant I have it all organized and Madeline has graciously allowed me to use the back offices at her place, while I'm waiting for my own offices to be finished. It shouldn't take too long."

"Won't that be uncomfortable for you and Phoebe?"

"I have worked with other women I've slept with, why would it be uncomfortable?"

"I just figured there's probably more to what you're feeling. I mean no woman's ever just outright rejected you before. I figured getting back in her pants was just an attempt to bandage up your wounded pride."

"My pride is not wounded in the least." His sourness penetrated through. True, Phoebe's rejection had kicked him pretty hard in the pride department, but last night had certainly assured him she did want him.

"You sure about that man?"

Jacoby most definitely didn't like the way Lawrence was acting so he decided to talk junk to throw Lawrence off. "Yeah man, if she doesn't want what I have to offer, that's her lost. I'm not holding my breath for any woman. She's not the only fish in the sea. There are plenty of them out there for me. Let's just hope Phoebe will be adult enough to not try to crowd me."

Lawrence chuckled in what sounded like almost relief.

****

Arriving at work a little past eight, she immediately took care of all email and voicemail problems. Afterwards, she had Simon finish shipping off the rest of the documents to their appropriate locations. They were given noticed by Latrice that Madeline would be arriving in Detroit about ten. That gave her and Simon enough time to do any last minute straightening up and preparations for the small office gathering Madeline had planned.

Soon as Madeline arrived she called Phoebe into her office. Business was discussed first, but Madeline's mind seemed a thousand miles away when she wasn't talking.

"Is everything alright, Madeline?" Phoebe asked reluctantly already getting a gist of what was preoccupying Madeline's mind.

"A little," Madeline said kind of sorrowful. "I kind of gave up my night thing, or he gave up me."

"Do you miss him?" she asked.

"Very much. I was kind of liking him," she said longingly. "I thought maybe we could keep it going, but I should have known it wouldn't go much farther. I'm old enough to know that a man's heart can never be captured. You remember that. Men say they love you, but they only love something about you and when it wears off, that's the end of their love, Phoebe."

"Did he say he loved you?" Phoebe felt that nausea starting to build up.

"No. Not once, but I thought if we continued, eventually he would and we could make it a more permanent thing. Although he was younger than I, but I figured age was nothing but a number."

"Did he know how you felt? Had you ever told him or even hinted to him?"

"No. We never discuss the arrangement. I guess that was the thrill about the whole thing. I felt we didn't need words to show what we felt. I just assumed he knew."

"How Madeline? How was he to know? Maybe you should have told him, so this would have never happened. He wouldn't have cut it off so abruptly."

"Oh yes," Madeline said sourly. "And have me hanging on, so he won't hurt my feelings? I don't think so, Phoebe. I refuse to be a man's crutch when he actually decides to get serious about another woman."

"What do you mean by serious about another woman?" Phoebe asked. "Did he say it was serious with another woman?"

Madeline shook her head. "He didn't have to. You could clearly see it on his face. Whatever this woman did to him, he was clearly enthralled by it and enjoying it. I don't hate him for what he did, but I sure as hell envy that woman who opened his nose."

Phoebe blushed furiously. Madeline noticed this and frowned. "You would certainly do well to find a man like him, Phoebe, so you can stop all that shyness when it comes to being with a man. Although Simon has mentioned to Latrice you've been quite happy these days and I must admit there is a certain glow about you. Has Daniel up and died mysteriously?"

Whatever glow was on her face instantly disappeared at the mention of her ex-husband's name. "Unfortunately he hasn't. He's become an even bigger problem in this past week alone."

"Then what has you so full of life? Is it a man?" Madeline saw the blush return on Phoebe's face. "Oh my, it is. Who is he and when can I meet him?"

"It was only a couple of dates thing. Nothing serious. I probably won't be seeing him again."

"Don't lay your cards out too soon. By the look of you, I'd say you really do want to see him again. He must have been a wonderful one night stand."

Phoebe shook her head, but it felt as if she were trying to convince herself of not wanting to see him more than Madeline. "I'm quite sure of not wanting to see him again."

A call came in and Phoebe was very grateful to get out of Madeline's presence and gather her wits about her. She couldn't believe how calm and collected she seemed as Madeline discussed being without Jacoby.

She couldn't possibly work here another week. Madeline would surely find out the truth eventually, because Phoebe doubted Simon could keep his mouth closed another week.

Chapter 17

At three, Madeline called in her office and let her know she would need Phoebe to come over to her apartment Monday to assist with the testing of the office's wireless software Lawrence's technician would be installing.

"I will also need you to get the back two offices on the other side cleaned out, so if you could stop by the cleaning department on your way out today, I would sure appreciate it. Lawrence just called and reminded me about you leaving early to help him out this weekend."

Phoebe wondered why Madeline needed the offices cleaned out, but she decided not to ask because she would eventually find out about it.

Her mother had also taken off early to help get the kids packed and a limousine pulled up on time. Of course Patricia was just too thrilled with the elaborate manners of Lawrence as he presented a dozen lilacs for her and a dozen roses for Phoebe. He even gave the twins Tootsie rolls lollipops after he graciously ask Phoebe if it was all right if they had sweets.

When her mother and the twins were inside the limousine, Phoebe turned to Lawrence and whispered, "You keep this up and she might start calling you son."

"Is that a bad thing?" he asked with a playful wink.

Phoebe felt a little uneasy wondering if he was serious. On their way to the boat, Lawrence was just too funny for the twins who were squealing in laughter at his playfulness. He didn't mind the noise they made. Patricia of course questioned him to death and Phoebe couldn't be more embarrassed, yet Lawrence answered all her questions humorously not at all minding her mother's nosiness.

Once they reached the boat, Phoebe knew it wasn't a boat at all. It was a beautiful yacht with two bedrooms and a dining room. There was a light brunch awaiting them and there was a private crew on board to serve it. Patricia was enjoying herself and didn't mind taking the twins off Phoebe's hands to give Lawrence and her daughter a little privacy up on deck.

"Impressed?" Lawrence asked, sitting very close beside her.

"Very, but not with all of this. Just at you."

"Why me?"

"Because you don't seem like the kind of guy who would care what other people think."

"That was the old Lawrence. I've turned over a new leaf."

She laughed, but his look read very serious. The smile on her face quickly faded. "Since when?"

"Since really getting to know you the other night. There was just something about you that I found myself thinking about you all the time, Phoebe. You're a woman that deserves the best in life."

"And are you saying you are the best?"

"I don't mind at all tooting my own horn."

Not at all liking how he decided to express himself, Phoebe became immediately defensive. "And me sleeping with Jacoby doesn't make a difference to you?"

"Should it? That was in the past, just like my own indiscretions. Are you going to hold them against me?"

"I probably don't know any of the women you slept with."

He chuckled. "It won't bother me, Phoebe. I swear."

"Won't Jacoby think differently?"

"Jacoby told me himself just last night that it meant absolutely nothing."

She tried her best not to let it show this affected her. "Well, why should it? He was only looking for a good time."

He studied her features carefully. Phoebe was excellent at hiding her true emotions. "He also said he didn't care that you rejected him. He said he could find a lot of other women who wouldn't mind what he had to offer."

"Good, because a man like that with an ego that arrogant needs to suckle on something or he might run back to his mamma, if she even wants him around," she snipped.

Lawrence chuckled. "Enough about him, let's talk about us."

"Us, Lawrence? When did I agree to an us? I thought we were only friends."

"Of course. Only friends," he confirmed.

Yet Phoebe had a feeling Lawrence wanted a lot more and she didn't think after spending yesterday with Jacoby she could give it to him. A promise is a promise and she did promise to help Lawrence this weekend. The kids and her mother were having a good time and that made it all worthwhile, so she couldn't complain. Their happiness made her feel a sense of peace.

Once they arrived at the home of Zane Quinn, a man, who reminded Phoebe of The Colonel without a cane and the bow tie, eagerly greeted them when they arrived. His grandson named after him, was there also and welcomed the twins with open arms. None of the other children were due until tomorrow, but the large eighteen-bedroom mansion was alive with excitement for the upcoming party.

Phoebe was shown to her room, which was connected, with her mother's and a nursery attached to the room, which had more square footage than her whole house. Patricia was given a private tour by the butler, while Phoebe put the twins to sleep after they had dinner. Lawrence joined her and even sung a bedtime lullaby for the twins.

"Do you have any children, Lawrence?"

Thoughtfully, as if longingly, he said, "Actually no, but I always told myself once I get settle in my business, I would find that right girl and have a family right away." That wicked sparkle gleamed in his nice brown cinnamon eyes. "You wouldn't happen to know any nice girls?" he winked teasingly.

She flushed at his teasing and guided him out the nursery into her own room. "I wouldn't dare introduce them to a charmer like you."

He pulled her into his arms molding her body against his frame. Phoebe was very aware that he was slightly aroused by their close contact and seeing the place they were at that moment, giving in to what he had in mind would be so easy if she wasn't thinking about Jacoby and then on top of that wishing he was here.

So when his thin dark pink lips swept down to take hers, as good as he kissed, she couldn't enjoy it because she knew she wouldn't enjoy another's lips again. Damn Jacoby, because even when she tried to concentrate on Lawrence's kiss, it didn't feel the same. No heat surrounded her, no difficulty breathing, no shuddering or shivering, nothing and Lawrence was a pretty good kisser.

When she pushed away, he was the one who was breathing hard and looking as if he couldn't believe what had just happened.

"I'm sorry," she said, feeling bad that she had not enjoyed the kiss.

"You have nothing to be sorry for. I'm the one who's sorry. I just couldn't help myself, Phoebe."

Moving away from him needing the distance, she said, "I should get some sleep. I'll see you in the morning for breakfast?"

He glanced at the bed, then at her. "Yes, tomorrow at breakfast, Phoebe."

She allowed him to lean forward and kiss her cheek. When she was alone, she went to the private lined phone, which Mr. Quinn had in each bedroom, and called her home phone to check her voicemails. There were several hang ups only, so she decided to check her work voicemail in case Simon had decided to spring some weekend project on her lap by surprise because he had gotten too lazy at the end of the day to complete it.

Simon's voice sprung on the line, "You won't believe who called here. Anyways, he went through the telephone computer prompts to find you and I just happened to be in your office. He asked for you and when I told him you had gone out of town for the weekend with a friend, he seemed very put out."

Phoebe buried her face in her free hand. She should have known Simon would do something like this. If he wasn't the most dipping man she had ever meet.

Simon continued, "In any case, I told him you'd be back in the office by Monday morning."

That was the end of the message, but not of Phoebe's misery. She couldn't believe this was happening to her. She should have told Jacoby about leaving out of town with Lawrence. There was probably no doubt he knew already, but it would have been nice if she had told him herself. Now it looked like deceit and that was the last thing Phoebe had meant to do. She knew exactly how she felt now after that kiss with Lawrence.

She loved Jacoby.

Staring at the phone, she wondered if she should make the attempt to call and speak with him. Assure him she was just doing this as a favor for Lawrence to help him get this account by buttering up the client with the children. Obviously the ploy had worked because Lawrence had come here just to ask Mr. Quinn for a trial period for computer services to his five different business ventures that needed server service. Yet by the end of dinner, Mr. Quinn was thinking about signing Lawrence's company to a five year a little over five million dollar deal. That would be wonderful for his company and Lawrence looked ready to pass out.

Picking up the receiver, she started to dial Jacoby's phone number, but then changed her mind. Even though Mr. Quinn had said it was all right to make long distance calls, she didn't want to over extend her privileges. Hanging up, she sighed wistfully with a grave sense of dread.

Lying down in bed, she glanced back at the phone wondering if she had made the right decision.

Chapter 18

They returned early Sunday morning and she put the twins to bed immediately then with her mother checked the house. Patricia called her to the back porch where there were overturned planters. They looked at each other knowingly.

"Do you think he knew we were out of town?" Phoebe asked worriedly, wrapping her arms around her waist from an invisible chill creeping through her senses.

Patricia started straightening up the planters. "I think so. I guess that alarm system did come in handy."

"Momma, why would he be watching us?"

"He's broke. He has nowhere to go. He thinks he can get back in like Flynn because of what he thinks he can do to you. Men are so one tracked. I know that ass like the back of my hand and in about a couple of days I bet he shows his broke ass up on our doorway making apologies." Patricia was clearly perturbed.

Phoebe had been thinking the same thing and didn't feel so bad to think such things now that her mother had said the same thing. "I'm going to unpack then check my emails. I'll cook tonight. You've had a long weekend Momma, get some rest, okay?"

"Yes baby." She kissed her daughter's cheek then looked into Phoebe's eyes as if trying to read her thoughts. "Can he get back in, Phoebe?"

Without hesitation, Phoebe said, "No, Mother, I no longer love Daniel or fawn over him. And I won't let him hurt me again." These words she was sure of.

****

Abraham Blue was a big man of six feet five and three hundred pounds. He missed no meals, and was the best negotiating lawyer Jacoby had ever met. He had a son and daughter, who were also lawyers and worked with their father learning how to be the best like him. Yet, as big as Abraham was, his looks belied his gentle side.

So it wasn't odd that when he met Jacoby and Desmond at Fishbone's in Downtown Detroit for lunch on Monday, he gave them spine breaking big bear hugs. His laughter boomed to the ceiling because he was very happy to see them and tell them of the wonderful time in Davenport, Ohio. He had the papers for Jacoby to sign, and the layout plans for Desmond to work on for new software and computer systems.

Desmond was slightly perturbed because of what Jacoby had done earlier that morning for Phoebe, but he kept his comments to himself being reserved and defensive. Jacoby didn't really care how Desmond felt about his relationship with Phoebe, but he at least expected Desmond to be a little happy he had found a woman he could trust and wanted to be with. Desmond was always saying how Lawrence and Jacoby needed to find good women and settle down like he was about to do, yet now that Jacoby had found one, it was as if Desmond was dreading that it had happened.

Jacoby concentrated on the meeting and not on what Desmond thought of his involvement with Phoebe.

"You bought yourself a steal. This company's on the cutting edge of setting up Internet research technology that people will pay big money for. There is so much information the company has, it was just never filed and managed properly. I figure with a great computer program, the information to cure the Ebola virus might be hidden in all that shit they've complied. Hey Jake, did you ever find yourself an office manager for Detroit?"

Jacoby sighed tiredly, "Not yet, but I had plans to steal someone in particular." A wicked smile graced his lips.

Desmond's eyes widened. "You can't be serious. Madeline would be a fool to let her go."

"Madeline doesn't know how to appreciate a good thing," Jacoby protested.

Abraham agreed wholeheartedly, "She sure as hell knows how to take advantage of people though. That bitch don't fool me with her pretty looks and soft style of speech. She'd screw the pope out of his robe if she needed it to make a penny."

"I think you all are being pretty harsh on her," Desmond said defensively. "Madeline's helped us in a lot of ways, with contacts, setups and so on."

"To get something out of us," Jacoby said, matter of fact. "You don't think she doesn't know we're using her? She's all business, Desmond. You're only charging her about fifty percent less than what you charge other clients. When she doesn't need us anymore, she'll throw us to the curb."

Abraham added, "Let's just hope we can get up and walk away if that happens too soon, but I can tell you now, I'm getting mine and getting gone before that bitch decides to throw me to the curb."

Desmond shook his head. "I haven't seen one deceitful bone in Madeline's body."

Jacoby asked, "So inviting me to stay at her place while I'm in town is no indication she is up to something? When we both have an understanding that we won't be seeing each other anymore."

"No. She's only being a friend," Desmond defended.

"My ass she is, Desmond. That woman's got something up her sleeve and I don't trust her."

"You don't trust any woman," Abraham pointed out.

"I bet you trust Phoebe," Desmond said quietly.

"Who's Phoebe?" Abraham asked, seeing the tension between the friends.

"Madeline's office manager that your client decided to dip his tool in, while dipping in the boss too."

"I didn't know she was her manager when I was dipping and I told you Madeline and I had an arrangement. I used her and she used me for one purpose."

"You mean that girl Maddie's been bragging she got for a peso, but she's worth her weight in gold?" Abraham asked, sucking greedily on some crawfish.

Jacoby was far from hungry and pushed his plate away. "Yes, the one and the same, Abraham."

Abraham looked grievously. "Damn Jacoby, does Maddie know?"

"Not yet," Desmond said.

"And when Maddie does find out, hopefully Phoebe will be out of that situation and getting paid what she should be getting paid."

"Maybe Phoebe likes it there and you just fucked it up for her," Desmond said angrily. "Maybe you don't know shit and you shouldn't be so selfish. There was life before you, Jacoby, and you should open your eyes before just going after people."

Jacoby had a feeling that Desmond was upset about something else other than what they were really talking about. He decided to change the subject and get Abraham out the way before talking with Desmond.

Once the meeting was over with, Desmond and Jacoby headed to Madeline's apartment not too far from where they had lunch. Madeline called Desmond on his cell phone to let him know she was on the way over to meet them at the apartment for testing.

"What the hell is going on?" Jacoby asked as they took the elevators to the fifteenth floor.

"I'm just saying, your involvement in Phoebe's life needs to be just business if you don't want to get hurt."

"Hurt by whom? Phoebe?"

Desmond took a deep breath of regret. "Both of you are my boys and I don't want to see any woman come between us, but she's playing both of you like a deck of cards."

The elevator doors opened as Jacoby was just catching on to what Desmond was trying to say. They arrived immediately at Madeline's apartment.

"What's going on Desmond that I don't know about?" he demanded to know.

"One day she's with you, the next she spending the weekend with Lawrence at Quinn's. She's got you so wrapped around her finger if she unwrapped you, I think you might fall so hard you'd never get up, but I can't keep my mouth closed another minute. I don't want to see the two of you hurt. Lawrence likes her a lot and so do you, but the way it looks, she could give a fig about either one of you."

The door to the apartment opened and Lawrence stood there innocently. "It's about time-" He was cut short as Jacoby's fist connected with his jaw.

Desmond held Jacoby back from taking another swing.

Jacoby exclaimed furiously looking heatedly at Lawrence, who was still in shock over the blow. "You son of a bitch, you knew how I felt about her and you still tried to move in on her!" Jacoby fought to be released from Desmond, but Desmond wouldn't let go.

"I'm the son of a bitch?" Lawrence said, coming to his senses and realizing what Jacoby was mad about. "I'm not the one trying to buy her pussy." He suckered punched Jacoby back in the jaw.

Desmond was knocked back from the force of the blow and released Jacoby. Jacoby wasted no time swinging back and landed several punches to Lawrence's mid section, before he was tackled against the wall and Lawrence gave him two sharp blows to the stomach.

They were oblivious to the fight until Phoebe's voice screamed, "Stop! Stop! Dammit Stop!"

They looked around to see Madeline, Simon, and Phoebe standing in the apartment staring at them as if they had lost their mind.

Jacoby shoved Lawrence away and faced Phoebe directly. "Was this all a game for you? Did you have fun fucking us both? How much did he have to pay for your pussy, bitch?"

The room was so quiet, a 747 flying above could be heard clearly.

Phoebe's eyes narrowed to slits as her hand came up and slapped him as hard as she could. The slap didn't seem to budge her, but the stinging in her hand was evident as she held it close to her chest. She turned and ran out the apartment.

Lawrence shoved Jacoby out the way and followed Phoebe out. Jacoby looked over at Madeline, then turned away and went into the bathroom not caring how Desmond decided to straighten things out.

Chapter 19

Phoebe made it down to the street looking around desperately for a cab as the tears fought to escape her. Lawrence pulled up beside her and honked the horn. She ignored him still searching for a cab.

"Get in, Phoebe," he ordered unlocking the doors.

"I don't want anything to do with either one of you. Just stay the hell away from me, Lawrence," she ordered, wiping her wet face with the back of her hand.

"You don't mean that, now get in the car and let's discuss this," he insisted blocking her from crossing a street by pulling his white Lincoln Continental, with burgundy furnishings interior, in front of her.

She knew the bus station was a long way from where she was and she had on heels instead of her walking shoes, she regularly changed into before leaving work. Reluctantly she sat in the passenger seat, but kept her eyes straight holding her purse close to her chest as if at any moment she would jump out the car and make a run for it.

He drove - slowly - going towards her office, which was two minutes from Madeline's new apartments.

"Look, I told you what happened between you and Jacoby meant nothing to me," he insisted. "I still want to be friends, Phoebe."

"It's not you, Lawrence," she said in all honesty. "I don't want to have anything else to do with Jacoby and since you're his close friend, I don't think we should see each other anymore."

"I value your friendship Phoebe. I don't want to lose that. Please don't deny me this little pleasure that I treasure." He pulled near the side of her office building, which was near Cadillac Square. "Plus, hopefully Desmond will work out what just happened and you'll be alright in Madeline's book. You did nothing wrong in my opinion to Madeline. How could you have known you were getting involved with a guy already involved with someone else. He's the one that needs to do all the explaining not you. I think he would be wrong to blame all this on you. You're the innocent one in all of this. Don't feel guilty because he should have made some indication to Madeline that he wasn't going to be just hers."

Phoebe bit her lip staring deep into Lawrence's cool brown eyes. What was Lawrence's game? Even though his words sounded sincere, he didn't sound as if he knew anything about Madeline and Jacoby's arrangement. Phoebe knew more than Lawrence did about the arrangement. Why was he trying to make her hate Jacoby? Did he really want to be with her that bad? Did he really have true feelings about her? Was that what he was trying to do and should she try to become more with him, since he didn't care about what she did with Jacoby?

Looking away, not wanting to show her doubtfulness to Lawrence, she said, "I just need time to think about us, Lawrence. You are a good friend, but I do have a lot of personal issues I need to work out before I even think about having close friends in my life."

He took her hand and kissed the back. "I understand. You'll call me though if you need anything?"

Glancing up at him and giving him a smile, she promised, "Yes." After lightly kissing his cheek, she got out the car and went up into her office. Simon and Madeline had yet to return and she decided instead of running away from Madeline, she would stay and face her boss. A little of what Lawrence had said was true. In the beginning, she had not known that Jacoby was Madeline's lover. There was nothing to tell her that he was and she should not be blamed. Now if Madeline knew about the second time when Phoebe did know who he was involved with, that would be an even bigger problem.

Madeline and Simon came back an hour later. Simon went straight into his office and Madeline stopped in Phoebe's and closed the door. Phoebe watched as Madeline went over to the window and looked out over the Downtown Detroit area. It was a beautiful view and Phoebe often loved to stare it at herself. The view was relaxing making her feel that she was not alone in this great big crazy world and that maybe her problems were probably small compared to others out there.

Phoebe made no attempt to start talking. She watched the tension in Madeline's back and wondered what her boss was thinking.

"Desmond explained to me what happened," Madeline said quietly. "If you want to know, I don't blame you. He did stress you didn't know. Neither were you aware of who he was when you were together."

Unsure of how much Madeline knew, hesitantly, Phoebe explained, "It was just supposed to be a one night stand."

"I know. You've already told me that." Madeline was silent for a long moment before she turned and said, "I can't really be mad at him either. It was an arrangement and no commitments were ever discussed. Plus, he didn't know who you were either." She sat down in front of Phoebe's desk. "Given that he is insatiable I don't blame him, but I am interested in how you met. Desmond said he couldn't really remember, but I knew he was trying to blow me off."

Phoebe chose her words carefully. Madeline had a bullshit detector and Phoebe would not be making alarms go off. "He approached me, gave me an offer too good to be true, I accepted and like I told you it was a one night stand."

Madeline gave a long hard look, but then relaxed. "It sounds like him and he is quite irresistible." She smiled to herself. "And to think I actually insisted you meet someone like him."

She wasn't sure if she wanted to discuss Jacoby with Madeline and hoped Madeline wouldn't do anymore prying.

"I don't want you to worry about your job. I'm not going to let a man come between my business. I never have and I never will." She stood up and asked, "I will see you Wednesday?"

"Yes," Phoebe assured her, but felt as if she was lying. Yet at least this reminded Phoebe tomorrow was the twins' doctor's appointment.

Madeline started to leave, but stopped in the doorway and said, "I see the system is getting full and this might be a busy week seeing that Thanksgiving is next week. Why don't you raise the purge to forty eight hours until Friday so we won't fill up too fast?"

This was a rare request, but Phoebe nodded. "I'll do it before I go."

"Why don't you just do it now while I'm standing here."

Phoebe felt a little tension, but moved over to the audio computer and obeyed Madeline's order.

Madeline seemed much happier about this. "See you Wednesday," she said and left out Phoebe's office.

Fifteen minutes later, Simon buzzed in Phoebe's office to say Madeline had decided to step out the office and would not be returning for the rest of the day. Phoebe didn't think this was strange since it was three o'clock nearing the end of the day.

Phoebe still felt uncomfortable about the casual way Madeline had taken the whole thing. She remembered Jacoby's words from the other night. Hell, it felt like she remembered everything all at once and was trying to fight this overwhelming sense of grief, as if she had lost something major in her life.

No, she told herself. She couldn't feel this way right now. She wouldn't think about him.

Yet, the idea that Madeline was going around bragging that she had gotten over on Phoebe really perturbed her. Going into Madeline's office she looked through the desk drawers until she found a locked card file box. Using a paper clip and a trick she had learned from Daniel, she picked the cheap lock and searched through the set of keys until she found what she was looking for. She removed the key she needed from the ring and replaced everything back in its place using a Kleenex just in case to wipe off all the fingerprints because Phoebe was really paranoid.

Quickly, she left the office and went back into her own office glad Simon had not caught her in the act because sometimes he was so nosey, he usually followed her shortly after every time she left her office as if he were spying on her. Knowing that this time he had not, started to gnaw at her brain. She walked quietly out her office and headed for the back offices to check to see if Simon was done with getting the back offices together per Madeline's instructions. Phoebe thought maybe Simon was so adamant about finishing the offices that he wasn't thinking about what Phoebe was doing. Just as she was getting to the door, she heard Latrice over the speakerphone inside the office, which were installed over the weekend.

"...I can't believe Phoebe would sleep with him for money!" Latrice exclaimed. "Does Madeline know that?"

"No, Madeline doesn't, but you know why she needs the money," Simon said.

Latrice giggled into the phone as if it were some deep dark secret. Phoebe quietly leaned against the wall and listened barely breathing so she could hear every word. "No reason Maddie called this afternoon and starting barking down instructions."

"What do you mean?" Simon asked.

Latrice sighed as if in regret. "She said she wanted me to call to inform security in your building that she would might need assistance this Friday at the office in Detroit. She was planning on letting an employee go and she thinks it might be disturbing. Can you imagine Phoebe being disturbed?"

Simon giggled now. "More like perturbed if you ask me. That's why Maddie was telling me in the car on the way back here that I needed to step up to the plate and take on more responsibilities because there was going to be big changes in the office."

"I just assumed it was going to be one of the typist?" She clicked her tongue. "I can't believe Phoebe could be so dumb as to believe all of Maddie's promises to raise her pay after she does a good job. I've seen that child jump through so many hoops for Madeline and Madeline keeps adding on things without giving her the raise. I thought maybe Phoebe would get smart after she made Madeline do everything in writing. It's about six different agreements each one Phoebe has kept and each one Madeline has broke. I think Madeline may owe her about a hundred grand in back pay. Phoebe doesn't even know the real pay Phoebe told the state she was promising to pay Madeline. If Phoebe wanted revenge all she has to do is get those agreements and take them to a lawyer."

"Where are they at?"

"There are two copies. One here in Lansing and the other in the locked employee cabinet in the copier room in the file room there in Detroit. Madeline keeps copies of all employees' stuff there for the politics. But in truth I think Madeline really thought Phoebe would fuck up any moment and Madeline would take great pleasure in rubbing the shit in her face, but Phoebe did everything perfect that I even heard Maddie say she should have hired Phoebe to run the office in the first place, so she wouldn't be in so much trouble with the state."

Simon inquired full of curiosity, " If she gets rid of Phoebe - and they like her a lot - won't she lose the state account?"

"I think that's a chance she's willing to take, but legally the state can't take the account away unless if ten or more reports come up missing with the exception to an act of God."

"What about the other accounts that love Phoebe?"

"Like I said it's a chance Madeline's willing to take because she is so pissed off at Phoebe. I didn't understand how much until you told me what happened, but now I know Madeline's going to make sure Phoebe can't get work to save her life in this city again. I just don't know how she's going to fire Phoebe and not have to pay the unemployment office. That would burn her up even more than having Phoebe on the payroll."

Simon gasped. "I know. She asked me to hold the Lansing package this afternoon, because that's the one that won't get to Lansing until Wednesday morning. If they aren't accounted for by the end of Wednesday they are officially lost and we would end up paying the doctors to do a rush report and that would come out of the company's pocket, not the state."

Latrice quickly caught on. "And that would give Madeline a good reason to fire Phoebe for incompetence."

They chuckled and Phoebe closed her eyes to control her anger as it was building by the second. Simon was supposed to be her so-called friend and as many times as she had saved his ass from getting fired by cleaning up his stupid shit, this was the thanks she would get.

"Well I won't worry about shit when I'm sitting in that nice office Phoebe's got because she took care of all the big problems. I won't have shit to do almost because she's cleaned up the mess. All I have to do is make sure the reports get out and answer any problems or questions the clients have." His voice turned harsh when he said, "And I won't be taking the shit pay Madeline gives to Phoebe. I'm not doing shit until I see it in my paycheck."

"Phoebe doesn't know about all that stuff I told you about her pay, does she?" Latrice said nervously.

"Of course not. She's so blind. Once I asked her why does she take all this crap and not get paid for it and she's going to tell me in some goody two shoe voice that good things come to those who wait. I wanted to tell her to wake up and smell the cappuccino because if you wait for Madeline to actually do something good for you, then you'll die waiting."

They had a very good laugh off of that one and Phoebe really fought for control. 'Am I really that bad of a character judge?' she wondered to herself. It seemed as if everyone knew she was being screwed, except Phoebe.

Latrice changed the subject to ask if Simon would be coming up for the weekend. Obviously now Phoebe was old news to them. As quietly as she had come up there, she made her way back to her office and cursed under her breath. Her mind was moving like a runaway locomotive and by the time she sat in her seat, she knew exactly what she needed to do in order to save her ass and make sure Madeline had a taste of her own deceitful medicine.

While she worked like lightening on the computer, keeping an eye on the phone, which indicated it was in use - knowing it was Simon and Latrice gossiping more - and keeping an ear on anyone coming down the hallway from the typing room, she called Leslie Cross, the Lansing supervisor.

"Hey kiddo," Leslie said happy to hear from Phoebe. "How's it going down in Detroit?"

"Stressful, but I don't have time for our usual talk sessions."

Leslie sounded really disappointed when she said, "Aw, that's really too bad, because I miss those."

Phoebe almost miss those days when they could sit on the phone and just talk like old pals, but she had only gotten in good with Leslie because she was trying to keep the account for Madeline and it had worked like a charm. Leslie would give her the inside scoop on what the administrators were getting upset about and what the other offices were saying about the reports. In all, Phoebe was well liked through all the FIA offices that she handled the reports for and she knew she could screw Madeline really bad if she wanted to, but instead she decided to save her own butt first.

"I need to ask you a favor," Phoebe said slowly.

"Oh this sounds juicy. You know you can ask me anything."

"I'm going to send you something special delivery through the email and I only want you to handle it. Don't even let your assistant know you received it because he will be asking you about it. I'm having a hunch about some things and I want to make sure before I make accusations I want to make sure it's the person I'm accusing."

"Will this make my doctor's upset?" Leslie's priority for her office was to make the doctors happy.

"Oh no, but you have to promise no matter how much shit hit the fan, you can't let on that you know the truth until I tell you. This involves my integrity. It has nothing to do with the doctors."

"Alright, give me the juicy details and we'll go from that, kiddo."

Phoebe quickly told Leslie her plan

Simon came into her office at the end of the day to ask when she would leaving just as she was sending off the last email to Leslie. It was ten minutes to five and everybody else was gone.

"I just have to take care of some reprints, then I'll be all done," she answered. "Then I have to wait until Leslie sends me a fax. It should be any minute." She tried to sound as cheerful as possible, without it sounding fake.

"You've had a long day. That fax will be here tomorrow and I'll personally take care of it," he promised.

She felt he was being a little bit too helpful. "I don't mind waiting, Simon."

"Then I can wait with you and help you out," he insisted.

Alarm bells went off like crazy inside Phoebe. Simon never liked working past five. It was against his own personal religion. It took all her control to keep a calm disposition in front of him. "No need, Simon. I'm just going to complete it and lay it on your desk, but since I'm off tomorrow I wanted to make sure it was complete."

"You don't trust me to do it?" he asked offended.

Her tone of voice was completely complacent. "Of course I would if I was here, but you'll be so overwhelmed and Leslie did ask me to help her out as a personal favor. You know how I am, I love to please."

Simon only smiled nervously. She could see he had run out of things to say to keep him there.

Phoebe asked innocently, "I didn't see the Lansing package on the pickup tray."

"Oh he came early just as I was done wrapping so I gave him what I had - which was Lansing. I'm sorry I forgot to tell you."

"Well, we would like to keep record of that. Did you sign the board for our records?" Usually Phoebe never cared if he signed the board or not and she would just go behind him and sign it.

She stuck an innocent yet flighty smile on her lips disarming him, as he said, "I'll sign it on my way out."

"Did Maddie tell you what's going on in those back offices?" she asked to throw him off. "I haven't had time to check them out yet because I've been so busy."

"Yeah," he said immediately perking up. Simon was a gossip by nature. He couldn't help himself and given any opportunity he could run his mouth until the cows come home. "She's having Mr. Knight use them for any of his business needs until his offices are ready next Monday." He snickered. "You think you can handle yourself around him until then?"

"I think I can," she said sourly. "Plus he's old news, Simon. You know that." Her voice was casual, but her brain was moving into outer drive and holding on to her turmoil of emotions was becoming difficult.

"That didn't look like old news to me this afternoon."

"Well, it was, but I couldn't help myself. I certainly wasn't going to allow him to speak to me that way a moment longer."

Simon smacked his lips as if he was very disappointed. "I just can't believe how he acted. After you left, he went into the bedroom's private bathroom, while Desmond told Madeline that a mistaken identity had been made and neither of you knew who the other was, but Lawrence had intentions on you way before then and Jacoby was being a sore loser."

"I wasn't a trophy," she said, letting her true emotions come to the forefront for just a moment, but then getting a hold on them and settling down taking a deep breath. "It doesn't matter. It's in the past."

"Obviously," Simon said, "Because Madeline went in the bedroom to speak to Jacoby. She closed the door, but by the time she came out she was beaming like she had won the Big Game Lottery."

Phoebe acted nonchalantly because she knew Simon had probably told her that to shock her. He was carefully studying her emotions and it was vital she kept good face.

"Can you believe how calm Madeline was in the office when she spoke to you?" he asked.

Of course the nosey prick would have been listening at the door. She didn't point this out to him. Instead she smiled a brittle, forced expression and said, "She must have been steaming on the way back here."

"Oh no," he lied blatantly. "She was pretty calm about the whole thing."

She wanted to punch him dead square in the jaw, but clutched the chair and grounded her teeth.

Simon checked his watch and cursed, but still seemed reluctant to leave. "If anything comes up, you'll call me, won't you?"

"You'll be the first to know," she promised with the most gracious smile plastered on her face.

Once he was gone, she deleted the emails for the entire day off the computer then went in the back and took them off the server. She signed on the server using Simon's name and password. She knew this because it was her job to know everyone's password in case something happened to them and no one could get into their computer, but along with that knowledge she wasn't supposed to use it wrongly.

Not a guilty bone in her body came as she used Simon's code to get in and saw that he also had administrative powers like her. Phoebe wondered when had his administrative duties had changed.

The computer allowed her to get in other computers and she knew exactly what do. Without Madeline knowing, she had taken computer software classes on the weekends, paying out of her own pocket. Phoebe had mastered the knowledge, of the program she used and had become certified without anyone's knowledge except her mother.

While she was at it, she checked Madeline's trash knowing the sequence to get into other computers in the office.

Maddie had shot an email to Desmond right before leaving the office today, telling him to block all of Phoebe's privileges by next Monday morning. There was also an email to Latrice in detail about what Madeline was planning and what Latrice needed to do in order for it to work. At the end of it all, Madeline ordered Latrice to delete this email messages and any other's concerning Phoebe in the next couple of days that would probably be sent.

Phoebe reprogrammed Madeline's computer emails to do secret CC's to her email at her private address. If Madeline didn't know how to read her e-mail's properly, she wouldn't notice this was happening until too late unless the email was re-forward back to Madeline.

She made copies of the emails and then closed down all the programs she had went into and signed off. Her presence in the computer would not be known, except without a thorough investigation, but by then she wouldn't care because she wouldn't be there.

The fax machine alarm to let her know a fax had come through went off and she went into the copier room where the fax was and took the fax Leslie had just sent her off the machine. There were several pages and Leslie had made notes in the margins pointing out the information that Phoebe had asked for. Along with the fax, she placed the emails in a folder and then she put this in her brief case along with the key to the personnel file. Tomorrow when no one least expected it. She would come into the office and look in detail in her file, hoping nothing would be changed and hoping that no one had thought of hiding the files.

Chapter 20

Tossing the remote control on the bed, Jacoby staggered over to the nearest chair to get his balance. He figured the eight shots of Corbel were the ones that had broken the camel's back tonight along with his intake of several beers and other hard liquors. It was a good thing he had only used the restaurant's bar because anywhere else and he knew he would not have made it back to his room.

Sitting in the chair before he fell on his face, he looked down at the bulge between his legs. Damn, he cursed sitting back in the chair. Tonight he had several offers from very beautiful women. Each one more beautiful and tempting than the other, yet he knew that none of them could satisfy him like Phoebe.

Soon as he got out of his clothes, he staggered over to the bed and laid down hoping he had gotten enough to drink to just pass out, but it felt as if he didn't because as he stared up at the ceiling, he found himself wishing she was here.

The phone by the bed rung loudly and he picked it up, grateful for the distraction. Before he could get anything out to say, Desmond came on the line. "Shut your mouth, cover the receiver and just listen, all right?"

He wasn't given a chance to answer as the line clicked then he could hear Desmond say, "No, I think I just missed her. I'll catch up with her later. So what were you saying about Jacoby?"

"Like I said, Jacoby couldn't go a second without having a woman. You know he's a sex addict. I haven't seen that man go seventy-two hours without being between some woman's legs."

"Which would explain why he was so irresistible to Phoebe?" Desmond asked.

"Jake doesn't deserve a woman like Phoebe. He wouldn't know how to treat a woman like Phoebe. You saw how he was with her."

"And you would?" Desmond asked doubtfully.

"Of course I would. I have. Jacoby doesn't know how to make any woman happy."

"Obviously he's doing something right. She slept with him twice."

This information seem to incense Lawrence, as he growled, "And each time he's had to pay. That's doing something right?"

"Are you saying if he didn't have the money, no woman would be attracted to him?"

"I think Jacoby wouldn't know how to get a woman if he didn't hide behind his money. Especially a woman like Phoebe."

"You sound pretty serious about Phoebe, but you've been serious about a woman before then you turned around and pretended you had no feelings for her."

"And I still don't." This was a pretty sore subject for Lawrence. "I'm going to go all the way this time."

"And what was last time? For practice?"

"Shut the fuck up, Desmond," Lawrence snapped. "If you're going to sit on the sidelines and watch to see who wins, you need to keep your nose and your opinions to yourself."

Desmond sighed gravely. "I just don't see why both of you are making an ass over a woman who cares nothing about either one of you. Yes, she's very beautiful, intelligent, and seems to have a nice personality, but that's no reason to make fools out of yourself."

"That's what you don't understand, Desmond," Lawrence said with relish. "Phoebe's different from any woman I've ever met and even though I haven't had a taste of her - but I will soon - I still want to just be with her."

"You've said this all before about other women. Plus, if she was so special why hasn't she been hounded by other men?"

"Desmond, why are you being so negative towards her?" Lawrence asked.

"Because I don't like what's she done to the two of you. You're letting some tramp come between two good friends."

"Who the fuck says Jacoby's my friend? He waves his damn money in everyone's face with a wink and a smile and expects to get the world. Well I'm tired of being in his fucking gratitude all the damn time. I wish I could tell him to take his money and shove it where the sun don't shine."

"So all this time when he thought you were his friend, you were really using him just to get the money to open up the business? Are you trying to say you were jealous of him all this time and wished we had nothing to do with him?"

"I sure as hell am saying that. If we didn't need the money I would definitely stay the fuck away from him."

"I think it's the liquor talking now, Lawrence," Desmond said. "I think you need to get some rest because without the money, the two of you are one and the same which is probably why the girl likes the both of you."

"Well, fuck you and the rosy ass horse you rode on Des. You wouldn't understand it all to save your life." The line clicked meaning Lawrence had hung up.

Desmond only chuckled which was his nature to do. He never took the verbal abuse seriously that Lawrence and Jacoby dealt out to him when they were upset.

"Why the hell did you want me to hear that shit?" Jacoby asked.

"To let you know Lawrence is just talking out his ass. He doesn't see the whole picture and you are going to have to tell Phoebe to stay away from the two of you."

"Why? Maybe Phoebe doesn't know the truth about Lawrence and I should be the one to tell her?"

As confusing as that sounded, Desmond did understand, but asked sarcastically, "Would it really make a difference to her, Jacoby? She's used the both of you and I don't think she really cares. Just let it go. Just leave her alone. I don't like what she does to the two of you."

"Like he said, Desmond. You really don't understand it all, but unlike Lawrence, I know Phoebe. I know what she feels and what she wants and what she really wants, is me. "

"That's the same shit Lawrence has been saying."

"Like you said, Lawrence is just talking out his ass." He hung up the line and now he really couldn't sleep. He had always known Lawrence had some animosity and jealousy for him personally not just his money. Lawrence wanted the money, but he could never understand how through all of Jacoby's life's trials and tribulations the money hadn't affected him. How people still wanted to be around him whether he had money or not. Lawrence was one of them even if he couldn't admit it.

Now his thoughts turned to Phoebe. She hadn't slept with Lawrence in all this time, but had what Jacoby done changed her mind. Was Jacoby responsible now for sending Phoebe into Lawrence's arms? Now she really wouldn't have anything to do with him.

Chapter 21

After the doctor's appointment, she came home and waited for her mother to come home. When Patricia came in the door, Phoebe was just about to start looking into the books. She had realized this morning, unlike all other mornings; Patricia had put the bill ledger up instead of it laying out on the end of the table.

"Don't you go worrying about the bills today," Patricia said, taking the ledger gently away from Phoebe and putting it back up on the shelf in the kitchen.

"I just wanted to see where we were?"

"You really don't need to have more to worry about Phoebe. I'll take care of these while you clear your mind about other things."

Phoebe sighed tiredly knowing her mother was determined to get her mind off of Jacoby. "Mother, my mind is clear about everything."

"If it was so clear, then you wouldn't look like someone broke your heart."

"No one broke my heart, Mother," she protested.

Patricia looked very doubtful. "So why did you avoid Lawrence's call last night?"

"I just wanted to spend time with the kids, plus I told you what happened yesterday."

"Are you still going to go back to work after what you know?"

"Until the end of this week. I don't want anyone to get suspicious about anything yet. Not until I get all the information that I need," Phoebe answered.

The doorbell rung followed by an impatient knock on the door. At the same time, Stephanie could be heard on the monitor awaking from her nap.

"You go check on Stephanie and I'll take care of the door," Phoebe said going towards the door.

When she opened the door, she was leery to see that no one was standing on the porch, but someone had left a dozen roses by the door. Opening the security screen door, she looked around warily and picked up the vase the flowers were in and went back in the house closing the door behind her.

Reading the card, it only read, "Missing you." No one had signed it, but she knew who the writing was from and dropped the flowers in the nearest garbage. Patricia was just coming down the stairs to see her throw away the flowers.

"Who sent those to you?'

"Daniel. I guess he thought I wouldn't know, but I know his handwriting." She handed her mother the card.

"Well it's a nice vase," Patricia noted getting the vase out and leaving the flowers in the garbage.

"Which he probably spent my money on," Phoebe snapped.

"No need to waste money then." Patricia took the vase in the kitchen.

Phoebe on rolled her eyes in exasperation following her mother. After asking about the children and getting a positive response she told her mother, "I going to the office while no one is expecting me until tomorrow to get some more files I need for me."

"Are you going to do what you spoke about yesterday?"

"Yes, but I do need some more information before I proceed and before they have time to trash anything."

Patricia kissed her daughter's cheek. "Be careful, Phoebe. I don't want you to get hurt."

Phoebe chortled. "Madeline wouldn't dare do something that could send her to jail. She would find that a waste to the half a million dollar plastic surgery she paid for earlier last year for her to look so good."

****

Arriving at the offices quietly Phoebe checked to see if anyone was there. She didn't bother to check the two back offices that had just been clean because she figured most likely he wasn't here. He probably didn't want to be around unless Madeline was around.

Moving quickly, she put her brief down on the nearby table in the copier room she got the key out and opened up the cabinets leaving her brief wide open to put the rest of the papers in there that she found today. Finding the file marked Phoebe Green, she opened it up and began to look through the papers.

Latrice always kept good files and Phoebe didn't have a hard time finding the agreements that had been signed by Madeline for a raise in pay for each accomplishment she had already done. Madeline always said the raises would come, but when they didn't Madeline would tell her the pay system was messed up and she would get back pay. Phoebe most times felt like a dog being led on a bone above her head too high for her to reach.

She hurriedly made copies of the agreements and other information that she would need, then found the past supervisor's file and made a necessary copies from that file. Just as she was about to close the drawer, her eyes landed on Simon's file. Picking it up, she briefly flipped through the papers until she came to an agreement form. Simon didn't have the skills to work in an office, but according to his resume he did have a good college background and had majored in a managerial field, yet why had he chosen to be an assistant if he was geared to do so much more.

Reading the agreement deep in her own thoughts, she didn't hear the footsteps behind her until it was too late. Screaming in fright, she whirled around to glare at Jacoby who stood directly behind.

"What the hell do you think you're doing?" Jacoby asked suspicious as the papers in her hand began to fly around.

Hurriedly she knelt down and picked up the papers glaring up at him as if he had just lost his mind. "Do you know how to announce yourself instead of scaring people half to death?"

"What are you doing here?" he asked suspiciously.

"That's what I should be asking you." She finished straightening out the papers and quickly put the file back in its place. Facing him, angrily she continued to glare up at him.

"Isn't it too late for you to be out? Mothers need to be at home with their children."

"Where I go is none of your business," she snapped.

He looked over at her brief to the papers sticking out. She picked up the papers she had just copied to avoid him from looking at them, but he snatched them out her hands and stepped away.

"Give them back!" she ordered.

"Why?" He was looking through them quickly.

"What are you? Madeline's spy and lover?"

Jacoby glanced at her for a moment and then went back to his reading. The frown on his face started getting even grimmer.

"This is none of your business!" she snapped.

"Good thing it isn't because I'd choke Madeline's scrawny neck if she did this shit to me. You're being paid fifteen grand less than what the last manager was getting paid and on top of that in the contract it states all managers are being paid forty five thousand dollars. I wouldn't choke her - I would shoot her. And I'm not her spy."

Phoebe snorted. "Just her lover?" She snatched the papers from him and stuffed them back in her brief case. Turning her back to him as she did this, she asked, "So you won't be telling Madeline what I'm doing?"

"Why should I? I am the one who gave you the advice to do this. And for your information, I'm not her lover anymore since our first night. I'm staying in the hotel. I'm sure you remember what hotel room, don't you?"

She stiffened as memories of their erotic last night together went racing through her mind. Jacoby had not brought up that memory for her to cause the stimulation it caused upon thinking about it, but instead, she assumed, he had brought it up to deceitfully call her another whore without even saying it.

He was only being vindictive and her animosity for him clearly rose to the surface. When he was nice, he could be so nice, but when he was mean, he definitely did that all too well. Jacoby knew how to hit way below the belt.

Facing him, narrowing her eyes, she asked, "Am I suppose to be grateful to you because you gave me that advice?" She wanted to call him a big fat liar because no man with his sexual insatiability could go too long without being without a woman. She refused to believe he was passing up sex with Madeline and was actually waiting on Phoebe. That would be too impossible to believe because that meant that he wanted only her. She quickly pushed this thought from her head.

"You should be appreciative." There was a wicked light in his eyes and she decided his proximity was started to effect her senses, so she left out the copier room and went into Madeline's office and began to replace the key touching as little as possible then using a Kleenex to wipe fingerprints off as she finished up.

He leaned against the door frame watching her quietly. When she was done, he said, "You do that well."

"If that's a compliment, thank you." Again she had to walk past him, but this time he blocked her way forcing her to look up at him.

"What do you plan on doing with this information?"

"Get money that's owed to me."

"What about her business? You sue her enough you could ruin her, take over her clients and get your own business."

The thought had crossed her mind, but this wasn't the kind of business she would like to have. "No thanks. I just want what's mine so my mother doesn't have to worry about money again."

He frowned disturbed. "When will it be enough, Phoebe? When do you actually think you'll have enough money?"

"When I don't have to worry about what will I be feeding my babies tomorrow. When I don't have to look into their faces and tell them we can't afford to buy them the things they see other children have or things on television. When they have to pretend to have the things they want. When I have to pass up the things in the store I need so bad just to make sure my babies live comfortably. That's when it will be enough. Their happiness means the world to me," she stated heatedly.

"And your happiness?"

She shrugged. "No one much cares about my happiness and I've stopped caring. It's not important. My children are my happiness." Phoebe pulled her worn brown coat around her shoulders and closed it up. "Goodnight Mr. Knight. Make sure you lock up when you are done."

Jacoby watched her until she was gone then cursed under his breath. He was wound tighter than a ball of yarn. Seeing her had made it even more difficult to concentrate on getting her off his mind, which had been his intentions of coming in this late into the office. He had fully thrown himself into his work today to keep him distracted all day, and it was working until now.

He swore if this kept up, he would have to jam ice down his damn pants to avoid an embarrassing bulge that would certainly draw attention.

Chapter 22

Simon came in her office Wednesday morning to let her know Carolyn and Rhonda's computers - two of the transcriptionists - were on the fritz and were locking up on them. He had tried to figure out what was wrong with them, but had no success. When Phoebe looked at them it was to see that somehow a file from both of the computers was deleted along with a years' worth of work plus their backup copies. She checked the server and saw that the reports were missing from there also.

"What are we going to do?" Simon asked nervously.

Phoebe frowned confused. It all seemed rather strange but she didn't feel like going into depth with this. "It looks like the current reports are still there. Reinstall the transcription programs so it will replace the missing files it needs to work, then do another find on their computers for the reports. If we still can't find them, we'll go from there."

Simon reported back to her right before lunch that the reports were gone. "Luckily though I've printed the reports they have already done today so we should be okay because we are all caught up."

This put Phoebe's mind somewhat at eased, but she did want to research it all just a little bit more wondering what had Simon done while she was off yesterday. She decided to forget lunch and check into the matter, but Lawrence showed up and asked if she was free for lunch.

"I really should work," she insisted.

He looked like a lost puppy dog. "You'll have me eat alone?"

"You aren't trying to start something again between Jacoby and you again."

Lawrence smirked. "I could care less about what he thinks. I even made sure he wouldn't be in the office when Madeline called me just a few minutes ago. So I ask again, can two good friends go out and enjoy a nice hour of lunch and good talk together?"

She agreed and he escorted her out. She needed a lift and Lawrence was a breath of fresh air when they spoke. He was the epitome of being a gentleman and he made her laugh relaxing her and getting her mind off of Jacoby and the office. She could deal with the office weighing heavily on her mind, but she really hated the fact that as much as Lawrence was a distraction mildly, any free second her mind had, her thoughts would turn to Jacoby. Seeing him last night had not deflated any feelings whatsoever in her body and her mind for him.

When Madeline called her up to speak with her after lunch, Phoebe thought for sure this was about what she had been doing the night before. Jacoby had told her he wasn't Madeline's spy, but she was positive he still hated her for something she didn't even do, but he was too stubborn to believe her from his own mind's machinations.

Her heart raced as she answered the phone. Simon had come into her office quietly so Madeline wouldn't know he was listening as Phoebe put Madeline on the phone's speaker.

"I was just informed by Kyle in Lansing that they are missing twenty six reports from Monday afternoon. Did that delivery go out?"

Playing the role, she checked her delivery sheet. Simon had not signed the board when he had left. She looked up at him accusatory, but she didn't want to let on that he was in the room, so she said, "I'm positive it did."

"Did you make sure?" Madeline asked. Her voice clearly said she was perturbed about something.

"No ma'am and I didn't check the board to make sure it was signed, but Simon told me that the FedEx man arrived early for the Lansing copies."

"And did you do a confirmation with Lansing?"

"We haven't had to do a confirmation in a long while."

"Well that's probably why Lansing is missing these reports and Kyle has reported them to me. How do you know the FedEx man made the pickup if you are just taking someone's word and not finding out yourself. I gave you a job, to do and I don't think I'm asking for too much. You do know your job don't you?"

This was clearly said to make Phoebe look dumb and if Phoebe didn't know what was going on, it would have certainly worked. "Madeline, I'll look into it."

"There's nothing to look into. I've checked the system and I can't find a report from Monday that was sent out. On top of that, the reports from Monday have been purged and we can't go back and get them."

"I'm sorry, Madeline," she apologized. "I'm sure I can request the copies from the girl's computers. Give me an hour and I'll look around for the numbers we need."

"One hour, Phoebe. If I don't hear from you in an hour you can kiss your ass goodbye." The line clicked and Phoebe looked at Simon.

"You are going to help me find these reports."

He smiled to comfort her. "I'll do all I can to help you out," he promised.

Phoebe decided to try to see if there were copies of the reports and learned Carolyn and Rhonda had typed all the reports that were needed. Her heart would have sank in disappointment if she didn't know what was going on. She went to the bathroom to give herself some privacy. Pacing the bathroom like a caged tiger, she cursed a vindictive at the ceiling fully knowing Madeline had arranged all of this to get her fired. Madeline was clearly going for the jugular with her sharpest blade of deceit.

When she returned to the office, Simon asked if she was all right. His concern was so phony she wanted to again punch him, but closing her fist so tight she felt her nails digging in her palm, she shook her head and went into her office to call Madeline back. Simon followed and sat down on the other side of the desk.

"What are you going to tell her?" he asked.

"The truth. The reports are missing. The computers they were typed on have crashed and the audio is purged."

"She is not going to be very happy."

"Well, I don't know what else to do."

"Why don't you lie? Say that Rhonda and Carolyn have to see if they typed at home or another typist has them. This should put everything off until Friday, but first call Leslie, Kyle's boss, and tell her you need until Friday in order to find the reports. She owes you favors, she'll give you the time."

If she had been in trouble, she would have taken this suggestion blindly thinking Simon had her best interest in mind. "Alright, thank you Simon."

"No problem. I only want to help."

It took all her control not to slap him, but instead she picked up the receiver and called Leslie.

"Hey kiddo, how's it going?" Leslie's perky voice asked.

"Hi Les, this is Phoebe about the reports you are looking for?"

"Yes?" Leslie said, matter of fact.

"I need to speak to a typist offsite. Can you give me until Friday at least?"

"No problem. Talk to you then."

Simon looked a bit perturbed and Phoebe was sure after she had hung up with Leslie, Simon had thought that Leslie would refuse. Phoebe called Madeline next to tell her what Simon had instructed her to say. Madeline seemed a bit put off, but with Leslie in agreement with Friday's date, that meant Madeline had to put off firing her until then. Phoebe would just have to pretend she was stressed out until Friday. That would be easy to do because she always looked like that around the office.

Patricia looked through the copies Wednesday night when Phoebe got off work and sighed tiredly. Phoebe had informed her mother of what was going at the office and Patricia was quite amused.

"This is over a hundred grand, Phoebe," Patricia noted after briefly surveying the papers. "I don't have a final total right now from just glancing it over, but the large numbers do stand out."

"I know. Can you add it up for me, including the payroll tax?" she asked.

Her mother was great at accounting, which was her part time job. Patricia had always wanted to have her own accounting company, but never had the money to do it.

"I can do you one better and even check with this payroll company that your company uses and see if there is any suspicious activities. I know a couple of people that work there."

Phoebe was excited because with this money she could give it to her mother to help her afford to work at home. "I need the car again to go into the office. No one should be there so it should be alright. I was reading something in Simon's file and the more I think about it, the more I think I should get a copy of what I saw."

Patricia looked skeptical. "You have enough here to go to any lawyer and get what you deserve."

"I still want to, Mother. I'll be back in a couple of hours." She kissed her mother's cheek. "Thanks for everything." Grabbing the keys off the desk she headed to the office. This time when she came in, she checked everywhere. No one was there and she went back into the employee's cabinet.

The agreement Simon was promised at his time of employment was that he was on an annual probation. If by that time, which was in a month, his performance improved he would be given a salary that would match hers along with benefits without any added responsibilities. On top of that he would be appointed co-manager of the Detroit Offices.

She had to wonder how had Simon gotten this agreement out of Madeline when he was about the laziest office assistant she had ever met. Staring at Simon's name, she frowned immensely wondering if her suspicions were true and went into Madeline's office. On the wall was a newspaper clipping from the Lansing Journal Newspaper of Madeline standing in the middle of two other people at a business awards dinner. Underneath the picture, the byline read, "...outstanding business woman of the year, Madeline Porter, stands next to Cynthia Reed, Editor-In-Chief of the Lansing Journal, and Joel Bowen, her co-business partner."

Cynthia Reed, a light blonde, deep tanned stick looked reluctant to be in the photo, but Joel looked ready to burst with happiness standing next Madeline. Phoebe went into her office and got online to look up Joel Bowen. His name came up as a wealthy investor living in Lansing. A picture of his family came up and her eyes went wide as saucers as she saw Simon standing next to his father, Joel.

Phoebe went back to the copier room and looked in the other drawers to find papers on P&B communications. Madeline only owned thirty percent of the company. Joel had put the money up for the business while Madeline had the know how to run it.

Phoebe's brain was going a hundred miles an hour. If Madeline was screwing Phoebe out of some money, Phoebe would bet her life she wasn't the only person Madeline was screwing. She searched more through the papers and decided that she needed her mother to have a look at all of this. Replacing the key to the file cabinet, she went to the back server and found herself in the Lansing offices computers by routing through the servers, which were connected. Finding Latrice's computer was easy because the technicians had set up the computers by name. There was a recently updated accounting spreadsheet. When she tried to go into it, the computer would not let her.

At first she decided not to press the issue, but it nagged her to death not knowing what was this spreadsheet about and decided to try Latrice's son's name Roger. The spreadsheet opened up and she printed the entire spreadsheet to the printer. It consisted of a three year record of the Detroit office payments for the FIA account, but why would Latrice need to keep record of the payments the FIA made to P&B Detroit offices when all the accounting procedures were outsourced. Latrice was just supposed to send the checks off.

A noise in the front of the offices startled her. She closed the programs down she had opened and signed Simon off the computer. Quickly packing up her things, she heard the fax alarm going off. She was going in there anyway to pick up what she had sent to the printer. Standing in front of the fax machine, Jacoby wore a nice pair of Bugle Boy khaki pants and a plaid shirt. He looked as if he had thrown on his clothes, but he sure as hell looked damn fine in those clothes. Phoebe stood there admiring the firm backside of him and enjoying the view as she became aroused at just looking at him.

He cursed quite violently and was about to yank the paper out the machine.

"I hope that's not your only copy," she said startling him.

An expletive shot out his mouth as he turned around to glare at her. "What the hell are you doing here?"

"We are not about to go through that again. Is that your only copy?"

"For now it is until I can get to my damn computer next Monday." His tone was sharp and filled with annoyance. Again he tried to yank the paper out the jammed fax.

Quickly she went over to him and moved his hands out the way. "You're going to tear it and break the machine too."

"Then you get the damn thing out." He stepped away from the machine to give her room to help him out.

She gave him her back as she properly removed the fax from the machine with a simple click. He reached around her once the machine was cleared and punched in the telephone number. Phoebe was very aware that a few times the front of him brushed up against the back of her and her breath caught in her throat. Her arousal was evident and she hoped he couldn't sense it.

Jacoby stepped back and watched as she feed the paper through the machine. He couldn't take his eyes off her backside and fought to keep his hands from touching the voluptuous portion of her body. His heart rate increased and his body came to attention as he imagined pulling that skirt up and moving the stockings away, then finding the warm moistness and hearing her cries of passion as she pressed back against his heat.

She turned abruptly and handed him his fax. "Even an stupid bitch can fax a report."

He had to swallow before he spoke. "I never called you stupid."

"You didn't have to, you just made me feel that way." Moving around him, she gathered her brief and coat by the door and turned back to him. "Make sure you lock up, Mr. Knight."

Just as she reached the glass doors to go out the office, she heard him calling her. He wasn't too far away she assumed without turning towards him, but not going out the doors, knowing he had followed her to the front of the office.

Jacoby's voice was almost a desperate whisper as he called her name again taking steps towards her. She turned to see him only inches away and his cinnamon brown eyes blazed with so much desire. There were no words needed to know what he wanted, so when his arms wrapped around her waist and his mouth engulfed the skin on her neck, she was not surprised.

There was a need coursing through his body so powerful it seemed to radiate into her own bloodstream and feeling his touch was almost a relief. Everything in her arms dropped to the floor as she pulled his mouth down to her own and their lips fused as if they were meant to be. They couldn't move fast enough opening a blouse here, unzipping pants there, lifting a skirt and practically tearing off her stockings and panties.

He cursed viciously in a very sorrowful tone of voice and she knew what he was feeling. Neither could deny they wanted each other badly, yet they both knew they would regret what they were doing. Even as this realization dawned on them, they could not stop the pleasure enveloping them as he pressed her against the glass partition and drove deep inside of her as if his life depended upon her. His teeth gently nibbled on each breast igniting her flames of passion way past the conscious level and she blissfully enjoyed the roughness, grasping him for dear life. The convulsions peaked inside her as her nails clawed his back and she felt him erupt deep into her. They were oblivious to the outside world as sweet pleasure and serenity surrounded them holding and bonding them together.

Phoebe didn't want this moment to end, but reality was cruel and she regained her equilibrium first. Releasing her legs from around his waist, she nudged him away. He carefully let her down releasing her only when he was sure her feet were on the floor securely.

She didn't look at him as she quickly fixed her clothes, but when she noticed the torn stockings she gave him an accusing look. He had already adjusted himself and smiled foolishly.

"I'll buy you some more," he promised.

"I don't want anything from you, Jacoby." She picked up her coat and brief. "Stay the hell away from me."

"Phoebe, it doesn't matter about the money. You know it doesn't make a difference and I didn't mind paying-"

She covered his mouth not wanting to hear another word. "Please just stop it. I don't want to hear another word about money for sex. I don't want your money anymore, Jacoby. It served it's purpose and this time was just ..." She couldn't find the right word.

He removed her hand smirking. "For pleasure?" he finished.

"Shut up!" she snapped angrily as he began to chuckle. Phoebe stormed out the office and decided to take the stairs wanting to get as far away from him as fast as possible.

Upon getting home, she went to her room to shower. When she had finished, she put Stephanie and Stephen to bed, and then came down unexpectedly seeming to startle her mother, who got up quickly from the kitchen table and put the ledger away as if she didn't want Phoebe to see what was going on. Phoebe was about to ask her mother why was she acting so strange over the ledger when the doorbell rung. It was ten o'clock at night and a very odd hour to be expecting guest.

Phoebe hoped it wasn't Jacoby because she didn't know if she could handle him when her bed was so close at hand.

"I'll get it," she said to her mother and went to the door.

Patricia went upstairs quickly as if she were trying to get away from Phoebe.

Opening the door, she looked as if she had seen a ghost. "Daniel?" she asked not believing her eyes.

Daniel had lost a considerable amount of weight, except in his stomach and he seemed frail. He was always lean of nature, but the man she saw now looked almost malnutrition. He had grown a thick moustache over his lips and his hair was unkempt. His clothing looked borrowed from the Salvation Army and outdated. On top of that he wore some old cowboy boots. Daniel never wore cowboy boots. Matter of fact, she had never seen him wear boots even in the wintertime.

"In the flesh, love," he said excitedly. "How's it going?"

"How's it going?" she asked tightly between clenched teeth. "You bleed me dry, you leave me penniless with two babies and drowning in so much debt, and you have the audacity to ask me how's it going?"

"Aw love, don't be like that," he said cajoling.

Placing her hands on her hips, she said, "If you don't get out of my face, I'm going to call the police."

"I just came here to help you out. I know it ain't that bad for you anymore. I saw your credit report yesterday. You're as clean as they come."

"What do you mean?" she asked confused.

"I mean, you got them rich niggars paying your shit off. What'd you do to them, baby?" He smiled wickedly and came closer to her. "You put a spin on it like you use to do me?"

Phoebe didn't know what he was talking about, but she didn't want Daniel anywhere near her or her children. "I don't need your help, Daniel. I've never needed your help. Because of you, I've turned myself into a tramp. I've degraded myself. I've had to lay down all the morals and values my mother instilled in me, just to get by because of you. I will never make that mistake again."

"Love, you know you're my first, my last, my everything. Remember that was our song."

"I will always remember that you're my first damn mistake, my last damn mistake and I'll always remember you will be the most stupid mistake I've ever made in my life. Get off my property now because I still have the restraining order against you." She turned to look behind her and yell, "Mother, call the police!"

"Aw love, don't be like that. We were so good together." He tried to touch her with his grubby hands and she stepped away.

"Daniel, I don't want anything to do with you ever again and I suggest you leave now, because since I do have a restraining order against you, I have grounds to shoot you. I won't go to jail as long as I shoot you in the front and plead self defense."

He started to get upset. "You're crazy! Why don't you just listen to what I have to say."

She looked behind her and yelled, "Mother, bring me my gun!"

When she looked back around at him, Daniel had bolted off the porch and was running down the street. The sorry ass couldn't even afford a car to get away in. She slammed the door just as Patricia was running down the stairs.

"What is going on, Phoebe?" she asked out of breath.

"That was Daniel at the door. I bluffed him and told him I was going to shoot him," Phoebe explained.

"I would have tried very desperately to find some kind of weapon to help you out," Patricia agreed.

Phoebe told her mother what Daniel had said. "He was saying my credit is all cleaned up. That someone had cleaned it up."

Patricia looked a little guilty. "How did he know?" she blurted out.

Phoebe frowned. "You knew. What is going on?" She went over to the ledger as Patricia immediately started to stammer. Looking at the totals, she saw that they were down to all zero. "Who did this?" she demanded to know. "Is this true?"

Patricia took a deep defeated breath and sat down at the kitchen table. "Yes, it's true."

"How Mother?"

"I didn't want to tell you too soon. They were paid with personal checks and I wanted to make sure they all cleared because I couldn't believe it all myself."

"Believe what?" Phoebe demanded to know. "That some mysterious person just swept in and paid my debts."

Patricia didn't answer. She didn't have to answer as the realization dawned on Phoebe's face of shock and bafflement all at the same time. Placing the ledger on the table she crossed her arms over her chest.

"How long have you known?"

"Friday afternoon, when I went to the bank to pay off the rest of the loans before we left out of town, I found out someone had come in and paid it off, so I checked other large debts and found out that same person had paid off those debts too. I requested your TRW before we left and they sent it yesterday in the mail." She got up and pulled out an envelope carefully hidden in one of the cookbooks on the shelf.

"How long were you going to keep this from me Mother? You were planning on deceiving me from the truth."

"Because I knew what Jacoby Knight does to you and I didn't want him to hurt you like Daniel did."

"But he wasn't, Mother. Don't you know what this means?"

Patricia scoffed. "It only means that he is trying to hold you in debt to him instead of the creditors. He's paying you to be his mistress."

Phoebe shook her head. "No!! Mother, he knows the money means nothing to me. He did it not to keep me in debt to him. He did it so I could finally put the hurt that Daniel caused out of my mind and get it out of my life so I could..." Her voice faltered as she remembered him about to speak about the money and the horrible things she had said to him. Covering her face with her hands, she moaned into them a long agonizing moan.

"Don't you dare feel guilty, Phoebe," Patricia said. "He said those mean things to you."

Removing her hands, she screamed in frustration more to herself than anything. "He thought I had slept with Lawrence, Mother. If I had known Friday what you knew, then you knew I wouldn't have went on the trip with Lawrence. I did deceive him, because I should have told him about going on the trip so he wouldn't get the wrong idea," she cried starting to pace. "I should call him. I should at least go see him again to apologize for what I said."

"What about what he said to you?!" Patricia cried.

"Mother, I deceived him! Don't you get it? He thought I betrayed him with his best friend."

Patricia sighed in frustration. "Alright Phoebe, I'm sorry. I thought I was doing right by you by keeping this information from you. I should have respected your wishes and kept out of it."

Phoebe calmed down and hugged her mother. She knew her mother was no more deceitful than her and that Patricia was only looking out for Phoebe's best interest because her mother cared so much for her. "I understand what you thought you were doing for me, Mother, but you have to understand that what is happening between Jacoby and I. You'll help me won't you, despite how you feel?"

Patricia stared long and hard into her daughter's eyes so unlike her own. Phoebe knew her mother was only concerned with her happiness and if Jacoby made her happy, Patricia would stick by her. "I don't want you to be hurt again, Phoebe."

With great relish, Phoebe said, "I know Mother, but like Jacoby said, in order to experience life, I've got to appreciate all that life has to offer. Up until now, despite Monday's events, Jacoby has been just trying to make me happy and I'm not expecting anything like marriage from him, I just want to live for the now and enjoy that."

Bowing her head, Patricia's shoulders slumped in defeat. "Fine, I'll stand by you, Phoebe and support your decisions from here on out concerning this young man, but the minute you aren't happy anymore, promise me you will stop seeing him."

Phoebe laughed as if the weight on her shoulders had finally been lifted. "Yes Mother," she promised.

Patricia hugged her again. "You won't be going out tonight to see him. You have a lot of work to do tonight for tomorrow. You should also get some rest before tomorrow when all the crap hits the fan. I've finished with everything and complied it all. I even made copies for you. In the morning I will do the necessary faxing and contacting for you."

"Thank you Mother. I love you so much. When this is all over I want us to use a little of the money and take a nice long trip with the kids away from here. Can we?"

"Yes, Phoebe," Patricia promised. "Maybe you can invite Jacoby along," her mother hinted with a wicked little grin.

Chapter 23

Coming in to work on Friday two hours early, Phoebe had not slept a wink. Madeline would be in the office that day and had shot an email to Phoebe Thursday night with a silent threat concerning those reports and her job. Phoebe had put the reports on disc after she had emailed them over to Leslie on Monday and now was coming into the office before anyone was to even think about getting here to print off those reports.

She knew this was judgment day and she wanted to rub all of this is Madeline's face. After putting the reports in the print queue, she checked all the offices and was surprised to see Jacoby in his office. He was speaking on the phone, but once he saw her, he hung up.

He had changed his clothes from the night before and was in a hand fitted Armani suit.

"I wasn't trying to bother you," she said.

"You didn't. It was my mother and I was really looking for an excuse to get off the phone. You're as good as anyone for an excuse."

Phoebe wasn't about to let his snide statements perturb her today. She had to stay focus. "Do you sleep here?"

"China markets are open at night and my father wanted to speak to me since he was there about some family decisions. He'll be selling the house in Lansing once I have found a house here. Do you know someone in realty?" He leaned forward on the desk.

She didn't know if he was being a smart ass or serious, but she was not in the mood to help him out. "No."

"I figured you would say that." Standing up, he came around the desk and looked at her up and down from head to toe. He didn't press his proximity to her, but he could still smell her sweet perfume despite the five-foot distance. Coolly, trying to ignore his arousal, he noted, "You didn't get much sleep either, Phoebe. Did you miss me?"

"Far from it, Mr. Knight." She said full of cockiness. As much as she believed he was still angry with her, he didn't look at all put out. Yet, knowing what Phoebe knew about the money he had paid on her debts and Jacoby's forgiving nature, he was more interested in being with her than anything. Now would be a perfect time to speak with him about what she had said the other night and her own selfishness. "I think we should talk." She closed the door ensconcing them into them in the office alone.

Jacoby raised a wary brow, but took full advantage of her need to be private. "Come a little closer and we can or are you afraid of me?"

She stepped forward until she was arms length from him. "I know what you did for me-"

He placed a finger over her lips to stop her from speaking. "How much time do we have until the first person gets here?" he whispered, removing his finger from his lips, but cupping her face in his hands.

"About two hours," she figured with a slight shrug to her shoulders.

Jacoby gently pressed his lips against hers in a simple kiss, but the look in his eyes told her a wealth of information. Moving her arms around his neck, standing on her tiptoes, she smiled knowing what was to come and the eroticism of everything was overwhelming.

As they kissed he turned her around to sit on the front of his desk. They took their time removing parts of their clothing careful not to rip anything knowing they needed their clothing for later.

He whispered in her ear, "I missed you, Phoebe."

She smiled, "I missed you too, Jacoby."

These words alone seem to unleash even more of his passion and he knelt down spreading her legs and burying his face down below her stomach. Phoebe was in pure heaven and didn't care about where they were as she cried out his name. She peaked several times before his oral onslaught was over with and when he stood up, his pants were already opened. When he entered her easily, Phoebe knew only he could make her so susceptible to lovemaking. There was no competition to keep his attention or make him stay, every touch with his hands, lips, and body told her that he wanted to be no where else, but in her arms. Making love to him made her feel like a queen in his life and there was no other place she would rather be than here in his arms.

An hour and a half later, she found herself sitting in his lap, while he rested back in the chair behind his desk. They were silent as her head rested on his chest and his arms wrapped around his waist. She listened to his heartbeat enjoying how the rapid beat was slowing down and would immediately speed back up whenever she wiggled around on his lap. He was still partially hardened deep inside of her and although he was spent, he was still aroused.

How they had gotten on the other side of the desk was completely obviously to her. She remembered him lifting her, but she was so consumed in pleasure, she really had not cared where they ended up.

Looking up at him, she used the tip of her finger and traced her fingers around the edge of his lips memorizing every centimeter of skin and the feel of it on her fingertips. When she would make her touch light as a feather, it tickled him and he would try to nip at her. Once he caught the tips in his mouth, she tingled as he suckled softly. She replaced her tongue with her fingers and immediately their passion was ignited.

Suddenly the door opened and Madeline stood there, eyes as wide as saucers and looking like a dark skinned Cruella DeVille.

"What the hell is going on in my offices?!" she screeched.

Phoebe didn't know what to say, but the feeling of Jacoby's arms tightening around her protectively made her feel a little secure.

"I can explain this, Madeline," Jacoby said. "This is all my-"

"This is all the workings of a tramp who can't keep her legs closed around my office guest to save her life," Madeline hissed.

"That's not true!" Jacoby protested.

"I'm guessing that with all your screwing around, Phoebe, you haven't found those reports," Madeline guessed.

Phoebe was too embarrassed to speak and only buried her face in Jacoby's neck.

Jacoby spoke through gritted teeth. "Give us some privacy please to get ourselves together, Madeline," he ordered.

Madeline's voice was clearly triumphant as she said, "She has five minutes to get in my office." She slammed the door behind her as she exited the office.

Phoebe groaned in his neck. "I can't believe this is happening to me."

"Quit now," he ordered.

Glaring up at him, she said, "I can't just go in there and quit." She kept her voice down so no one would hear their voices.

"Yes, you can. Then you can come work for me."

Narrowing her eyes, she snipped, "I won't be your mistress." Moving up and off of him, she started to fix her clothes.

"I don't want a mistress." He stood up adjusting his own suit. "I need an office manager."

"You've lost your mind again, haven't you?"

"No. I know you're smart and highly motivated. You'd be perfect in running the office, while I'm not there and you can help me with my growing clientele. Keeping them happy while I'm gathering up new clientele. I know you'd make a great manager and I won't have to worry about anything as long as I have you there."

"I won't be your whore either, Jacoby. You won't pimp me to your friends."

"I think you need to calm down."

"Calm down?! Madeline caught us. Doesn't that bother you?"

"No. Why should it?" he asked.

She huffed in frustration. "Does anything bother you, Jacoby?"

He kissed her nose. "You do, but in a good way."

She started toward the door trying to put on her shoes as she walked.

"I'll pay you forty thousand. The amount she was supposed to be paying you."

Looking back at him over her shoulder, she shook her head. "I won't work for you, Jacoby."

"Fifty."

"No."

"Sixty."

"Stop that." Phoebe faced him.

"Seventy five and that's my final offer, plus full benefits and a company car."

"You're crazy." Calming herself down, she leaned against the door and shook her head not believing she was actually considering another offer from him. "This has nothing to do with sex, Jacoby."

"I told you I never mix business with pleasure. I don't hire you for sexual reasons," he stated firmly. "I hire you on your business skills and determination to do a good job."

"Let me handle this crisis first, then we'll talk." She started to open the door, but he grabbed her and pulled her in his arms kissing her hard.

"What was that for?" she asked breathlessly when he finally released her.

"Luck and later." A wicked twinkle in his eye clearly told her Jacoby was a man filled with desire for her, but he also was filled with admiration for her knowledge and intelligence.

Gathering her courage like a thick coat around her, she prepared to face Madeline. Going first to the printer where the reports were all run off, she gathered them off and placed them in an envelope, then went and grabbed her briefcase. Going into Madeline's office, she looked at the corner of the room to see Jacoby standing by the window out of the way with a sympathetic look on her face and Simon sitting in front of the desk with a triumphant look on his face just like Madeline.

"Are you ready to explain where the reports are?" Madeline asked. "We have Leslie and Kyle on the phone already. Kyle has informed me that they are missing reports from Monday. Do you have an explanation?"

"Yes, Phoebe," Simon butted in. "You do have an explanation, especially for taking so long to find them."

Phoebe shot Simon a loathing look. Sitting down in front of the desk, she found herself very able to speak now that she wasn't so undress.

"Before anything is said," Jacoby interjected, "Maybe I should leave."

"Oh no, Jacoby," Madeline beamed. "I would like you to stay."

Phoebe knew Madeline wanted Jacoby there and Jacoby looked over at her feeling a bit uncomfortable. Obviously, Madeline must have explained the situation and Jacoby couldn't find any good reason to get her out the situation she seemed to have dug herself in.

"I would like you to see that Phoebe has incompetently failed our client. With her gross negligence and stupidity she has lost over twenty reports and then never told anyone what she has done." Madeline leaned forward toward Phoebe. "Now you expect me to pay out of my pocket to doctor's and the transcriptionists to re-dictate and retype reports that you lost. I don't think so." She pulled out some papers from a file she had on her desk. "According to my calculations, you owe this company ten thousand dollars for your ignorance. How do you intend to pay it?"

Phoebe looked at Simon and then Jacoby. Returning her gaze back to Madeline, she said, "I don't intend to pay it, Madeline."

"Then I suggest you give us your resignation now or would you just prefer I fire you for incompetence."

Phoebe ticked her tongue. "I think neither would be feasible for you."

"Feasible for me?" Madeline cackled. "Have you listened to a word that I've said? I don't owe you a dime, Phoebe Green."

Taking the information out of her bag that her mother had complied, Phoebe handed the packet to Madeline. She had three more copies. With those she handed two to Jacob and Simon, then kept one for herself. "According to this packet, you owe me a total of one hundred and twenty thousand dollars in back pay including bonuses and the use of a vehicle which you quoted in the FIA agreement of what your office manager would be making and having. In the total I have put in the cost of transportation, extra expenses I have incurred because of what you have not given - this includes late fees for daycare and nonpayment of bills because of decrease living expenses or unable to make payments because I was too busy at work."

"Are you forgetting the issue at hand? You lost reports!" Madeline screamed standing up. "You have yet to explain what happened to those reports."

Phoebe tossed the reports on the middle of Madeline's desk. "I emailed those reports personally to Leslie Monday afternoon because I knew your deceit would know no bounds. Those reports are where they are supposed to be - with the doctors. I asked Leslie to send those reports off and didn't inform Kyle that I had sent them. All you can fault me on is miscommunication, and you can't fire me because of that. I got my job complete and that's all that needs to be said."

Jacoby chuckled. "According to these agreements, Madeline, if Phoebe gets a good employment lawyer, your ass is grass."

Stiffly Madeline said, "This does not concern you, Jacoby. You may leave."

"And miss the going down of the Titanic? I think not." Jacoby crossed his arms. "I really want to see this."

"Furthermore, I think Simon's father would be very interested in hearing about how you have misappropriated some of the funds that the FIA has been sending you," Phoebe said continuing. "You deliberately deceived the state in issuing out two checks. One for the regular reports and another one for the extra reports requested, then you over billed for those reports from the state."

Leslie spoke up. "I would also be interested in that as well."

Madeline picked up the entire phone and threw it against the wall ending the call with Lansing. "Shut up!" she screeched. "You stupid, bitch. You think you can come in here and mess up what I have worked so hard to create."

"You deceived everyone, didn't you Madeline? You did anything and everything to get your way, but I won't let you get away with it another moment. I'm taking all I have to the state and Joseph Bowen. You'll go to jail for what you-" Phoebe was cut off sharply as Madeline seem to leap over the desk and enclose her long fingers around Phoebe's neck strangling her.

Phoebe fell back from the force of body weight on her and Madeline followed all the way to the ground. At this same moment security arrived along with Lawrence to see Madeline choking Phoebe. Jacoby was above them, trying to pull Madeline away, but she had a death grip on Phoebe's neck.

With all her might and what was left of the strength inside her body, Phoebe delivered a fist to Madeline's right jaw sending the older woman careening off of her. Phoebe stood up with Jacoby's help as Madeline jumped to her feet on her own. Phoebe was still coughing, but when Madeline charged at her and swung the claws she called nails, Phoebe ducked and Madeline viciously scraped Jacoby's neck with her nails.

Phoebe bawled up her other fist and delivered a full body weight punch to Madeline's chest followed by a right to her eye. Madeline fell back over the chairs. Phoebe turned to Jacoby to see if he was all right as Madeline barely was able to stand up on her own.

"Arrest her!" Madeline sneered. "Call the police."

"But you were landing the punches," one of the security officers said.

She sneered, "This is my office and I demand that this slut be thrown off my property."

Phoebe was sick and tired of Madeline's petty name calling. "I'll show you some throwing, Bitch," she sneered lunging for her, but Jacoby grabbed her around the waist and held her against him. Madeline ran behind Simon, who now stood with a daze and confused look on his face.

"Take your hands off of her," Lawrence ordered.

Jacoby gave Lawrence a warning glance. "This isn't the time, Lawrence."

Phoebe rolled her eyes heavenwards and moved away from Jacoby to turn the attention back to her ignoring Lawrence's displeasure. "Simon you better start talking, unless you were apart of this. In that case, I intend to tell your father about your involvement on having me fired."

Simon was sweating like a stuck pig as he blurted out, "It was all her idea!"

The room was quiet as all eyes turned on Madeline, whom Simon was pointing an accusing finger at.

"She said we could get away with it all if I didn't tell my daddy and I'd get a boatload of money."

"Just how much money is involved here?" Jacoby asked bothered.

"Over a million dollars in overages alone, not including the money for the office personnel that she supposedly told Bowen that was employed here. Looking over the accounting records," Phoebe said, going over to the desk to flip through the packet, "She has four bogus employees here that don't exist, but their checks are being cashed and put in her account."

Jacoby was astounded by the extent of Madeline's deceitfulness. "I'm sure Joseph Bowen deserves to be called on the matter."

A large man of over six foot came through the door. He was a larger replica of Simon's short lean nature.

The giant was puffing on a thick Cuban and not at all looking too pleased about being there. "What should I be called on?" he demanded to know.

Phoebe knew exactly who he was. He looked bigger than the picture on the wall portrayed him, but she remembered that voice clearly from the voicemail she had made late last night and he was right on time. "Mr. Bowen, I'm Phoebe Green, I left a message on your machine last night."

He shook her hand. "So you're the little lady who left that vague message on my machine last night to be here at ten. I wasn't about to come until I saw that fax early this morning on the FIA spreadsheets," Joseph said, looking over at Madeline warily.

Phoebe smiled confidently knowing her mother had faxed over the spreadsheets and other information to Joseph Bowen and Leslie Cross.

"Whatever this tramp has tried to convince you I've done, Joseph, she's a lying whore and should not be trusted. I have every intentions of firing her for incompetence and she just wants to get back at me," Madeline said.

Joseph gave a long puff on his cigar before responding. "Seems to me, Maddie, you might be talking about yourself. This girl had enough information about your double dealings to put you away for a long while with the State of Michigan and I'm going to make sure you never try to screw with me again."

At this time two Michigan State Police Officers appeared at the door.

Madeline gasped. "Joseph, how could you believe her? We're partners! She's nothing but a disgruntled employee who thinks we owe her."

"And we do. I was never aware that you weren't paying her what she deserved or even close to what you turned in on annual reports to me. I have had my suspicions that something wasn't smelling right over here, which is why I insisted that my son worked here." He looked over at Simon who looked about ready to pee on himself. "If I had known you would involve yourself in scamming me as well, I would have just done a private investigation myself, but I thought as my son, you would at least have the heart to come back and tell me that my partner was deceiving me."

"She convinced me that we'd be rich if I participated in it, Dad, and I was going to tell you all about her taking the money once I got the money," Simon nervously explained.

"How much was it going to take, boy?" his father asked, coming very close to losing his temper. "Because fifty thousand dollars was already transferred into your bank account from Madeline's personal account two weeks ago. I think that was more than enough time to come to me."

"You got to believe me, Dad. I was convinced this was the right thing to do," Simon begged. "I didn't realize-"

"You didn't realize what?" his father exploded cutting him. "I damn well raised you better than that, you spineless son of a bitch. The only thing she convinced you was that you were as greedy as she was." He turned to the officers. "Take my partner and my son into custody, officers."

Madeline gasped, "How could you do this to me, Joseph?! I am your partner," she exclaimed as one of the officers started to put handcuffs on her wrist. "We've known each other for so long! Please Joseph. Please don't do this!" she begged.

Simon only lowered his head in shame as they led him out, but Madeline continued to plead, but all her shouting fell on deaf ears. Joseph Bowen turned to Phoebe.

"If you had suspicion something was going on, Mr. Bowen, why did you wait until she had taken so much?" Phoebe asked.

"Because I had no proof. I did secret searches on the server, but I never guessed that Latrice was also in on it." He took her hand in his. "Thank you for all your help."

Phoebe frowned very uneasily. "Why didn't you suspect me?"

"I did," he admitted. "And I had the investigators look into you as well, but they couldn't find a thing that could link you to the embezzlement. Only Latrice, Madeline, and Simon were involved. Madeline was only going to have you as a temporary because the FIA account was in jeopardy of going bad and she didn't have anyone who could help her get the money and also keep the account going. So she hid everything from you, while Latrice took care of the money. It was too easy." He smiled gratefully. "I didn't have any real proof of what she was doing until now. I was very glad that you were not apart of this, Phoebe. You have been a great asset with this company and now that I need someone to really run this office, I was hoping that you would assist me in this matter."

Phoebe took a deep breath and looked back at Jacoby. Before she could answer Joseph though, Jacoby spoke up saying, "You have a month, Mr. Bowen to find yourself a new manager for this office. Phoebe has accepted my offer to become my Detroit office manager."

Joseph looked highly disappointed. "I do apologize for any loss wages you may have suffered because of all of this. You'll be paid for every cent you should have been give, Phoebe," he promised. "I give you my word and if you ever need anything, I'm at your beck and call."

"Thank you, Mr. Bowen," Phoebe said gratefully.

With a defeated sigh, Joseph said, "I had better get on the job of getting someone dependable here, but I must admit you'll be a tough act to follow Phoebe."

When he left, she turned to Jacoby, who looked as if he were going to burst with pride. Before she even got a word out her mouth, he swept her up in a big hug almost crushing her.

Looking over his shoulder she noted that Lawrence was still in the room with them just leaning against the windowsill. Pushing away from Jacoby, she moved towards Lawrence.

"You did a good job," Lawrence said quietly. "I'm glad you did that." He looked over her shoulder at Jacoby and then he looked back at her. "Do you need a moment alone?"

Lawrence just naturally assumed she wanted to be with him and not with Jacoby. It was quite arrogant of him and he was being "gracious" enough to allow her to speak with Jacoby alone. The idea that he could be so arrogant didn't shock her, but she wondered when had she given Lawrence indication that she didn't want to be with Jacoby. Or did he just naturally assume that she would do his will, rather than Jacoby's.

She looked over her shoulder at Jacoby with a look of sympathy. He knew what she wanted, but it didn't look like he really wanted to give it to her. Reluctantly, he left out the room to give them some privacy. The security officers followed him closing the door behind them.

"Lawrence, I think we do need to talk," she said feeling quite guilty.

"There's nothing to say," he said, coming up to her and pulling her in his arms. "You'll be working only as his office manager, nothing else. I can accept that."

"Can you accept us only being friends?" she asked.

"Of course. Jacoby probably won't like it, though."

She frowned in frustration and pushed away from him. "I think you are misunderstanding the matter, Lawrence. I was speaking about you and I."

The deflated expression on his face was very evident. Phoebe didn't want to hurt him, but she did not want him to get his hopes up and think that there could be something more. "Jacoby doesn't know how to treat a woman like you, Phoebe. You need tender loving care and I can give you that."

Biting her lip, she decided to be evasive in her relationship with Jacoby. "This has nothing to do with Jacoby, Lawrence. I have already told him I don't want a relationship. I just don't want you to think that there could be something more between you and I, when I know there won't be. The last thing I want to do is hurt you, Lawrence."

Lawrence looked towards the door warily. "So you have no intentions of being with Jacoby either?"

Phoebe bit her lip confused not really wanting to discuss how she felt about Jacoby right now. Looking out the window to gather her thoughts, she said, "I really can't answer that question right now. I'm not sure how I feel."

He gently rubbed her cheek. "Like I said, I don't want to pressure you about it. I'll always be there for you."

She had a feeling Lawrence was highly disappointed and had expected a lot more than just friendship from her. Yet she smiled at him and said, "Thank you so much."

Lawrence leaned over and kissed her cheek very close to her lips paused a moment then left. In her heart Phoebe felt she was right to tell him the truth about her confusing feelings for Jacoby. On one hand she was very much loved what he did to her sexually and emotionally. She enjoyed the times she was with him and when he wasn't around she found herself still thinking about him. Yet, she was terrified. Terrified of getting hurt and terrified that she would hurt him.

So she did love him, but was too proud and too terrified to admit it to anyone.

"Penny for your thoughts," the man on her mind whispered in her ear.

"I think you've given me enough money, Mr. Knight and who gave you permission to talk for me?" she asked, turning around to face him folding her arms across her chest and looking highly upset.

"I assumed you wanted me to give you the opportunity not to answer him directly and you probably didn't figure Mr. Bowen would assign you as director of this office. Plus I wasn't going to lose the best thing in my life. Did I assume wrong, Phoebe?"

Dammit if her heart didn't skip an extra beat. Was he talking about his business life or personal life? Phoebe pushed the thought of her actually finding him attractive even more out of her mind. She just needed right now to get home and away from this irresistible man to think over the days events.

"No you assumed correct, Jacoby."

Immediately, he asked, "Will you accept my position at my office?"

"I would be a fool not to. It's too good to be true and you know I need the money. Why do you always have to do that?" she asked perturbed more at herself than at him, but he didn't know that.

"Do what? Use money in order to get you?" Jacoby questioned. "Phoebe, you've made it no other way to have you." His voice was almost desperate.

Filled with apprehension, she asked, "What do you want from me personally, Jacoby? You've got everything. What could you possibly want from me?"

"Haven't I made it obvious?" he asked as if she should have known, but the look on her face made it apparent that she had no idea what he was talking about.

"Thank you for paying off those things for me," she said. "Is that what you want to talk about? I will pay you back all that money, I promise, now that Mr. Bowen will give me the back pay."

Angrily he said, "I told you before it wasn't about the money. It was never about the money and you should know this by now."

"Then what?"

He looked at her seriously. "I can't believe all this time you didn't know. Phoebe, have you been that hurt that you can't see when a man really likes you?"

"Likes me? Daniel liked me, but that didn't stop him from hurting me," she sneered.

He cursed under his breath. "There is no convincing you is there? You will never be able to put down the hurt Daniels caused you, will you?" he asked. "Why can't you just accept what today has to offer you, Phoebe?"

"And what has today offered me?" she asked incredulously.

Jacoby stood there for a long moment as if just staring at her would make things better. Yet it seemed the harder he stared the more she just didn't get it? Shoulders slumped in defeat, Jacoby went to the doorway, stopping before he went completely out of it and turned back to look at her. "Me," was all he whispered before turning back around and leaving out the door.

Phoebe sat down in the nearest chair covering her face in her hands hoping the best thing in her life had not just walked out the door.

Chapter 24

Phoebe went through life at the office like a robot. She had always done her job well whether she wanted to be there or not. Of course, Joseph still continued to offer more money to get her to stay, but Phoebe wanted no part in P&B Communications anymore.

Lawrence called her often and came by as much as he possibly could to cheer her up, but it was hard to cheer her up when he couldn't figure out what was bringing her down. Patricia was still enamored of Lawrence, but had stopped trying to convince her daughter on what a mother thought was good for Phoebe. Instead, Patricia kept all her comments to herself about the situation.

Two weeks passed and Jacoby had not called Phoebe. Lawrence mentioned by the middle of the second week, Jacoby had gone to Chicago to secure another deal and in the middle of it, he was called away to go to the Philippines to see his parents. Apparently, his mother had fallen ill, but with it being right before Thanksgiving, Jacoby had intentions of seeing them anyway, although usually his parents came home for the holidays. Lawrence seemed in high spirits with Jacoby out the country.

Phoebe was not that out of touch with everything. She knew Lawrence wanted to start a relationship with her and if she had not met Jacoby, she would very seriously consider being with Lawrence, but she had met Jacoby, and her heart and body was in desperate need for him.

At night after she had put the twins to bed, all she could do was think about him, wonder where he was and hoped she had not destroyed her last opportunity of happiness. On top of this, knowing his insatiable nature, she was deeply envious of the woman who could be satisfying his needs now and Phoebe wished desperately it were she getting his attention at that moment in time.

At the beginning of the third week, a package came to the office for Phoebe. The new office manager, Amy Tarre, had brought the package in Phoebe's new office, which was Jacoby's old office space. Amy looked very excited and it made her oriental eyes close even more. She was a real nice girl, thirty years old, and very able to take over the position at the office.

"Hurry up and open it," Amy said.

Phoebe pulled out two envelopes of varying sizes. She opened the skinny one first. It was a letter from Jacoby addressed to her in a professional manner along with some other documents.

Ms. Green,

Welcome to your new position as office manager for Knight Marketing. In this envelope you have just opened, I have enclosed everything you need in order to get you started as a new employee. Although, I will be away from the office most of the time, we will always be able to keep in touch. My previous office manager, Cathy Reese, in Lansing, will also assist you in setting up all that you need in order to get things under way in Detroit. Please fill out these forms enclosed and send them to back to Cathy in the envelope provided as soon as possible.

The other envelope contains the necessary items you will need in order to run the office in Detroit and to stay in contact with me. Cathy will explain to you all the priorities and what I will expect from you, but please don't worry, I know you will do well in the position as my eyes and ears when I am not around.

Cathy's number is enclosed in the other envelope. She will be expecting your call in the next few days. Please don't disappoint her.

I'll be speaking with you when I come back in town late Monday afternoon. Good luck, Phoebe.

Jacoby Knight

'Why had she expected him to say more?' she asked herself. He had thrown the ball in her court and all she had to do was hit it back, but it was so hard to put herself out like that. Phoebe felt he was rushing things. Even though she had forgotten about Daniel and couldn't get Jacoby out her mind, she still felt it was much too soon to proclaim her heart to Jacoby.

Even though this letter wasn't personal, she found herself reading it over and over as if there was some hidden clue inside the letter to make it personal. When she laid it down on her desk, she wanted to scream more at herself than anyone else.

Amy picked up the letter and read it over. "He sounds like a nice boss."

"He seems like he's going to be, but wish me luck," Phoebe said, trying to hide the hurt in her voice that seemed to be seeping out of her heart like a slow leak.

****

"The heart wants, what the heart wants," her mother said quietly late Friday night after she had gotten off the phone with Lawrence. He had wanted to see her tonight, but she told him she was busy and rescheduled a date with him for Saturday morning.

Phoebe had been moping at the table, staring down at the food she was never going to eat. Patricia was looking highly disappointed in Phoebe. Phoebe had to blink several times to come from her daydreaming to understand what her mother said. "Why are you saying that to me?"

"Because you reminded me of that night when you first started seeing Jacoby and couldn't understand why you continued to see him. Don't you listen to yourself, Phoebe?" Patricia chuckled at her daughter's baffled expression. "Your heart choose him a long time ago, Phoebe, it's your mind keeping you from him. The more you try to deny it, the more terrible you'll feel."

"I'm not feeling terrible, Mother," she lied.

"If your lips goes any lower it will be dragging on the floor, girl. I'm your mother; you can't lie to me. If you're that worried about it all, just ask him. Whatever his answer is will help you get on with your life and you'll stop all this moping around the house."

Phoebe knew her mother was right and seeing him this Monday would conclude everything. He'd be all business, she was sure of it.

Lawrence came over Saturday and along with the twins, they went out to a nice family restaurant giving her mother a break. The twins were always well behaved in public. Lawrence complimented her on her parenting skills. "Most single working women don't find the time to mother their children like you have, Phoebe, and still have a bond with their children even though their not babies anymore."

Phoebe flushed under his praise. "I do my best, but I must admit, my mother has been a wonderful help. I just wished my father could be here as well to see them."

Lawrence had a sympathetic ear for her and they talked all afternoon. When they returned home, Patricia invited him in for coffee. Phoebe gave her mother a warning look as

Patricia tried several time to encourage Lawrence to stay close with Phoebe.

Patricia took the twins on up to bed giving Lawrence and Phoebe a little privacy. They decided to watch a movie together and she ushered him over to the couch and sat by him. When she sat down, he moved over until he was sitting right beside her with his thigh touching hers. His arm moved around to rest on the back of the couch behind her head while his other hand moved on top of her hands that were resting on her lap.

"So how's it going over at the office?" he inquired to make general "safe" conversation.

"I've been working at both offices to make sure one is working well when I leave and the other is working well for when I come. It's been a lot of hard work, but I know it will pay off in the end."

"I can see the enjoyment in your face." Lawrence tried to hide his disappointment.

"The more I think about it, the more I would like to really thank Jacoby for the opportunity he has given me," Phoebe admitted sincerely.

He looked at her suspiciously. "How do you want to thank him?"

She blushed thinking clearly about how Jacoby and she had been together the last time. "Lawrence, maybe there is something more you need to know about Jacoby and I."

"Whatever it is, I know that it is in the past and it doesn't matter, Phoebe."

"It's not that far in the past."

He looked a bit confused, but Phoebe thought this was as good as any time to let him know the real deal between Jacoby and herself.

"Jacoby and I have made love more than one time, Lawrence. I'm not going to lie to you, but I loved being with him." She stopped to hear his reaction to this admission.

Lawrence frowned. "Well I have heard of his sexual appeal and I clearly understand your attraction to him, but I must admit, it takes more than sex to make a relationship. A true match is one where you can be friends and lovers, Phoebe. I am that man for you."

She shook her head. "Lawrence, maybe you don't understand me all the way. Not only do I enjoy being with sexually, but also I enjoy his company. I can't explain it, but I think I know now from these past weeks of not seeing him. I do love him." She stopped as Lawrence stood up to get away from her. His back was to her, but the tension was evident. "Please understand that this happened all too quickly and I have tried to deny what he does to me. I ended up hurting him as a result of my stubbornness."

He turned around steeling himself. "You think Jacoby is actually hurt by you not wanting him when he's a sex addict? If you've rejected him, there's no doubt that he's found someone else. Has he even tried to tell you he's hurt? Has he even made an effort to call you or anything?"

She shook her head. "I just assumed it was because he had tried to convince me so many times that he was different than others."

"Different?" Lawrence questioned incredulously. "Jacoby Knight is no different. He's probably even worse. He throws his money around and expect people to bow down to him. You really want to be with a person like that. A person who thinks he can buy whatever he wants? I've told you in the past he doesn't deserve a woman like you. Jacoby only cares about himself."

Phoebe was very confused. From what she knew about Jacoby personally what Lawrence was saying didn't sound like the Jacoby she knew. Could Lawrence be that jealous of Jacoby to the point that he would say or do anything to get Jacoby out the picture with Phoebe? "Lawrence, Jacoby really has nothing to do with our friendship."

"He has everything to do with our friendship, Phoebe. Can't you see? If you're going to always think he could possibly have feelings for you, how can we be together?"

"That's the point Lawrence, I couldn't be with you even if I had not been with Jacoby. I am not romantically attracted to you."

He pulled her in his arms as if the more they touched she might think differently. "Things change, Phoebe. People change. Tomorrow could be different."

She shook her head. "It won't, Lawrence. I know time won't change how I feel for you."

"You don't know," he said disappointingly releasing her and giving her his back.

"I don't mean to hurt you, Lawrence."

"I know." His voice belied his feelings though, but it still could not make her change her mind.

To make him feel better, she said, "I do appreciate all you've done. Your friendship has made it easier for me understand how I feel about Daniel. I think you are a great guy, Lawrence, and you'll make some woman very happy."

He turned around and in disappointment said, "I was hoping that it would be you."

She pulled him back down to the couch. "Well as friends, let's finish watching the movie together."

He sat back down and she allowed him to pull her to him as they finished watching the movie together.

Chapter 25

Jacoby watched as Lawrence left out the house. She came out on the porch with him and gave him a hug. Jacoby gripped the steering wheel so tight the leather squealed in protest. Once Lawrence had pulled off, he got out the car and came up to the door. She had gone inside and lights were being turned off down the stairs.

He was so angry at himself for wasting his time speeding all the way from Metro Airport in order to see her thinking maybe if she saw him, she would see what a foolish mistake she had made.

He was the fool to think she could actually appreciate the attempt he had made. Getting back in the car, he slammed his fist down on the steering wheel and then drove off cursing himself.

****

Phoebe thought she had heard someone on the front porch, but knowing Lawrence was gone, she quickly went upstairs to her room and looked out the window to see a car pulling away across the street. Daniel was probably still after her.

Moving away from the curtains she sighed with relief that she had gotten everything out to Lawrence. She had a feeling he would still continue to try to pursue her and she didn't feel she could continue to keep Lawrence as "a friend" for much longer. He seemed too adamant in them becoming closer.

About an hour later as she was getting out the shower, Daniel called her. Phoebe was in full capacity of her senses and angrily answered the call once she knew that it was him.

"I wanted to know if I can see the children," he said.

"I'm going to press charges against you, Daniel," she announced not even bothering to respond to his statement.

He became exasperated. "I sent you flowers!"

"Which I probably paid for with my money."

"Why Phoebe?"

"Did you forget that you stole from me?" she asked. "Once the prosecution finishes gathering all the evidence against you, including the camera at the ATM that shows you stealing the money there, will be a warrant for your arrest."

"Dammit Phoebe, I'm coming back so we can be a family again. They're my kids too," he sneered. "I'm their Daddy, Phoebe."

"You may have fathered them, Daniel, but you are not their Daddy. Daddies provide for them, hold them when they're scared, wipe the tears from their eyes, tuck them in at night, encourage them, and would never leave them. Any man can be a father, but it takes a real man to be a Daddy." She slammed the receiver down hard and then dropped on the bed trying to calm herself down.

The phone rang again and angrily she answered, "Daniel, quit calling me. I don't ever want to speak or see you again."

"I'm not Daniel. Do you want to speak with me?" Jacoby asked calmly.

Phoebe gasped. "What's wrong?" she asked highly concerned very off centered.

He seemed mildly amused. "Shouldn't I be asking you that?"

The frustration in Phoebe's heart washed away as she relaxed a little. "He was being a pest if you must know."

"I don't care to know, unless you wanted me to know, Phoebe."

Phoebe was quiet for a moment wondering if he was trying to say something else. In his background, she heard some weird voices. "How's your mother?"

He sighed before answering and Phoebe had a feeling he wasn't speaking of the subject that was really on his mind. "She's getting better. There was inflammation in her pancreas and she couldn't leave the hospital until she was able to eat. We're flying home tonight on the red eye. She'll need a lot of rest."

"You're a very good son. She's blessed to have you." Phoebe complimented him, loving how deep his voice became as he spoke about his mother. "Although she hasn't been near you all your life, you seem very close to her."

"She's an extraordinary women Phoebe. I hope you can meet her soon."

Phoebe used his words back at him. "Only unless you want me too."

He chuckled more to himself, but didn't respond to her statement. There was this weird tension between them and she was positive there was a lot more that needed to be spoken about, but neither he nor her wished to speak about it.

Phoebe didn't think now was a good time to speak personally about anything. "Why did you call me?"

His tone of voice became very serious. "To let you know Abraham Blue, my attorney, is going to come into the office to deliver some information. I need you to fax it to me in Lansing as soon as you get it. I have a meeting with some Chicago people up here early Monday morning and I need a copy of what Abraham has. Can you do that for me?"

"No problem. Will there be anything else?" She did not think this was a good time to speak with him about her personal feelings at this time.

"No, Phoebe, I should make it into town late Monday morning, but as you can see I have a lot of meetings all this week. Did you make all the necessary arrangements with each one?"

"Yes. The conference rooms are booked down at the technology center just like you wanted and I've set up the account with them. I made sure all the copies are made and I've set up the catering as well."

"I knew I would not be disappointed in hiring you."

"I'm glad I could keep your confidence in me, Jacoby."

"Goodnight, Phoebe."

Before she could respond, he hung up and Phoebe was left holding the phone staring at the receiver wondering what she could she have said to make him see how she felt. He said he never mixed business with pleasure so when would be a good time to fit a personal situation in with the business.

Lying down in bed, her last thought was that this was why she never got involved with office personnel and she should know way better than to be involved with her boss.

Chapter 26

On her first day at work, she didn't mind the quietness of the office. Cathy had helped her set up the email system for the office and Desmond had come over during the weekend and made sure all of her electronic equipment was working correctly. Cathy had told her there was a stipend to hire temp's if needed for any extra typing or filing, but Jacoby was very organized man and his marketing team - which he referred to his other employees - were very hard working and hardly at the office. It was her job to make sure they received any communication that Jacoby had for them and each team member was in charge of a certain client. Phoebe was needed to make sure that if the team member's assistant couldn't complete something, they would come to her for help.

According to Cathy, the assistant's came into the office more than the team members who preferred to either work at home or on the road. Cathy had everything organized and properly address for Phoebe, so she had no problems finding things.

Jacoby had left a list of instructions of things he needed for upcoming meetings. Cathy would still assist her for about another month if she needed anything.

Phoebe was nervous knowing she was going to see him late that afternoon until he shot her an email around three to let her know he had something personal to do up in Lansing and would not make it down for their meeting. Checking his calendar, she saw that he would not be getting back in Detroit for another week to attend the marketing meeting unless he made a special trip, which she didn't think he would do on her account. Not after what she had done to him.

Throughout the week, there was not even a hint that he really wanted to speak to her except for business purposes. He called every morning at nine on the nose to get any messages he had missed or any e-mail's he needed to know about. He was always saying "please" or "thank you," and he never got upset, but Cathy had told her this was his natural behavior when Phoebe questioned her about it.

"You can fuck up so bad you want to bury your head in the ground, but he's not one to get upset. If you tell him you can't fix something, he'll help you out. He's cool like that,"

Cathy explained. "Just don't try to hide anything from him. That pisses him off."

On Thursday afternoon when it was getting near the end of the day, Amy called up unexpectedly. She updated Phoebe on what was going on. Madeline, Latrice, and Simon would be prosecuted to the full extent of the law for embezzlement and fraud. Amy said the rumor was that they would get up to thirty years apiece if convicted.

"It's been pretty quiet otherwise although I was shocked that Joseph bailed Simon out of jail. Simon is not on this property or in any of his father's other business and just has to sit around and wait for trial. Madeline and Latrice are broke and couldn't make the million dollar bail that the judge ordered."

"That is terrible, but why would Joseph get his son out of jail?"

"It's his only boy, what do you expect? But you better be careful, because I heard Joseph and Simon arguing about you. Joseph was telling Simon to stay away from you. Simon called you a few choice names. There might be some repercussions."

"I'll be careful," Phoebe promised. "Thanks Amy."

"So how's the dream job coming?" Amy asked excitedly.

"It's a dream, if you must know."

"You do sound bothered though. What's up?"

"It's personal Amy." Although she had known Amy a short time, Phoebe felt comfortable speaking with her about her present dilemma. "There's this guy who I think I hurt badly because I was too hung up over the hurt my ex-husband did to me. Now that I'm over the hurt, I think I might have done too much damage to this guy to even get back with him."

"Did you hurt him on purpose?" Amy asked.

"Oh Jesus, no Amy. I never meant to hurt him. He does things to me that I never want him to stop doing."

"Have you told him what he does?"

"I don't think it will help."

"What's the worst that could happen?"

Phoebe snorted unladylike. "He could laugh in my face. He could tell me exactly where I could put my heart."

"He could hug you to death and kiss you all over, but at least you tell him."

Phoebe sighed. "My mother said the same thing, but it's not as easy as it sounds."

"How so?"

"He's my boss."

Amy chortled. "You're in love with your boss."

"I never said it was love," Phoebe protested weakly mad at herself at admitting this out loud.

"You didn't have to. Just your tone of voice and the intensity you've expressed yourself easily tells me that you love this man, but your boss Phoebe? You know dating office personnel is never a good practice unless it's your husband. Now that wouldn't be so bad, but Jacoby Knight is not a man who intends to marry too soon."

"That's what makes it so bad. On top of that I never can find a good time, since everything we do is all business. What am I suppose to say? If that's all the notes you want me to take we can adjourn to the couch and bump uglies."

Amy laughed so hard, it became contagious and Phoebe couldn't help herself at her own silliness. "Now that's a good one," Amy said through her howl of laughter. When they were able to calm down again, Amy asked, "How did he get to you if I may be so bold to ask?" Phoebe giggled more to herself blushing from head to toe. Amy must have sensed this embarrassment and asked, "Not all the juicy details, but what was it about him that made you so attracted to him."

Phoebe didn't have to think hard about that. "It's the way he made me feel like a queen in his arms and when we are together, I'm so happy that I want to scream which I think I've done quite a few times."

Amy snickered. "Do you think he feels as intensely as you do about him?"

"I think he did until I hurt him. Now all I get is business talk. How am I supposed to even try to get close to him again when he doesn't mix business with pleasure, Amy?"

"Sometimes you have to make him break the rules, Phoebe. Seduce him. If you do to him, what he does to you, any small seduction will work."

"Amy, you're confusing me."

Amy described in detail what Phoebe should do and although it had Phoebe's cheek blazing, Amy had a pretty good idea on how to drive a man crazy.

Chapter 27

Desmond only raised a brow at the outburst that shot out of Jacoby's mouth. It was so unexpected that he couldn't believe Jacoby had said it and the look on his face told Jacoby clearly Desmond thought he had just past through the Twilight Zone. "Come again, brother? Stick my opinion where?"

Jacoby sat back in the chair and huffed. "Just forget it."

"Do you know for the past three weeks, you've been sounding like a sailor?" Desmond pointed out.

"If you don't like it, then quit talking to me," Jacoby snapped.

"That's another thing. You're so damn snappy."

"I'm not snappy!" Jacoby snapped.

Desmond chuckled. "If I didn't know better, I'd say you weren't getting your daily rations of sex."

Jacoby didn't say anything and if a feather had touched Desmond, he would have fallen over as if a Mack truck had hit him.

"You're pulling my leg, Jake."

Jacoby closed his eyes and leaned his head back. "If I were, I'd have enough strength to yank it off about now. I feel like I'm wearing my pants to damn tight, but if I go back to that damn tailor anymore the man's just going to adjust my pants to the next size."

"Are you trying to say you haven't had sex in a while?" Desmond asked.

"A while?!" Jacoby snapped. "Dammit, I haven't had sex in over a month." He looked at his watch. "If you want me to be fucking exact I'm at one month, five days, eight hours and fifty four fucking minutes as of three seconds ago."

Desmond burst out laughing so hard tears streamed down his face. Jacoby found nothing funny and sat there glaring at him with no expression on his face. This made Desmond laugh even harder.

"You've got to be kidding me, Jake," Desmond said when he could be understood. "Is this over Phoebe?"

"What do you think?"

"I think you're wasting your time on her, which is the same thing I said to Lawrence who's lost his marbles."

"I haven't lost any damn marbles."

"You have if you're saving yourself for her. Like I told him and you, she doesn't care what the two of you feel."

"That's not true, Desmond."

Desmond sighed. "Is this why you've been hiding in my office all week instead of going to Detroit? You're the one who offered her the position. If she's not working out then fire her and get another person."

"But that's the problem, Desmond, she's working out great, but I think if I go around her I might attack her."

"You can't hide from her, Jacoby. That's not normal."

"I'm just trying to stay away from her enough for her to come to her senses."

"What senses?"

"To realize she loves me," Jacoby said simply.

"Now I think you've lost your marbles for real. She's deceiving the both of you."

"How so? Just the other day you told me she admitted to Lawrence she still has some feelings for me she just couldn't explain it. Trust me Desmond, she's coming around."

"But at this rate you're going to wither and die if it isn't soon."

Jacoby huffed knowing Desmond was right. "I just need something to make her see Lawrence is a bad choice."

"I take it she doesn't know the truth about Lawrence."

Jacoby smiled wickedly. "I think you've given me the answer to my problem, Desmond."

"You wouldn't!" Desmond gasped.

Jacoby flipped through Desmond's address book to find the number to Lawrence's previous address. "All is fair in love and war, Desmond."

"So you love her?"

"Damn Skippy, but I'm not admitting it to her until she admits it to me."

Desmond sighed exasperated. "This is ridiculous. If you know she feels the same as you do, why don't you just tell her."

"Because I'm too damn stubborn and I've waited so damn long that I think I deserve a damn good I love you from her before I allow myself to give in." Jacoby smiled brightly as he picked the card out the Rolodex he was looking for.

Desmond blocked Jacoby from picking up the receiver to the phone. "What about Lawrence? Why don't you just go beat the shit out of him instead of ruining his life?"

"Beating him within an inch of his life has crossed my mind a lot, Desmond, but I figure now that you've given me this idea, beating him won't be as cruel as sending out the hounds to him." His laughter was nefarious as he knocked Desmond's hand away and picked up the receiver.

"This is not going to accomplish anything," Desmond grumbled.

"It damn well better or I'm going to kill someone with this damn hard on."

****

Saturday felt so weird. It was the first time in so many years that she had the weekend off and even though she was on call, there was no one pestering her about problems. Jacoby had emailed her and let her know she would only be called if she was really needed, but he was pretty set for anything that he had planned and that he would see her Tuesday at the employee meeting. She knew at that time they still would not have a moment of privacy together because the rest of his team would be there.

Today was such a nice day for the weekend before Christmas that she took the twins with her on errands leaving the company car Jacoby had provided for her at the house, while they took her old Chevy out and about. Stephanie and Stephen were so excited about being out with their mother; they were on their best behavior.

Phoebe's cell phone rung and it was from one of the assistant's asking if she could go to the office and send a fax to California that had been left on the desk. Phoebe told her she didn't mind doing this and headed downtown. She had finished the errands and had been heading home so it was no problem. Plus the day was still early being a little after one in the afternoon and parking was easy since it was on the weekend.

She helped the twins out the car and took them up to the office telling them to stay put in the lobby area until she finished what she had to do.

"I'm hungry, Momma," Stephen complained. It was more like a whine in his most babyish voice.

"We'll stop wherever you want after this," she promised.

The twins looked a bit tired and disappointed that they were going somewhere boring, yet they didn't protest.

Chapter 28

Jacoby didn't know why he had come down to Detroit, but he decided if he was going to be there and keep to himself, he would get some work done, but after an hour of staring at the walls and doing absolutely nothing he decided to go into Phoebe's office and sit at her desk. He could smell her scent throughout the office. She had left a scarf hanging on the back of the door and he held it up to his nose.

'This was crazy,' he told himself as he closed his eyes, relishing in her scent. 'Damn her!' He cursed in his head over and over again. Opening his eyes, he looked at the desk to the picture of the twins. Beautiful children that looked just like their mother. Picking up the picture, he stared into eyes so dark and brown he could just drown in them and wondered how did it feel to have double the unconditional love.

The time he had spent with his mother made him realize his true feelings for Phoebe. He knew without a doubt how he felt and what he wanted. His mother had begged for his forgiveness for their stupidity.

"You will never know the feeling of having a child wrap their arms around your neck and knowing you are their security, their world, the love of their life. I'm sorry I took that away from you, Jacoby. I'm so sorry."

He told her he had forgiven her, but she still said it, even in her worse pain, she screamed it until the doctors had to give her something to calm her. Jacoby stayed by her side the whole time as she held his hand in his.

Putting down the picture, he had to blink twice as the same adorable faces in the picture now stared at him on the other side of the desk. Jacoby had not heard anyone come in the office, but he had been in his own thoughts for so long, he couldn't have heard much.

"Why are you in my momma's office?" the little girl spoke bravely and quite articulate for what she looked to be about three years old or a little older.

"And who is your mother?" he inquired.

"Phoebe Green. Who are you?"

"I'm Jacoby Knight. I'm your mother's boss."

The little boy scooted behind his sister shyly and whispered something in the girl's ear.

"My brother said you're too big."

Jacoby frowned. "He did, did he? Is he scared?"

The little boy whispered something else in his sister's ear and she relayed this information to Jacoby. "Stephen says he's not scared of nobody. Why are you sitting in my momma's chair?"

"Where is your mother?"

"She said she had to fax something and we are supposed to be sitting down in the lobby because she said we aren't supposed to be here."

"But you aren't where your mother told you to be," he pointed out not believing he was having this conversation with a three year old.

Stephen whispered in his sister's ear again and she relayed the message. "Stephen says Momma keeps snacks in her draw."

Jacoby opened the bottom drawer on Phoebe's desk and saw a box of oatmeal cookies. "These?" he asked showing them to the children. Their eyes lit up like Christmas lights.

"Stephen! Stephanie!" Phoebe's voice called frantically as she appeared at the doorway of her office then gasped seeing Jacoby sitting there. Jacoby hurriedly tossed the scarf in her drawer not wanting to be caught with it.

"Jacoby?! What are you doing here?" She rushed over and took the twins hands. Before he had a chance to answer she turned to them, "I told the two of you to stay put."

"We were hungry," the girl protested. "Stephen knows you had food in your desk like the last office."

"I told you we would eat when I got done."

"It's alright," Jacoby said standing up.

Phoebe looked at him sharply. "It's not alright, Jacoby. They disobeyed me and they know they aren't suppose to."

"Please don't be so hard on them. They're just hungry."

She narrowed her eyes at him not use to anyone telling her how to be a parent except her mother. "I'm more upset at myself. I shouldn't have brought them here, but Yvette asked if I would fax something to California for her that was left in the office."

He nodded. "Ned called and asked if she could bother you today. I told him you probably wouldn't mind, but if you were busy then he would have understood."

"Not busy. I was done with all my errands for the day. I just have my hands a little full," she said referring to the children.

"Why don't I take you out to lunch for your extra effort? Are you guys hungry?" he asked the twins.

They nodded eagerly, but then looked up at their mother for approval. Jacoby almost envied her at so much respect pouring on her from those beautiful brown eyes so like their mother's.

"I thought you would be in Canada this weekend entertaining," she said, trying to think of a good excuse that wouldn't make him think she didn't want to be alone, with him. Although technically going out with the children wasn't being alone since they couldn't talk about what she wanted to discuss with him.

"I thought so too until my client's son came down with a case of chickenpox," he explained quickly. A bit too quickly in Phoebe's mind as if he had hurried up and come up with the excuse, but this meeting couldn't have been planned by him, because why would he go through all the trouble of canceling a meeting, getting down to Detroit, and break his neck to be here at the office when she got here and act as if it were absolutely nothing when the children were here.

"I have the whole day free if you must know, so if you want we can shoot down to-" He had to quickly think of a restaurant where children could go downtown and not a bar. "Sweet Georgia Brown over in Greektown."

She looked wary, but then nodded. "They are hungry," she justified.

"And of course you are doing this for them?" he asked.

Phoebe met his cinnamon brown eyes knowing that remark was purely sarcastic, but she decided she would not try to argue with him, not with the twins present. "What are you doing in my office?"

"I thought maybe there might be some messages you forgot to give to me," he lied quickly.

She looked insulted. "I never forget."

"I can tell." He moved around the desk until they were arms length apart. "Are you ready?"

Phoebe knew she had to keep her thoughts to herself, especially with the children present. The children were always quick to see when she was bothered, especially

Stephen who was attuned to everything around him even though he didn't speak much.

"Were we taking the People Mover?" she questioned. The People Mover was a transportation device built on a high rail system above the street to make it easier for people to get around in Downtown Detroit.

He was caught off guard as Stephanie came up beside him and put her hand in his. "Yes," he said a bit flustered. "That would be perfect since we're right by it."

Phoebe tried to take Stephanie's hand, but the child seemed adamant on holding Jacoby's hands. "I'm sorry," Phoebe apologized. "They really never take to strangers, especially male strangers, so openly."

"It's alright. Maybe I just have that affect on people." He was looking at Phoebe when he said it and the intensity in his eyes made her shudder. Phoebe quickly looked away leading Stephen out the office. She wasn't going to respond to that quip either.

He followed with Stephanie grasping his hand in a death grip. "So she isn't so responsive to Lawrence's attention, either."

"She's like me, Jacoby. She knows something doesn't smell right in the Garden of Eden. Stephen always goes with the flow unless he knows I'm really upset. I think he's only intuitive of mine and his sister's emotions. Sometimes my mother, too."

He snorted. "And you think Lawrence is up to something?"

"I don't know, but he doesn't seem like the type that likes friend's leftovers."

He opened the door for her. Stephen skipped a little ahead and pushed the button to the elevator to go down. Obediently, he returned and took his mother's hand.

Stephanie didn't let go of Jacoby's hand for one second.

When the doors to the elevators were closed on them inside the elevator, Jacoby said, "You were not leftovers."

She only shrugged.

Just as the doors opened again at the floor they were to get off at, he said, stepping out, "I'm not done with you yet."

Phoebe was almost stunned, but the doors closing and Stephen tugging on her hand knocked her out of her shocked state. "What is that supposed to mean?" He only gave her a wide-eyed innocent look. "Are you using the children to avoid talking?"

He smirked to himself as they waited on the dock of the platform for the train with this weird smile on his face. "I don't know what you mean, Phoebe."

"I mean you are deliberately trying not speak of what we need to speak about."

"Would I do something like that?"

Phoebe couldn't believe he was actually trying to be funny and she couldn't yell at him because it would upset the children. In a forced calm voice, she said, "I can't believe you are not taking this serious."

He continued to keep the levity in his voice. "If I didn't keep a sense of humor about this entire thing, Phoebe, I would have beat the sh-" He stopped himself remembering the kids were present and rephrased his words, "crap out of Lawrence a long time ago, but I've come to the conclusion that Lawrence is a pathetic welsh that tries to destroy what he envies." His look was filled with confidence as he said, "I'm hoping he doesn't win, but whether he does or not, I will still pity him because no matter what he does, he can never get away from his past mistakes."

Phoebe thought this was a rather evasive omission of some kind, which she wasn't supposed to get, but she had a feeling she might be finding out this information sooner than she thought.

Throughout lunch, the twins were a good distraction. Stephanie, who was usually the shy one opened up to Jacoby completely. She was enthralled by him asking him so many personal questions it was almost embarrassing, but Jacoby was so entertained he answered them, his patience never wearing thin to the adorable little girl.

When they boarded the People Mover to return back to the office, the twins fell asleep almost immediately.

"Do you work all the time?" Phoebe inquired.

"It helps get rid of the boredom. It keeps me out of trouble and it's a great distraction for me personally," Jacoby answered keeping his eyes forward and not looking at her at all.

Phoebe had noticed throughout the entire lunch he had purposely not made direct contact with her. Matter of fact, he seemed to speak to the children more than he spoke to her.

Never had Phoebe felt more hurt than now. It was as if to look at her would kill him.

When the People Mover stopped, he lifted the sleeping Stephanie into his arms and offered to carry Stephen as well to her car. They went straight to the parking lot where she had parked, but she stopped dead in her tracks when they were five cars away from where she normally parked.

He followed her eyes to the old Chevy. The car was in good condition, except there was a large hole in the middle of the windshield.

"It would seem the vehicle would be difficult to drive like that? Please don't tell me you drove it around like that," he teased looking around cautiously.

Narrowing her eyes at him, she said, "I don't find your levity funny anymore, Jacoby."

Jacoby wiped the grin off his face. "Who would do something like this?" he asked handing Stephanie to her to free his arm to get to his cell phone.

"I don't know." She opened her car and gasped. Someone had cracked the column and slashed at the seats of the car with a knife. It smelled as if someone had tried to start a fire, but was unsuccessful, but her radio was stolen and the pedal off the accelerator looked as if it had been hammered down.

"This was deliberate malicious destruction," she said getting out the car, slamming the door closed in frustration.

Jacoby called his car to his location and looked into the car himself. After assessing the damage, he waited with her for his car to arrive. "No one suspicious comes to mind?"

Sarcastically and angry, she responded, "You do, but you have an alibi."

He finally looked directly at her. "You think I would hurt you?"

"I don't know what you're up to, Jacoby. One minute-" she stopped almost saying something she knew he would just use to hurt her with. "Since I don't suspect you, I would suspect Simon."

"He's in jail, just like Madeline, isn't he?"

Phoebe would have figured he knew where Madeline was. "No, his father bailed him out. Don't ask me why Joseph did this, but Simon was ordered to stay away from me by the judge personally. I received a call just yesterday letting me know I would be needed to testify at all three of their trials."

"You think he might do something extreme?"

"Simon doesn't seem like the type on the outside, but if he could deceive his own father, who is to say he would do anything to stay out of jail."

"Even hurt you?"

"Oh, he's hurting me good. He knows hurting my pocket book is always painful."

A black limousine pulled up. Jacoby took the car seats out the Chevy and the driver assisted in placing them in the back of the limousine. While the driver placed the twins in and securely strapped them down, Jacoby turned to her keeping arms length away.

"My driver will take you home and I'll stay here for and have this towed to your home."

She took a deep breath filled with a feeling of disappointment. "I don't know how I will ever pay you back, Jacoby. You've done so much for me and my family."

"It's not about paying me back, Phoebe. It never was and you know it."

Phoebe held back what she wanted to say so bad and turned away to get into the limousine. He grabbed her arm and turned her around holding her shoulders tightly.

"Dammit Phoebe say it! Say what you have to say or I swear I'm going to go insane."

She bit her lip and searched his eyes that were filled with so much pain and anger. Yet all she could think about was today when he had deliberately avoided her eyes, chances to touch her when other times he had, and how now it seemed to pain him to even get this close to her. Why should she speak her mind or her heart when she knew he wouldn't care? Maybe Lawrence was right? She probably wasn't the only woman on his plate. Why should he care about her feelings for him?

"Nothing Jacoby," she forced out, using every bit of strength not to collapse in his arms and mold her body against him. "There's nothing to say." She moved out of his arms and quickly got into the limousine.

Jacoby was barely able to control himself as the car pulled away. He slammed his fist down on the hood of her Chevy creating a large dent in the middle. Cursing violently, he paced trying to get his temper down.

If that woman didn't come to her senses soon, he swore he would end up raping her where she stood.

Chapter 29

When Phoebe got home that night, after telling her mother what had happened at the parking structure, she went to her phone book and found Amy's home phone number. Amy wasn't home, but called her back after an hour.

"What's up?" Amy asked concerned.

Phoebe told her what happened with her car, then asked, "Do you think it was Simon?"

"It may sound like something Simon would do, but that would be impossible since his father put him into a drug rehab Friday night when the sheriff busted him at a rave party with a bunch of teenagers."

"What was he doing there?"

"Getting high on Ecstasy, I suppose. Don't really know the real details, Phoebe. Do you have any other enemies?"

"None that I know of. This is all very confusing, Amy."

"Did you report it to the police?"

"I was going to make a report, but I wanted to speak with you first."

"You be careful," Amy warned. "Not to change the subject, but what happened to the affair with the boss you were talking about with me the other time?"

"I never got the chance to do what we spoke about because he's been avoiding me like I'm the plague. I don't know what to do, because I don't know what he really feels. Maybe I've hurt him too much for him to like me again. I had a chance, but I don't want to be disappointed, Amy."

"That's part of life, Phoebe. You're going to have to deal with whatever he feels for you now in order to get through this. If you keep it all bottled up inside of you, you'll hurt even more."

She got off the phone with Amy thinking more about Jacoby than the destruction of her vehicle as the minutes passed. Phoebe didn't sleep well Saturday night. When the morning came and Patricia asked if she would like to go out to Great Lakes Crossing Mall, she declined feeling every muscle in her body screaming for rest. Patricia let Phoebe know she was only taking Stephen with her because Stephanie was still asleep.

About one in the afternoon when her mother had yet to return, she heard Stephanie coming awake and decided to crawl out of bed and get something to eat. After making a light breakfast for the both of them, she started to clean the kitchen.

When the telephone rung, she answered it by the third ring with a tired, "Hello?"

"You sound exhausted," Lawrence said on the other end. "Are you up or still curled up in bed?"

"I've been up for awhile."

"Is working for Jacoby that exhaustive?" he asked.

"No, someone wrecked my car on purpose."

"Are you all right?" he asked quite concerned.

"Yes, I'm fine. Jacoby took care of all the details. He even put the car in the shop."

"Jacoby was in Detroit yesterday?" he questioned quite shocked.

"Yes, he was at the office. He said the appointment he had canceled because his son was sick."

"But he was supposed to be in Canada with Thaddeus Newman, right?"

Phoebe only shrugged. "I guess so."

"Mr. Newman doesn't have any sons. His wife, Skye just had a daughter. That's their first child together. He lied to you."

Phoebe frowned. "Why would he lie? He didn't know I would be in the office. Seeing me was very unexpected."

Lawrence changed the subject. "I was wondering if I could come over and speak to you about some things that I think we should talk about. It's really important. I wouldn't stay long if you didn't want me to."

She really wasn't in the mood to entertain, but decided today would be a good time to tell Lawrence that they shouldn't even be friends. Phoebe knew he wanted more than just friendship and today she would really put her foot down about them spending time together and her true feelings for Jacoby would be revealed to Lawrence so she wouldn't feel as if she were pulling him along in some kind of game. Although she had made it evident to Lawrence that she had no intentions of taking their relationship any further in the past, she felt he would be a hindrance in her pursuit to get with Jacoby with his negativity. "I'll see you in a few minutes?"

"Sure."

Just as she hung up the phone, the doorbell rung and she put down Stephanie in the playpen to answer the door. An

Amazon dark chocolate woman about five feet eleven stood in the doorway. She would be beautiful, almost angelic if it wasn't for that horrendous frown on her face. Her light green/gray eyes glared down at Phoebe as if she had committed treason in the United States. Either that or Phoebe was standing in the door naked.

Phoebe looked down at herself to see if she was dressed appropriate. Today she had only dawned on some jeans and a sweater because she had no intentions of going anywhere. The cooking glove was still on her hand and her hair was still undone from sleeping restlessly.

"Are you Phoebe Green?" the young lady asked vehemently.

Phoebe was unsure if she should answer her, but curiosity was killing her to know why this woman wanted her. "Yes, I'm Phoebe. Do I know you?"

"It doesn't surprise me that you wouldn't know who I was or you wouldn't care that you're breaking up a marriage."

"What are you talking about?" Phoebe demanded to know.

"I'm talking about you and my man being together shamelessly in public while his wife sits at home five months pregnant." Suddenly the woman burst into tears. "I've tried to keep our marriage together. I've known he's been sleeping around. We only married for convenience, but instead of him helping his wife run a business, he decides to start another business. He understood if my daddy found out we weren't running the business together, he'd come and take my business away from me. He knew this yet he's still going to file for separation." The sobs became louder.

Stephanie, who was just in the other room, began to whimper in distress.

"Who are you talking about?" Phoebe asked.

The woman suddenly stopped crying and asked incredulously, "Are there so many men in your lives that you don't know one from the other?"

"No!" she exclaimed. Flustered and confused she said, "Why don't you come in and have a seat."

The woman came in and Phoebe found some Kleenex for her while ushering her to a seat in the living room. Phoebe didn't even bother closing the main door to the house too eager to hear what this woman had to say.

Phoebe thought to take it from the top so she could get an understanding of what was going on. "Let's start all of this back over, Miss. You think that I am seeing your husband and that I'm breaking up your relationship."

"I know you're seeing my husband and I know you're breaking us up because a lawyer, Abraham Blue called yesterday to ask for my social security number so he could file the separation papers. I knew you had to be different from all the others, because even though he sees other women he's never made any attempt to leave me until now." She broke into another round of loud sobs.

Phoebe didn't know how to handle this. Abraham Blue was Jacoby's attorney and if Jacoby was married...the thought of it made the room spin and Phoebe had to sit down across from the woman to keep from passing out.

"I swear to you I had no idea he was married."

Spitefully the woman asked, "You don't think he gets his money off of trees, do you? He used my money to front the money for part of his business. He wouldn't have become a partnership if it wasn't for me."

"But Jacoby doesn't have a partner," Phoebe pointed out completely perplexed.

The woman stopped the sniffles and sobbing. In an about faced disgusted tone, she spat, "I'm not talking about that sex maniac! Any woman crazy enough to even sleep with that man won't walk straight for the rest of her life. I'm talking about my husband, Lawrence Ripley."

Phoebe's jaw dropped wide open. "You're Lawrence's wife?"

"Yes," the woman sobbed. "I'm Natalie Ripley." She touched her stomach tenderly. "And this is Lawrence's baby I'm carrying."

"You're pregnant?!" Phoebe was feeling more nauseous by the second. Even though it was the second time the woman had stated that, it was now that it really hit home.

Proudly, Lawrence's wife said, "Five months."

Patricia chose that time to enter the home carrying Stephen. She seemed oblivious to Natalie as she spoke, "You'll never guess whom I found outside," she sang merrily. "He pulled up at the same time we pulled up."

Lawrence came around the corner. "Hi Phoebe, I was..." His words trailed off as he saw both women glaring up at him. He looked from one to another speechless.

Patricia noticed the horrified look on Lawrence's face and then looked at her daughter. "Who is this, Phoebe?" she asked.

Phoebe stood up. "This is Lawrence's wife, Natalie Ripley, Mother."

It was Patricia's turn to look shocked.

"You little bitch, what the hell are you doing here?" Lawrence snarled.

Natalie stood up and snapped, "I wouldn't be here if you had not broken your promise."

"What promise are you talking about? I never broke any promise to you!"

"Oh and Abraham Blue, your lawyer, doesn't plan on filing separation papers tomorrow morning."

"Abraham Blue isn't my lawyer! That's Jacoby's lawyer," Lawrence pointed out.

"So why is he calling on your behalf?!" Natalie demanded to know.

"I DON'T KNOW!" Lawrence screeched.

Phoebe saw Stephen about to get upset and decided to calm the situation down. "Mother, please take the children up to their room and close the door." Patricia was still stunned. "Mother!"

Patricia startled and picked up Stephanie from the playpen and took both twins upstairs as fast as she could so she could return.

"Lawrence, why didn't you ever tell me you were married?" Phoebe asked angrily.

Flustered, he looked from her to Natalie, then back at Phoebe. "I was going to. That's why I was coming over here to speak with you. I wanted you to know everything."

"So she was special enough for you to leave me?" Natalie cried.

He huffed. "No, dammit, Natalie. Stop twisting my words around."

"But you did keep it from me, didn't you, Lawrence?" Phoebe questioned.

"Yes, but only because I thought you probably wouldn't understand our arrangement."

"Arrangement? Is that what you call this marriage between you and her?" Phoebe asked. "Does this arrangement have any provisions about children? Your wife is five months pregnant."

He looked at Natalie seething in anger suddenly realizing something very terrible. "You lying bitch!"

"You're the one who's lying!" Natalie shouted.

"You told me nothing happened that night!" he accused her. "You drugged me on purpose to get me to sleep with you."

Natalie looked very guilty. "I wanted to make sure you didn't break the promise. I wanted to insure that we stayed together because you knew what the consequences would be if we didn't."

"How the hell do I know if that's my child?"

Natalie slapped him as hard as she could and then burst out in loud sobs.

Lawrence looked only a little bit sorry, and then looked at Phoebe for help.

Phoebe moved between Lawrence and Natalie saying calmly, "I think you should leave, Lawrence. It would be best."

"You're going to believe this bitch. She'd do anything to ruin my fucking life-"

The backhand Phoebe delivered was more a blow to his conscious than for pain, which made him stop talking. "Get out, right now," she sneered through clenched teeth.

He actually looked as if she had broken his heart before he turned around to leave.

Natalie quickly stopped her crying after he left, dried her eyes and moved to the door. "I should go. I've caused enough problems."

Phoebe didn't respond to this still somewhat stunned over what had occurred.

Natalie came back over to Phoebe and pressed something into her hand. "This is for yesterday. I'm sorry. Just write in the amount of the cost of damages and send me the receipt. You know how love goes, don't you, sweetie?" She didn't give Phoebe time to respond, nor time to see what was given to her before she left out of the home closing the door behind her.

Patricia came down the stairs. Mother and daughter eyes met and Phoebe looked down at her hand to a signed check with no amount put on it.

"And you wanted me to start a relationship with him?" Phoebe asked her mother incredulously.

Patricia was still speechless.

Phoebe knew she would sleep well tonight because when she saw Jacoby tomorrow she would do what Amy had told her to do. What's the worst that could happen.

Chapter 30

Desmond looked over at Jacoby with much annoyance. Jacoby was drumming his fingers so hard on the table at The Whitney the crystal water glasses were starting to vibrate.

The Whitney was a high-end restaurant housed in one of the enormous historic mansions in Detroit. On Woodward Avenue, The Whitney hid behind large brush and on the outside had this forbidding feel. Most people believed the place was haunted.

"Do you have to?" Desmond asked quite annoyed.

"Yes," Jacoby snapped not even looking over at Desmond. He kept his eyes at the Whitney's restaurant doorway. This was one of Thaddeus Newman's favorite spots other than the damn cafe he loved to visit on the outskirts of Detroit. Yet with it being December, Thaddeus choose closed quarters and the Whitney would definitely put him into a better mood since he might be a bit perturbed at Jacoby for standing him up Sunday.

The doorway stayed empty as minutes passed and Jacoby was about to conclude that Thaddeus had probably decided to stand them up. Jacoby knew he really didn't have to watch the doorway for Thaddeus. The room of people would indicate Thaddeus's arrival when their heads would turn, gasps would follow and whispers would be abounded. Thaddeus was no ordinary man with a height of over six and a half feet and a thick brawniness about him. On top of this, he had a face that women couldn't help but drool over. He was an ex-University of Michigan two time champion before his knee busted on him in his junior year and he was forced to immediately find something else to pay his bills. Going into the construction business had been a good idea and his company was internationally known for its high quality and excellence in building structures. He had worked with nationally and internationally known firms and architects including a locally known Davenport architect named Abigail McPherson.

The steady drumming of Jacoby's fingers became harder and harder as the minutes passed.

"How can you be nervous? This is your friend," Desmond stated. "You aren't the one begging for an account with his construction firm."

Jacoby choose not to answer him too on edge to not give a harsh answer and Desmond's sense of humor was starting to piss him off. He had decided not to be around anyone since he was so tense inside he knew he would not be good company for anyone.

Thaddeus and Jacoby had been friends since college and Desmond had begged for this meeting to get more revenue into the company. Jacoby knew Thaddeus wouldn't be that mad because Thaddeus had stood Jacoby up in the name of love several times in the past.

Plus, yesterday's meeting was only a small friendly get together at the Windsor Casino. Nothing spectacular, although Thaddeus had insisted on speaking with Jacoby privately about Desmond and Lawrence's computer firm and if Jacoby had confidence they could handle Thaddeus' company.

As told when their guest arrived, the crowd did turn heads and many people recognized Thaddeus Newman as he entered the room. The host went up to meet him, but Thaddeus brushed him away and came straight for the table because Jacoby was no hard man to miss either.

Soon as Thaddeus arrived at the table, the frown on his face completely went lax as he sensed the tension in Jacoby immediately. "What's got your boxers in a bunch? I haven't seen you like this since college finals. Not getting any, Jacoby?" he teased.

"How did you know?" Jacoby blurted out.

Desmond chuckled. "Does everyone know when you aren't getting any, Jacoby?"

Jacoby shot him a murderous glare.

Thaddeus had a seat as he said, "I know when Jacoby's not getting any because of the way he acts and looks. He used to deny himself around finals time because he said it made him study harder. I guess it worked since he graduated in the top five percent."

"Is this meeting about me or about other things?" Jacoby snapped.

"Now I see why you stood me up yesterday, Jake. You aren't in the best of moods are you?" Thaddeus guessed.

"I'm not in any mood to be teased, if that's what you mean."

"Don't tell me you have women problems. Not Jacoby Knight." Thaddeus chortled in amazement. "I didn't think I would live to see the day when you would actually have women problems. What are you saving yourself for?" This was a joke, but the look on Jacoby's face clearly said Thaddeus had hit the nail on the head.

"I don't believe it either," Desmond said.

"I'm not in the mood to hear your comments, Desmond," Jacoby snapped.

"I'm just trying to tell you, she's not all that, although I do commend her on handling Natalie very well."

"You sent Natalie over too her?" Thaddeus asked. Even he knew of the meddlesome, troubled wife of Lawrence from all the stories Jacoby related to him over the years. "Was she still standing afterwards or did she wither from the fire Natalie spouted out her mouth?"

Jacoby had to chuckle and then said proudly. "According to Desmond who heard from Lawrence, Phoebe handled the situation quite well and actually got a compliment from the fire breathing dragon wife if you call being called sweetie a compliment, but in Natalie's book that is almost like being placed on a pedestal."

"Who the hell is Phoebe? And how did you meet her?" Thaddeus inquired.

"He paid for her, almost like you did for your wife, so you two should have something in common," Desmond blurted out.

Jacoby thought to straighten the matter with Thaddeus. "Not as extensive or complicated as your situation, Tad, I assure you."

Both men shot Desmond a potent glare, who all of a sudden decided the ceiling was looking very interesting about now.

"Details, Jake, I'm quite intrigued," Thaddeus said after everyone ordered a drink.

"None to tell. She's intelligent, beautiful and wants nothing to do with me or my money."

"Is she blind and frigid?" Thaddeus asked.

"No, but she'll change her tune tomorrow when I see her."

"What are you going to do?" Desmond asked poking his nose in again.

"Now that she knows that Lawrence is a slime, she'll come running to me."

"How so when she thinks you're upset with her over her seeing Lawrence behind your back?" Desmond asked. "You haven't said anything about forgiving her."

"But if she truly knows me, she'll see that I've already forgiven her and she just has to admit to me that she really loves me."

"And if she doesn't do that? Then what?" Thaddeus inquired.

Jacoby didn't want to think about that and changed the subject, but since he really didn't have to be there mentally at the meeting, just physically to introduce them and get the discussion going, this gave him time to think about Phoebe more and what he would do if she decided to be involved with him. He didn't think he could take this abstinence much longer without killing someone in a rage of passion.

Chapter 31

Every nerve in Phoebe's body was on edge as she awoke Tuesday. She had been on pins and needles yesterday, but since she had not heard from Jacoby, she slept almost all the way through the night. His calendar was booked all Monday and she was busy assisting in another employee's project.

The employee's meeting wasn't scheduled until five and the conference center that was booked for the meeting was right down the street on Woodward from the office building where Jacoby's business occupied. She had already made sure yesterday and early this morning that everything was going to go like clockwork and she didn't have to be there until the last minute, which was at ten.

So when she arrived at the office from the conference center at eight, she was surprised to see Desmond at the front lobby desk making some adjustments on the computer there for the new permanent office help that was to start next week. Business had picked up considerably in the last weeks that she had been there and instead of using the temporary companies every day, Jacoby decided to have her hire someone on a permanent basis, so she could handle more stuff outside of the office for him.

"Good morning, Mr. White," she said about to walk past him to go to her office. She knew Desmond did not care for her at all because he assumed she had played both friends.

"Phoebe, can I speak with you?" he asked casually.

"Can you?" she questioned sarcastically, stopping and turning to him.

"I know you have a meeting in a couple of hours and I didn't want to take away the time you might need to prepare for it."

"I'm already prepared."

"Good." Desmond stood up and moved in an awkward spot so her back was to the office. "I just wanted to know what you intended to do."

She frowned. "What do you mean? About what?"

"Jacoby. You've got him about to burst. He hasn't had a woman since you and it's driving him crazy. I think you should talk to him, Phoebe."

"He hasn't had a woman?" she asked in disbelief.

"He believes himself to be saving himself until you come to your senses. No matter how I have tried to convince him that this is a foolhardy idea, he believes you will one day, but I don't think I can wait until you decide to drive him to the nut house. Jacoby is my good friend and I need him to be in good spirits especially for my wedding in two weeks. You two need to speak and I want to know when."

Her shoulders sunk in defeat. "I know, Desmond, but there's been no time lately with the new office and since he doesn't mix business with pleasure, I never know when to speak to him and..." Her voice trailed off.

"What?" Desmond asked impatiently.

"I really don't know what to say. I've been given a lot of ideas, but whenever I think about doing them, it's all wrong or it doesn't feel right."

"Like Saturday?" he asked.

She looked a bit perturbed that he would know about Saturday, but they were all friends so most likely he also knew about Natalie as well. "Yes, Saturday. I wanted to tell him about how I felt, but I didn't think it was the right time. Maybe it will never be the right time, Desmond. Maybe I shouldn't even try."

"Don't even think that way, Phoebe. I think if you expressed the feelings I think you have for Jacoby to him, then you wouldn't have any problems with him. Bottom line is I think the two of you need to talk. He really wants to know how you're feeling."

She looked now a little wary. "Why are you so concerned? I know that you have some animosity towards me, Desmond, because of the kind of person you think I am, but I always made my feelings known to both of them. I never led them into believing there was more."

"But have you really told Jacoby the extent of how you feel?" he asked.

Phoebe didn't really want to answer his question. Not until he answered hers. "You first Desmond. Why do you care?"

All of a sudden his confidence faded a bit and he stuttered slightly. "Like I told you, Jacoby's my friend and he's starting to get on my nerves with his touchiness."

She smiled, which relaxed him and decided to answer his question. "No, I haven't told him anything about how I presently feel because like I said he doesn't mix business with pleasure."

"He would make an exception to this rule for you, Phoebe, trust me."

This took a lot of weight off of Phoebe's mind and heart and a brilliant smile came to her lips. Desmond seemed memorized as she approached him and kissed his cheek.

"Thank you, Mr. White," she said.

He took a moment and swallowed before he said, "Desmond, please call me Desmond."

"Thank you, Desmond."

"No, thank you. He's been a sour puss for the longest." He nodded towards Jacoby's office. "He's in there right now probably biting off people's heads."

She gave him another kiss and rushed to Jacoby's door. Before opening it, she took a deep breath and closed her eyes. Suddenly she remembered the intercom red light blinking on the phone in the lobby.

Looking back at Desmond, she saw how he was just standing there very sure and confident. It was a plan. All planned, Phoebe realized. That son of a bitch was probably sitting in his chair gloating wanting her to come back to him and confess that he wanted her, and then what? What did he have planned?

The office phones rung and she decided to answer it before going in the office. It was a team member letting her know he had arrived at the conference center early and was wondering when Jacoby would be coming down. She let him know they still had an hour and a half left before Jacoby had to be there. The team member then asked if she could add something on the itinerary.

She agreed and wrote down what he needed for Jacoby to address at the meeting. When she was off the phone, she decided to go into Jacoby's office and give him a piece of her mind about how he was trying to deceive her.

Phoebe should have suspected Jacoby was the mastermind behind all of this. First her car, then that horrible Lawrence and Natalie situation, and now Desmond purposely trying to convince her when she knew Desmond could care less.

Stubbornly, she decided to go in his office and be perfectly professional to him and not give in first. That was what he wanted, she was sure of. He wouldn't have gone through all this trouble if he didn't want her to concede first. Phoebe concluded that two could play his game.

Going in the office, Jacoby was just getting off the phone. She paused at the doorway and remembered some of Amy's words on what to do. Shoulders back, breast thrust forward and a walk so sexy he couldn't help but stare. With the wicked knowledge that he wanted her, Phoebe came in with the confidence of a woman bent on seduction.

Late last night, she had put some reports on his desk that he needed to have looked over by the time he went to the meeting. He had a pencil in hand for corrections and as she got closer and closer to the desk, the grip on the pencil became tighter and tighter until his strain on the wood broke the pencil in half.

He hissed an expletive dropping the pencil on the desk. Jacoby's cinnamon sensuous eyes were liquid pools of passion seeming to visually caress every inch of skin from her head to her toes. She couldn't help herself knowing her heart rate increased at her proximity to him.

Leaning over the desk, she placed the message in front of him, but his eyes never moved from her, especially as she leaned over revealing a very open neckline.

Phoebe was enjoying herself immensely as she had to repeat her message over to him that she put in front of him. He looked very perturbed now. It took all of Phoebe's control not to laugh at him and his present "hard" dilemma.

"Did you need anything, before leaving for the meeting?" she asked simply.

Whether he knew it or not, he was not viciously gripping the arm of the chair. "You don't have anything else to say to me?"

Phoebe pretended innocence as she stood up and came around the desk. "Well there is one thing I did want to tell you."

"What?" he asked on the edge of his seat.

She paused a moment, then said, "You weren't going to address Campbell about New York were you when he isn't completed with all three club openings yet, were you?"

The deflated look in his face was evident and Phoebe gloated on cloud nine.

In a strained voice, through tightly clenched teeth, he snipped, "No, I had no intentions, especially after reading his report. Was there anything else?"

"One more thing," she said leaning down again, and wrapping his tie around her hand. "You weren't going to wear this tie were you?"

He gave her a look as if she had lost her mind. Unwinding his tie around her hand, he sneered, "My tie is fine, Phoebe."

"Well then, I'll be seeing you at the meeting then." She moved from around the desk and started for the door.

"That's it!" he exclaimed, jumping from the chair and coming around the desk.

She faced him. "What more were you asking for, Jacoby? This is business."

"Dammit Phoebe. I don't give a fuck about the business right now and you damn well know it."

Looking insulted and confused, she asked, "What do you care about then?" she asked.

He ran a frustrated hand through his hair glaring at her knowing what she wanted. "You are nothing but a stubborn anal woman."

"And you are nothing but a conniving deceitful man, Jacoby Knight, and there's nothing for us to say." She went to the door and opened it.

He was beside her in a flash, slamming the door back closed. "Dammit, I love you, Phoebe. I Love you!"

"And I love you too, Jacoby, now get off the door!" she hollered back, just as frustrated and hurt.

So confused and disconcerted, he opened the door to let her leave. Phoebe gave him a look of disbelief. She couldn't believe that was it. He was going to just let her go! Wasn't this where he was supposed to take her in his arms, carry her over to the desk and make good love to her?

Stepping out in the hallway, she decided to just walk to her office and cry. Halfway down the hall, he came after her, grabbed her arm and swung her around.

His mouth captured her own so possessively, as the wind was knocked out of her as she was slammed against his chest. Breathlessly pulling away for a moment, he asked again filled with uncertainty, "You love me?"

Phoebe was too out of breath to speak and only nodded. This was all he needed as he kissed her hard and long. Her mouth couldn't keep up with his, as he seemed to drain her senses and then fill them up again with a need to have him so overwhelming their surroundings were forgotten.

He swept her up and carried her to his office, never breaking the kiss as he kicked the door hard behind him. Jacoby didn't stop until he got to the desk and knocked whatever was on it off.

"The reports," she warned, opening his tie and then his shirt.

"Who cares," he muttered, kissing her face and neck. His hands were everywhere holding, gently squeezing, and undressing her.

Phoebe relished in his touch and took great measures to remember the smoothness of his skin, the velvety feel of his hardened manhood, the tightness of his butt as she gripped the muscles holding him closer to her.

Wanting her very ready for him, Jacoby wasted no time once they were free of clothing preparing her for him. His mouth made her ready, but he didn't stop there, not when she was begging for him to be inside of her. He continued to arouse and please her until she was a whimpering mass of sensitive nerves. As he joined with her, his body over hers, he whispered sweet words in her ear on each thrust deep into her.

"You're my everything, Phoebe. My sun, my moon, my stars." He licked her neck up to her earlobe where he briefly nibbled the soft cartilage. "You've given me purpose," he whispered in her ear. "And being with you is so beautiful. I promise to never ever hurt you."

Phoebe couldn't help the tears of joy slowly slipping from her closed eyes as she felt him explode deep into her loins with her, filling her with his love. This man was much too wonderful and she knew her heart, mind, body and soul would always belong to him.

Amazingly, he was first to come to reality. "Phoebe, look at me."

She opened her eyes slowly to look up at this handsome man, who had just made her so happy.

"I'm going to prove to you for the rest of your life, you are my world," he promised.

"The rest of my life?" she asked. "In that case why don't we just get married if you're going to waste your time like that?" Phoebe was teasing and her tone of voice clearly said so.

He smirked moving away from her and finding his jacket on the floor. Phoebe sat up on the desk and looked down filled with curiosity at his strange behavior. He dug through the inside pockets and pulled out an old velvet green box.

Moving to one knee, he opened the box and looked up at her. "Since you suggested it, why don't we?" he said simply.

Phoebe gasped as if he had cursed at her covering her hands over her mouth. "Jacoby, that's a ring!"

He chuckled and gently pulled her down to him. When she was on her knees in front of him staring at the ring like it was going to jump up and bite her, he asked, "I want you to be mine, Phoebe, because I'm already yours. I've been yours from the beginning and I'll be yours until the end. I'll make you so happy-"

"Shut up and put the ring on my finger!" she cut him off.

He did, and giddy with joy Phoebe threw her arms around his neck. She had never imagined getting to propose to by a naked man in the middle of his office, but love has its way of making things so weird.

"Jacoby, you already make me happy when I'm with you," she admitted with a brilliant smile on her face.

He laughed in relief as he laid her down on top of their clothes. This time when they made love, it was much slower and she could tell he was relishing everything as if they were making love for the first time. He made her mindless in pleasure and she reciprocated this time until he too didn't care about the world around them. Phoebe wantonness for him made her feel like a queen and he was her king reigning pleasure through every vein in her body.

When their second love session ended, he asked, "What about the meeting?"

"What meeting?" she asked then gasped, remembering they were supposed to be somewhere. Checking the clock on the wall, she saw they still had five minutes to get down to the conference center and smiled. "I think you should call them and let them know you might be late."

"Might be? Who's to say I'm finished here?"

She blushed feeling his hardness still deep in her. "Jacoby, this is the office and just because I agreed to marry you, don't think I'm going to allow you to break office decorum all the time."

"Only when I want you?" he asked.

"Only when you really want me," she teased.

"Hell, that's all the time. We'd never get any work done."

She burst out in laughter at his silliness as he nuzzled her neck. "We really should get dressed," she insisted. "I promise we can take all afternoon together, if you get through with this meeting although you had lunch with Desmond planned and he might get jealous."

"I think I can afford to make Desmond a little jealous." He helped her up, agreeing to her terms. "Go in my private bathroom and get freshen up, while I call down to the conference room and let them know we'll be a little late. They know how to start without me and then I'll meet you downstairs in the car. Deal?"

She nodded and picked up her clothes quickly. Before he let her in the bathroom though he gave her a fervent kiss as a promise to what was to come in the afternoon. Phoebe couldn't wait.

Chapter 32

Phoebe called home about seven that night to let her mother know she was going to be home late - as if she couldn't guess already. Strangely, no one answered her phone. Not even the answering machine had come on.

Jacoby had taken her to his apartments he was renting in Harbortown right after one of the quickest employee meeting he had to date. His team was not worried about his strange behavior and Phoebe knew a lot of them would be getting back to him with questions about their reports being so messed up.

"Let's take my car to your home," he suggested.

"Stephanie would love that. She has asked about you."

His face lit up. "She has?"

Phoebe nodded. "My mother says she thinks my daughter may have a crush on you, but I'm going to have to disappoint her."

"Are you jealous?" he teased.

She giggled. "Yes, because I don't like to share my man with anyone."

He kissed her gently. "Say it again."

"What? I don't like to share my man?"

Obviously that was it because he kissed her again, holding her close. They soon dressed and made it to his rented green Jaguar. On the way to her home, he asked, "What do you think your mother will think about us getting married, Phoebe?"

"After Saturday, you are certainly looking good to her. She said yesterday she couldn't wait to meet you, although she is still in a bit of a shock over what Lawrence failed to tell us."

Upon arriving at her home, Phoebe was suddenly reluctant to get out the car. Anyone else looking at her home wouldn't think anything was strange, but Phoebe immediately sensed something wasn't right. The front picture window curtains weren't opened and her mother had pulled in forwards. Patricia hated pulling out of the driveway backwards and always took great effort to pull in backwards.

"What's wrong?" he asked seeing her reluctance.

"Can you call my phone inside the house?" she asked.

He used his cell phone to dial her number. "No ones answering it. Could she be sleep?"

"My mother never sleeps during the day and most likely the ringer has been turned off along with the answering machine." She got out the car. "You stay here and call the police."

"Why don't I come with you first, Phoebe?" he suggested worrying.

"No, I'll be fine. She could have just been doing something and just forgot. I don't want her to get embarrassed if she's walking around naked. If I'm not back in a couple of minutes then come in." She closed the door and went up to the front door. Checking the door she found it unlocked.

Alarm bells went off in her head, but she still proceeded inside of the home. Patricia's coat was left on the stairs going up and the house was completely quiet. Rushing up the stairs, she went straight to her mother's room. No one was in there so she went to the nursery to find her mother was lying face unconscious with a lump on the right temple.

Phoebe's heart lurched in her chest praying that her mother was not dead and that the twins were okay.

"Momma!" she said frantically, moving down and lightly shaking Patricia.

Patricia slowly opened her eyes and groaned. "H-He...he took...babies...heard you...coming." She grabbed at Phoebe's arms desperately. "Go...Go get them."

Phoebe went to the back down the stairs and to the back of the house.

"Stop right there!" Daniel said as she rounded the corner into the kitchen.

Phoebe wouldn't have stopped, but she did when she saw the gun pointed at Stephanie's head. Immediately she halted and put her hands up terrified now. Stephen tried to run to her, but Daniel was gripping the child's arm so harshly his dark skin was starting to turn a bright red.

Daniel looked as if he hadn't eaten in several days. His eyes were partially sunk into his face with dark lines under it. She could also smell that he hadn't taken a bath in a while either and his clothes looked worn and dirty. He was a man at the end of his rope and getting to her was his last option, since he probably had no one else. This was the only way to get to her - with the children.

She knelt down and gently ordered Stephen to calm down. "Momma's right here."

"He hurt Grandma!" Stephen cried. "He said he's gonna hurt Steppie, if I don't be good."

It took all her strength to keep from crying so she wouldn't alarm either twin. Stephanie was almost the epitome of control staying calm, but there was so much worry in her eyes and Phoebe knew the child didn't trust herself to speak.

"Are you okay, Steph?" Phoebe asked.

Stephanie only nodded and held her brother's hand for support.

"Ain't no fucker coming in to daddy my kids!" Daniel sneered.

Phoebe stood up and seethed angrily, "Daniel, you're scarring the kids."

"Ain't no fucker coming in here to daddy my kids, Phoebe," he repeated louder, pressing the gun harder against Stephanie's temple. The child closed her eyes and whimpered in pain.

"Alright Daniel. What do you want?"

"I want my kids! I want my family back together like it used to be Phoebe. Why can't you see that?"

"Daniel, this isn't right. This isn't the way to do it." She edge closer slowly.

"Shut the fuck up. You don't care. You don't see that you need me."

"What is it you want me to do?" she asked humbly. "What is it you need me to do to make things better, Daniel?"

"You can shut the fuck up, bitch! I'll kill her. I'll blow her fucking head off! Then I'll shoot him too. If I can't have them Phoebe, no one will."

"Daniel, no," Phoebe pleaded forcing a sob back. "Don't hurt our babies. Please don't. They aren't apart of this," she pleaded now within arm's length of him. "What do you want me to do, Daniel?" She was desperately trying to think of anything to make him stop.

He let go of Stephen's hand and reached in his back pocket to pull out a rumpled piece of paper and a pen. "You sign this paper, bitch."

She looked down at the child custody agreement papers. It was to give Daniel full custody of the children. He wanted her to sign over the children to him. Tears wielded in her eyes. "Daniel, please don't do this"

Daniel pointed the gun at her forehead. "You sign those papers bitch and maybe just maybe I'll let you see the children from time to time for a price." He looked her over lustfully, making her skin crawl in disgust. "Even if you don't have the money, I'll let you sneak a peek for a piece of you. Sign'em!" he ordered.

Taking the pen, she scribbled her name at the bottom and handed the paper back to him, but kept the pen.

He leered evilly as he backed to the side door of the house with both the children. "Their mine, Phoebe, and soon you'll be," he said triumphantly.

Phoebe watched in horror as he turned the knob to the door because she had a feeling she would never see her children again. Sobs of pain encompassed her chest. The tears she had tried to fight now flowed down her chest as he got the door opened partially.

Just as he was about to turn to open it all the way, the door was kicked opened, slamming into Daniel's nose. A ghastly crunching noise was heard as the gun dropped to the floor. Phoebe didn't waste a second kicking the gun toward the living room far away from them, while screaming for the children to run and hide. Stephanie grabbed her brother and ran under the kitchen table for cover as Jacoby entered the doorway of the side door.

Phoebe wanted to jump into his arms, but Daniel was between them. Daniel held his nose in one hand and swung his free arm at Jacoby's face, but missed. Jacoby didn't miss with his hard fist as it connected to Daniel's jaw, sending her ex-husband across the room out cold.

She ran to the phone and called the police. While she was giving them her address, Jacoby dragged Daniel to a kitchen chair and tied Daniel's hands to the chair using his own tie.

Stephen saw what Jacoby was doing and ran to the broom closet and found some rope. As he handed the rope to Jacoby, Phoebe saw how Stephen glowed in pride at Jacoby.

When she got off the phone, Jacoby was done securely tying Daniel and came over to her with the custody paper in hand. After tearing the paper to shreds, she collapsed in his arms for comfort for a brief moment. She didn't realize how scared she was until now and knowing he was around gave her so much relief, she shook as she felt the security of his arms wrap around her waist like a warm blanket from the cold.

Stephanie and Stephen came over to them and hugged Jacoby's legs in thanks. Jacoby and Phoebe looked down at them.

"I think you have to very grateful children in your debt," she said now looking at Jacoby.

"And their mother?" he asked.

She briefly kissed him. "Will always be in your debt," she promised. "I hope to have forever to make it up to you."

"You will especially when I add all the interest," he teased.

She knelt down to kiss and hug her children. Stephen tugged at Jacoby's hand for the larger man to kneel down. When he did, Stephen hugged him tightly. Stephanie followed.

Phoebe smiled in compassion as she met Jacoby's confused, yet emotional frown. "They're trying to tell you thank you," she explained.

Jacoby relished the feeling of having the twins in his arms and he knew at that point besides making their mother happy, he would enjoy giving them the world as well.

Chapter 33

The day before the New Year was Desmond's wedding and Phoebe was set to go to it. Patricia had suffered minor bruising and recovered quickly, but Daniel had sustained a broken nose and a fractured jaw. He would stay in prison until his court date for felonious assault and attempted kidnapping.

Phoebe was in high spirits over her engagement. Jacoby had insisted they marry as soon as possible, but she managed to put the date late in the summer of next year. Spending Christmas with Jacoby had been very special and now she was going to spend the New Year with him and his friends. Lawrence had come to the pre-wedding dinner last night only because he was the best man. Jacoby had no hard feelings for Lawrence, so Phoebe had to concede especially once Jacoby told her everyone really feels sorry for Lawrence for marrying a wife that is obsessed with him, which he doesn't love and now, with a baby on the way by him, he was really in deep - too deep to file for a divorce.

On the way to the church, Jacoby didn't waste time in the back of the limousine exploring Phoebe and became doubly excited upon finding out she wasn't wearing any underwear under her peach velvet dress with matching shoes. She had to hold him off though because she wanted to look presentable at least when she walked in the church and had to spend a moment inside the limousine after it arrived at the church, fixing her makeup because he had been intent to kiss her, which was hard to avoid and even harder to resist.

"When we're done saying hi, we still have fifteen minutes before the ceremony starts," Jacoby mentioned. "Why don't you excuse yourself and I'll meet you in the back room of the church near the bathrooms?" he suggested wickedly.

"Jacoby!" she exclaimed. "You are so bad. This is a church!"

"And? You think I'm going to actually sit through the whole thing feeling like this."

"You won't be sitting, you'll be standing," she pointed out. "You are one of the groomsmen, remember?"

"How can I forget in this ridiculous tuxedo?" he grumbled.

Phoebe giggled getting out with him to go into the church, when she had finished her makeup. She thought she had seen a familiar face in the crowd of people as they entered the church, but shrugged it off. Joseph and Amy were there and she was able to meet Thaddeus and Skye Newman again. She had met them at Christmas with Jacoby, along with their beautiful newborn named Theona Skye Newman, who was too adorable for words.

She also learned how Skye and Thaddeus met and couldn't believe Skye had been so shy. Thaddeus often called her his diamond in the rough and it had taken meeting him in order to bring the brightness out in her. Skye would only roll her beautiful lavender eyes that contrasted against her deep caramel skin as her husband spoke benevolently about his wife.

Skye had been involved in an illegal drug experiment by her own doctor and Thaddeus had been asked by the police to help go undercover and find out who was behind all of it, which turned out to be a very powerful crime boss the police had been trying to get for a very long time.

Once they greeted everyone, Patricia, who had come in a separate car, pulled Phoebe aside to tell her that somehow a patch of white powder was on the back of her dress. She thanked her mother for saving her and excused herself to go to the bathroom. There was someone in there, so she found the room that Jacoby had mentioned, which had a small sink in there. She wet a piece of tissue and turned slightly away from the door to wipe the back of her dress.

She heard the door open and close. Assuming it was Jacoby, she didn't bother to look as she said, "I said we were going to wait, Jacoby, until after the service is over, then you can take care of me."

The cold click of a .38 caliber seemed overwhelmingly loud in the quietness of the room as it sent fear chills down her back. Slowly, she turned around and couldn't believe her eyes.

"I'm not your lover boy, Phoebe, but you can bet your pretty ass I'm going to take care of you," Simon sneered, placing a silencer over the end of the gun and aiming it back at her.

"You really plan on killing me and getting away with it, Simon?" she asked, trying to remain calm and reasonable. "You are already going in for embezzlement. Murder will certainly get you life."

"Shut up!" he screamed. "I'm going to make sure no one knows I was here. No one's seen me and no one will ever know."

"You don't think they're going to suspect you?" she asked.

Footsteps could be heard coming to the doorway and Simon moved around her and held the gun at her temple. Jacoby appeared in the doorway with a look of disbelief on his face.

"What the hell is wrong with you?" he asked, looking directly at Phoebe as the door closed behind him. He didn't sound as upset as she felt he should be. Matter of fact, he almost sounded as if he were about to laugh. "Should I be worried you're going to drive me insane like all these nut cases you seem to attract?"

Phoebe chortled in incredulity. "You have got to be joking. You think I do this to them?"

"Two in one month, woman, I have to wonder."

"Shut up!" Simon ordered. "I have the gun and you need to hush up before any one else comes this way."

"Does he really plan on using that thing on anyone?" Jacoby asked Phoebe.

"He says he is, but I told him what the consequences were. He told me to shut up."

"Quit talking to me like I'm not here!" Simon exclaimed.

"Okay," Jacoby said through gritted teeth. "What were your plans now that you have both of us?"

Simon looked very unsure of himself.

Suddenly, the pounding at the door startled all of them, especially Phoebe who thought the gun had went off against her skull. When she opened her eyes to see Jacoby still standing in front of her and she didn't see her brains on the wall, she loosened up a little bit.

"Dammit Jacoby, I know you're in there and you might as well put your clothes back on. You are not about to make me late getting married for your erotic insatiable needs!" Desmond yelled on the other side of the door.

"Do I answer him?" Jacoby asked.

"Why are you asking me?" Simon asked.

"Because you have the gun, asshole."

"Tell him not to come in," Simon ordered now very nervous.

Phoebe knew she would have a headache come morning from how hard Simon was pressing the end of the gun into her temple - if she made it to morning.

"Don't come in," Jacoby called out, but he knew Desmond would not listen.

The door slammed opened hard. Desmond and Thaddeus were crowding the doorway as if they were coming to save her.

"Who the hell is that?" Thaddeus asked.

Phoebe could feel Simon shaking in fear.

"Simon?" Desmond asked assessing the situation. "What the hell are you doing with that gun?"

"Didn't I say don't come in?" Jacoby asked.

"When do I ever listen to you?" Desmond asked.

"Is he going to use that thing?" Thaddeus asked.

Everyone looked at Simon, except for Phoebe who was in the grip of fear. It seemed the more men that showed up at the doorway the more nervous Simon became and she was terrified that he would really find the balls to pull the trigger.

"There's no way you can kill us all, Simon," Jacoby said calmly. "Just put the gun down and I will allow you to walk out of here on your own two feet, but I won't promise I won't beat the shit out your face."

"I'm damned if I do or don't, right pretty boy?" Simon asked. "I know what you're thinking. I'll kill her if you touch me."

"I'll touch you worse if you kill her," Jacoby promised.

"Could we hurry this thing up?" Lawrence asked now at the doorway.

"He is right," Desmond said. "I would like to get married sometime today."

"This bitch isn't going to send me back to jail!" Simon said frantically. "I'm not going back there."

Jacoby took off his jacket saying, "Why don't I send you to hell, so you won't have to worry about jail?"

Phoebe could see he was starting to get very angry and knew then Jacoby had never really been upset with her because she had never seen him with this frightening murderous glaze in his eyes. A man his size should always have full control of his own strength and emotions, but right now, Jacoby's control was slowly slipping away. If Simon didn't do something fast, Jacoby had intentions of taking it all in hand. Phoebe just prayed she would live through it all, so she could hit Jacoby for scaring her like this.

"I've got an even better idea," Lawrence said, coming in standing next to Jacoby. "Simon, why don't you kill Jacoby for me?"

"You'd like that you son of a bitch, wouldn't you?" Jacoby sneered, now looking at Lawrence.

"Hell yes, because until the day I die, I will always know Phoebe didn't give a flying fig about her feelings for you until I stepped into her picture."

"And I'm suppose to show you some gratitude?" Jacoby asked in abhorrence. "You've got nerve, you son of a bitch?"

Lawrence swung at Jacoby, but Jacoby ducked his fist and delivered two jabs to Lawrence's stomach.

Simon screeched in madness and turned the gun away from Phoebe's head to aim at Jacoby. Jacoby's movement was like thunder striking, as he was close enough to grab Simon's arm and aimed the gun up at the ceiling at the same time it went off. The bullet hit somewhere above the doorway of the room as Jacoby's rock hard fist struck Simon's face dead center, and Jacoby's other fist slammed into Simon's chest knocking the breath out the smaller man. Simon fell to the ground, along with the gun.

Phoebe only stood there shivering in fear, eyes as wide as saucers not believing she was still alive. She was still frozen in fear as Thaddeus used a handkerchief to pick up the gun and left out to call the police, while Desmond and Lawrence dragged Simon's unconscious body out the room.

"Thanks for the distraction, Lawrence," Jacoby said gratefully.

"You didn't have to fucking hit me so hard and twice."

"Yes, I did because I'd probably killed Simon if I hadn't expended the energy on you."

Lawrence's eyes narrowed to slits. "Glad I could be so fucking helpful."

Laughing in relief, Jacoby turned to Phoebe to see that she was still standing there gripped in fear. Immediately he moved to her and held her. As his large arms wrapped around her, she collapsed against him weeping almost hysterically.

He whispered comforting words to her until she calmed down. Jacoby lightly planted kisses on her tear stained cheek and neck. Phoebe started to forget her near death experience as she became aroused to his kisses.

Desmond cleared his voice at the doorway. "The police are here. They said they can wait until after the ceremony to ask questions. Is that okay?"

Phoebe drew partially away from Jacoby blushing hard. "That's fine."

"I'll give you a minute to gather yourself and then we'll start," Desmond said. "Did you hear me, Jacoby, I said a minute?"

"I heard you," Jacoby growled, turning around to face Desmond. "I can tell time."

"I know how you are," Desmond said suspiciously.

"Then it won't surprise you when I do this," Jacoby said, slamming the door and locking it.

Phoebe giggled as Jacoby drew her in his arms again kissing her amorously.

"He's going to be highly upset. The wedding, Jacoby!" she insisted as he buried his lips in her neck.

"He said a minute," Jacoby said moving her dress up way past her hips. "I'll just blame you when it's all over."

"Why me?" she asked.

"Because you know I can't get enough of you, April."

She laughed, remembering the name she had given him that first night.

His mouth encompassed hers, making her breathless and filled with a wantonness to have him as much as he wanted her.

"Say it, Phoebe. Let me hear those sweet words, please," he begged in her ear.

"I love you, Jacoby. I love you so much."

He groaned in mercy as he moved to his knees and Phoebe's back pressed against the door.

Before Phoebe could protest again, Jacoby was sending her into the heavens with his wonderful mouth, as they both ignored the incessant knocking Desmond was doing on the other side of the door.

THE END

Related characters in the book, Thaddeus and Skye Newman:

Dreams Of Reality

Skye Patterson - 24-year old entrepreneur trying to make her way in the world all by herself since she was orphaned at birth - finds herself the victim of a mind controlling substance.

Moving to Detroit, was a big step emotionally, but she never thought it would be a big step mentally. The mind controlling drugs invade her life enveloping her in a world she never thought she could experience and a love that was too good to be true with one of her clients,

Thaddeus Newman, a powerful construction business owner. When she begins to experience the too real dreams she tries to convince herself they are not real, but as the dreams become more vivid, she delves deep into a world of pimps, businessmen, doctors, and murder, until she finds out what is really happening to her. With Thaddeus by her side, she is able to face her reality and conquer her fears. Dreams of Reality touches on the new age drug, GHB in the revitalization of Motown, where a woman tries to make it alone and finds that in order to survive she has to make her dreams of love, into dreams of reality.

http://SylviaHubbard.com

Get more of this author's books at her website.

About this author:

Detroit Native, Sylvia Hubbard, is a diehard romance/suspense author. In 2005, Sylvia Hubbard was the recipient of The Detroit City Council's Spirit of Detroit Award for her efforts in Detroit's literary community, voted Romance Book Cafe favorite author and her book Stone's Revenge was voted best African-American Mystery by Mojolist.com.

The Author is also founder of Motown Writers Network, which offers literary education and events in Detroit, Creator for The Michigan Literary Network Radio Show and speaks on Internet Marketing and Promotions for Writers and Authors.

She resides in Detroit as a divorced mother of three.

She writes a blog called How To Love A Black Woman, which is described as her manual for loving her, and speaks on Creative Intimacy for couples.

She's written over 35 novels with more to come and always available to speak at any event on literacy, writing, publishing and mommying!

Related Links:

http://MotownWriters.com
http://HowToEbook.org
http://MotownMomMusings.com
http://HowToLoveABlackWoman.com

Connect Online to Sylvia Hubbard:

Twitter: http://twitter.com/SylviaHubbard1
Website: http://SylviaHubbard.com
My blog: http://SylviaHubbard.com/blogs

Want another book to read now?

http://sylviahubbard.com/fictionbooks